Robert Kroetsch

Robert Kroetsch was born in Heisler, Alberta, in a homestead shack. He worked for six years in the northern bush and has since been a professor of English at the State University of New York at Binghamton and writer in residence at the University of Calgary, Lethbridge, and Manitoba. He is now professor of English at the University of Manitoba in Winnipeg. He is the author of numerous works of fiction, including: *But We Are Exiles, The Words Of My Roaring, The Studhorse Man, Badlands,* and *What The Crow Said.* He has also published five books of poetry: *The Ledger, Stone Hammer Poems, Seed Catalogue, The Sad Phoenician,* and *Field Notes.*

Bruce St. Clair

Bruce St. Clair was born near Galt, Ontario, in 1945, studied at the Ontario College of Art and now lives near North Bay, Ontario. In addition to his regular solo and group shows at the Aggregation Gallery in Toronto, St. Clair's work has been shown in numerous public gallery exhibitions and is represented in many important private and public collections across Canada and abroad.

New Press Canadian Classics

Distinguished by the use of Canadian fine art on its covers, New Press Canadian Classics is an innovative, much-needed series of high-quality, reasonably priced editions of the very best Canadian fiction, nonfiction and poetry.

New Press Canadian Classics

newpress CANADIAN CLASSICS

Robert Kroetsch

Badlands

 General
—PAPERBACKS—

New Press Trendsetter edition
published in 1975

PaperJacks edition published in 1976

General Paperbacks edition
published in 1982
2nd printing 1983
3rd printing 1988
4th printing 1991
ISBN 0-7736 1170-3

Printed and bound in Canada

for Harley and Hugh and Gerry,
companions with me on the Red Deer River

But suddenly a joyous impulse seized him: the joy of having his wife again overwhelmed him. He jumped to his feet and rushed over to embrace her. His wife cried out, "Stop! Stop! Coyote! Do not touch me. Stop!" Her warning had no effect. Coyote rushed over to his wife and just as he touched her body she vanished. She disappeared—returned to the shadowland.

> "Coyote and the Shadow People," *Nez Percé Texts*

> this is a strange country
> desert flows around us death &
> breath makes us wary

> bp Nichol, *The Martyrology*

CHRONOLOGY

Summer 1916:   The Dawe Expedition enters the Alberta Badlands via the Red Deer River to collect dinosaur skeletons.

October 1916:   William Dawe visits his wife for two days and two nights, then leaves again, a custom he is to continue for twenty-seven years.

October 1926:   Dawe makes his annual fall pilgrimage to his wife's bed, and this one time stays a third night.

July 1927:   birth of Anna Dawe, while her father is in the field collecting dinosaur skeletons.

October 1942:   Dawe goes home to visit not his dying wife but his daughter.

September 1962:   death of William Dawe.

Summer 1972:   Anna Dawe, in the company of an old Indian woman, Anna Yellowbird, enters the Alberta Badlands, carrying in the trunk of her Mercedes-Benz two cases of Gordon's gin and a cardboard box half-full of her dead father's field notes.

Anna Dawe

I am Anna Dawe. I am named Anna because my father, eleven years after that season of 1916, remembered the Indian girl, Anna Yellowbird, who had, he explained to my mother, saved his life. What he did not explain to my mother was how that Anna — by what violent surgery of the spirit—healed him back onto his feet of clay.

I don't know that I ever received a letter from my absent father. He sent us instead, left us, deposited for me to find, his field notes; God help us we are a people raised not on love letters or lyric poems or even cries of rebellion or ecstasy or pain or regret, but rather old hoards of field notes. Those cryptic notations made by men who held the words themselves in contempt but who needed them nevertheless in order to carry home, or back if not home, the only memories they would ever cherish: the recollections of their male courage and their male solitude.

We read those field notes, mother and I; together we went through those long and slender notebooks, designed to fit a denim pocket rather than a coffee table. We read in those sun-faded and water-wrinkled books, read not only the words but the squashed mosquitoes, the spiders' legs, the stains of thick black coffee, even the blood that smeared the already barely decipherable words. And the message was always so clear that my mother could read, finally, without unpuzzling the blurred letters or the hasty, intense scrawl. She could read her own boredom and possibly her loneliness, if not his outrageous joy.

2

I am Anna Kilbourne Dawe, 45, unmarried, conceived by William Dawe out of the woman he was no longer living with but upon whom he occasionally imposed himself, especially after he had been in the field for a season and could return to Ontario and, for a few hours, or perhaps for as much as a couple of nights, plead deprivation and repentance and lust. Then my mother would feel, for an evening's relief from her boredom, perhaps even for two nights, that she had been mistaken in her memory of the man, and she would allow him into her bed. And then her boredom, again, would seem preferable to the man she had married out of boredom. And out of that union, if it might be called such, out of that version of wedlock, I was born into my own silly inquiring.

Why it was left to me to mediate the story I don't know: women are not supposed to have stories. We are supposed to sit at home, Penelopes to their wars and their sex. As my mother did. As I was doing.

And yet I was not Penelope because no man wagered his way towards me. The one who did, ever— the man who violated my inherited dream of myself, if not me—assuming I did not seduce him into it— was gone, not travelling, but into death. And I was alone and I sat in the house inherited from my mother, who inherited it from her mother—a winterized summer place on the shore of Georgian Bay where William Dawe might sit and dimly apprehend across the water, through the coming storms, the west he found and denied; and I was there alone with only my parents' financial acumen to guard me, and I bought my gin by the case, bought and read my books by the parcel, imagined to myself a past, an ancestor, a legend, a vision, a fate.

3

Web was the man I imagined most often. He was the one person whom my father could never destroy; possibly because there was nothing inside him, nothing behind that penis of his, that was destructible. Weber was his last name, and if he had a first name other than Web my father never bothered to write it down. And if he had a home other than "the shack that fucking bastard lived in," I never heard of that either. I only know, dimly remember hearing, that his father kicked him out saying if he was going to eat enough groceries for two men he could earn them with his two hands, and Web saying he left that day and went back that night, put a match to the shack and left again before he found out if his old man got out dead or alive, and then, his way lighted by the burning shack, headed down the road and kept going. "There is no such thing as a past," Web, his father forgotten, said to mine.

There is nothing else, Web. That you should misunderstand is unfortunate; on that one issue, on that issue only, my father perceived correctly. And he went out and looked for that past. Appropriately enough, with a pick and a shovel and an awl and a chisel and a hammer. And shellac to seal it with and burlap and plaster of paris to wrap it in. And museums to sell it to at a handsome profit.

1. *Web's First Discovery*

Web combed his fingers through the abundant grass, carefully picked the berries. When his left hand was full he raised up his head, he let himself rest, his haunches on his heels, the ferocious red of the heaped berries held almost to his darting tongue. He glanced around before eating: and only then did he notice about him in the growth of new poplars, not just the one low roof he remembered vaguely having bumped, but the scattering of roofs. They were set a few inches off the ground, on stout pegs, each narrow unpainted roof six to eight feet in length, one of them partially shingled, each constructed of boards that were weathered grey now. Web stood up: and there in the green light of June, the odour of balsam sweet and sticky on the air, he might have come to a buried village, only the roofs left visible to the hot, climactic sun.

He was pushing the heaped strawberries into his mouth, staining red his blond, three-day mustache, when he noticed behind the ragged edge of a gooseberry bush the hump of fresh earth. He saw the mound, what seemed to be a mound of fresh, newly opened earth, then looked again at the low roofs, saw on one end of one roof a small wooden cross, on another roof, another cross. They were not in rows, the few crosses, the roofs, and that too had fooled him; they were scattered. But not quite at random. And he held the berries in his mouth, the berries sourly sweet, and he could not swallow. He was relieved and even delighted to be off the flatboat, away from the other men, away from the confinement of the flatboat's moving, unsteady, rectangular deck. But he could not swallow. And he knew also, guessed without knowing, he was come to an Indian or Métis burial ground; the small roofs were intended to keep coyotes and wolves from unearthing the bodies. And still, even so, it was he who first walked towards the shallow depression beside the fresh mound.

"Dawe," he shouted. Web tilted up his head, closed his eyes against the blaze of noon sun that came in under the brim of his dirty cap; he seemed to cough blood into the air: "Dawe!"

2. *William Dawe in Command*

William Dawe, hunchbacked, small, made smaller by a broad-brimmed black hat, moved stiffly off the open prairie and into the stand of poplars. If he saw the scattering of graves, of roofs, he did not let on; and yet he saved his shins from their grass-hid corners, marched in abrupt irritation through Web's strawberry patch and stopped at the base of the mound itself, stood combing his black beard with his fingers, watching while Web put out a hand in preparation to grasp and then lift up the apparition that he, Web, could not quite believe in.

Dawe, watching, deciding.

And the woman also, the girl, watching, staring with luminous eyes at the tall man who bent over her, the hunchbacked man at his side; and they, not she, might have been the apparitions, spirits at or even from the surrounding graves that were themselves fading back into prairie and bush.

"Well stay there then," Web said. Willing to be dissuaded.

Dawe stepped onto the heap of sod and clay. The girl lay apparently at ease in the small rain of dirt set loose by his boots, her own moccasined feet somehow too small for standing or walking. Dawe, on the mound, struggling to unfold what seemed to be his folded wings.

"Do you know the river?" He gestured over his own right shoulder. "Not Tail Creek. The Red Deer River."

"Yes," she said. Perhaps she was in awe of his twisted back, his magical hump. He wore it, under his dusty and wrinkled and elegant grey suitcoat, like some talisman of splendid good fortune; he pointed not so much at the river as at the hump itself. "No," she added.

"Can you tell us," he said, Dawe said, with condescending patience, "where the bones are?"

The girl, watching, her luminous eyes not quite indifferent, not quite concerned: "What bones?"

But a third man came out of the coulee, came limping up onto the flat prairie at the point where the prairie itself broke and disappeared; he stopped, waited, put out a hand and helped onto the prairie's lip an old chinaman. They stood comically together, lame McBride, the chinaman, for all their dusty clothes looking like two swimmers who had only just made it ashore; they saw their companions and started towards them; they saw the small, unlikely roofs and stopped again.

And Dawe, his audience assembled: "The bones of the big reptiles." He would make it clear to these poor souls, the uninitiated, the ignorant, the vulgar: "The long bones—"

And then even he, William Dawe, originator and financier and leader of the Dawe Expedition, was at a loss to explain his own compulsion to recover the past, his maniacal obsession: "Dinosaur––" He stopped again. As if for a moment he recognized he was about to risk his boat, his crew, his own life. "We are looking for the bones of the dead. We must find them."

"You are going to the place of the dead?" the girl asked.

William Dawe, not understanding her, as he refused to understand his wife, his friends, anyone who was not his equal in madness, answered, "Yes." Dawe whose whole existence was become a veritable and deliberate wager, a gamble, a bet that he could in one season find the rib or femur or skull that would insinuate to him, however grotesquely, the whole truth; the one gigantic and perfect skeleton of his dreams that would cast man out of everlasting vanity and conceit. And that for a profit too. With fame thrown in as a bonus. . . . Dawe, crippled, shrunken, confined to a drifting flatboat with a little old chinaman who might on occasion cook or fish but who would never, except when not spoken to, speak; a lame dirt farmer who claimed to have journeyed––"sailed," he said––down one part of this Alberta river one time before; a big and homeless man named Web or Weber or something who might, in spite of the flies, the storms, the heat, be strong enough and healthy enough to dig up the skeleton once he, Dawe, had found it––Dawe agreed: "We are going to the place of the dead."

The girl, inside the bright Indian blanket she wore

8

over her shoulders, moved an elbow, moved into a sitting position. She wrestled against the sliding earth, trying at least to get her knees under her body. She had, in her own fevered wandering and isolation, not only found nothing to eat but deliberately had not eaten. "I will go with you," she said. "I must find my husband."

"Do you know where the bones are?" Dawe repeated.

"No," the girl said. "You know the way. I will go with you."

William Dawe turned abruptly to his waiting crew. "Let's get on with it," he commanded them.

Web wiping his hand on his trouser leg, reaching again, fastidiously; Web both defying Dawe and apologizing to the silent girl: "Come—"

"We have no place for women," Dawe said. "Let's get on with the task I hired you bunglers to perform."

3. *Flatboat with Crew*

And they departed, the four men together, left the burial ground and walked in single column through the buckbrush and the wild roses along the lip of the valley; they turned down into the coulee, scrambled and slid down through the sparse grass on the steep hillside to the first stand of spruce, to the nearest beaver dams; they crossed over on a dam, stepped over some beaver-felled balsam poplars. And they were on the flats where Tail Creek held in loose assembly 100 cabin sites, the cabins themselves burned by a prairie fire that had swept into the valley eighteen years previously, the hunters gone because the last buffalo herd had vanished, thirty years before the fire, into its own extinction. The four men walked in silent order. Dawe leading, Dawe by a combination of intensity and arrogance enforcing the silence, Web and McBride letting the chinaman follow behind Dawe, making their own acceptance of that silence not a surrender but an accident of order. They marched in diligent haste past the mounds of clay and stones that had once been fireplaces, the trembling aspens already grown tall inside the clay-marked boundaries of the burned cabins; they returned to the river itself, pushed their way through the man-high willows on the swampy ground, speaking now only to curse the sudden swarms of mosquitoes; they stepped from the sucking mud onto the gangplank, Web waiting to be last, waiting to free the stern, and as he did so, looking back to watch the skyline.

They slid past the small, low island at the mouth of the creek; and they were not so much on an island of their own as on a badly managed stage, the plank deck measuring twelve feet by thirty and dominated in its middle by a large white tent.

The rectangular flatboat itself was designed to draw hardly two feet of water when loaded with eight tons of fossils, designed to be powered only by the current of the river, for this would be a one-way trip, into the Badlands empty and out the other end loaded, presumably, with a season's plunder and loot; designed to be manoeuvered by means of two oar-like sweeps each twenty-two feet in length, one on the stern where Web held domain next to the chinaman's cast-iron cookstove, one on the bow where McBride must work close to the water's edge, the hand-capstan, not to mention the white wall of the tent, crowding him from behind. The boat, supposedly running light, was already loaded with enough food to last four men for three months, with cooking equipment and excavating equipment, with sacks of plaster of paris, with tins of shellac, with kegs of nails, with lumber for building crates for the as yet to be discovered and excavated fossils.

McBride, on the bow, found the main current and held it, the river there below the site of the Tail Creek Settlement angling south as well as east, towards the bald prairies; the glacier-cold water already beginning to warm, turning muddy and brown.

William Dawe sat down on a keg of nails and dug in his pockets for his pencil and field book. He wrote on the long, narrow, lined page: *Tuesday, June 27. Arrived Tail Creek shortly before noon. Climbed up out of the valley intending to find a farm or ranch, buy some fresh food, send off some letters.* And then, either to amplify his heroic endurance or to underline his disappointment, he added: *Encountered a pitiful young squaw who seemed to think—* He broke off the enlarging sentence, surprised at his own unscientific noting of the world. He scratched, righteously, pompously, in his cramped hand on the next line: *she would accompany my expedition.*

And all afternoon they floated downriver, Dawe watching the banks, watching every new slide that might have betrayed a buried bone into daylight; they put him ashore, let him hammer and brush as if to smash and then clean the continent itself, the boat drifting while he crawled, walked, leapt; Dawe on board again and watching every cutbank or rilled butte, the tumble of scree at the base of a sandstone cliff; they tied up that night at the head of an island where driftwood was available and a breeze kept down the mosquitoes while they ate supper and then listened to the coyotes and then slept; they followed the morning sun into waking, were scolded awake by the myriad birds and the fuzzy, raw light on the white canvas roof and walls; and all morning they drifted again, put Dawe ashore, picked him up, drifted on past dinnertime and into early afternoon. Web watching the skyline.

4. *Chinese Cook on Open Deck*

Web arguing: "We can beat her."

McBride, at the forward sweep: "No chance in the wide world. This current and a headwind to boot, we couldn't stay ahead of a porcupine. We're lucky to make two miles an hour."

Web, at the stern sweep: "She's got to sleep sometime. Can't see in the dark, unless she's a mole. So that's the trick. We run all night tonight, get ahead of her, then she'll give up. Indians got no staying power. Leave her twenty miles behind and get that shadow off our tail."

McBride arguing. Claude McBride, seeking the channel, avoiding the snags, the mud cutbanks, the gravel bars, the boulders bigger than a kitchen stove yet hardly visible, the shore itself. "Get ahead of her hell, give her half a chance and she'll walk right past us." McBride, in bib overalls and a straw hat on the bow of a flatboat, who only wanted to make a few

12

dollars, a summer's wages, then return to his homestead at Red Deer Crossing, to his wife, his four kids, the crop that was supposed to grow and ripen while he was away.

"Fuck her," Web said.

Then in response to his own comment: "I'd like to."

"Or she falls asleep," McBride said, "sleeps all night and half the next day. All she has to do is keep on walking and sooner or later she'll find us again. Where are we going?"

"Away," Web said.

"How?" McBride said.

The chinaman, bending to dip water from the river, lifted his pail and laughed.

"Grizzly, what do you think?" Web driven to that last refuge by McBride's logic. To the man whose name they would not bother to learn, but whom they nicknamed Grizzly because the first night out, the dark falling, he had tried to tell them a story of a time in the Rocky Mountains when he, Grizzly, was camped somewhere near the source of the Red Deer River, cooking then for a crew that was making a topographical survey. The story had held Web even while he despised the teller, because he had never thought of that flatlands river as having its source in the mountains; and that first night out of Red Deer Crossing, having heard the chinaman's jumbled tale of what had, apparently, been an encounter with a bear—that night he, Web, dreamed he was on an upriver trip: he was looking for the hidden and pristine lakes that are the river's source, the sky-high and dazzling glaciers that feed the originating lakes.

"What do you think, Grizzly?" Web tried again, on the silence. Wanting the old chinaman to say they should not even tie up to eat a meal.

Grizzly knelt down. He filled his strangely rounded old felt hat from the river and lifted it and turned it over on top of his own head, his pigtail. Then he began to clean the goldeyes he had caught while the flatboat moved slowly with the current. And into that silence—the knife moving, scraping, the fish scales shining still and mica-bright on the washed deck—Dawe sat up. Dawe, who was either dozing or pretending to doze in the afternoon sun, awkwardly lifted himself up off the canvas cot he had brought out from the tent:

"I don't think you saw her up there on that damned cliff to begin with, Web."

Now it was Web's turn to be deaf.

"But run all night if you want to," Dawe added. "Nothing for us in this stretch."

Web, granted his extravagant privilege, stumbled for ways to have it denied. "Risky," he said. "Risky. Can't get ahead of her anyhow."

"Just might," McBride said. "Why're you changing your mind, Web?"

"I'm not," Web hollered. Over, around the tent. "I'm weighing the possibilities—"

And while they argued, debated, watched for a place to tie up and watched it slip away behind them, Grizzly finished cleaning the fish. He chopped a piece of driftwood into kindling and started a fire in his stove, moved the pail close to the fire, afraid an encounter with shoal water might tip the coals and the flames onto the plank deck, or onto the tent

14

itself. Web and McBride surveyed and rejected an island that would involve them in a long crossing; Grizzly lifted the filets out of the pail of water, into flour and pepper and salt, into a frying pan.

"What have you gentlemen decided?" Dawe said.

McBride stared at the river as if he must not ever lift his gaze to land. Web, at the stern sweep, did not take his eyes from the slant of sandstone cliffs at the sky's edge, the jumble of rocks below the cliffs, the mudslides that reached out into the river from steeply sloping hills, barren hills studded with sage.

The valley itself, there below Tail Creek, falling apart. Heavy stands of spruce on one side as if the boat might be slipping down a river through northern bush; eroded and baked and parched hillsides on the other, as if the desert was coming to swallow the slant of water. And the shoreline everywhere sliding down, the earth shapeless, the trees cracked and twisted and leaning away from the sun.

Grizzly served the fish, served the biscuits. He went his quiet rounds, carrying a tin plate to each man, then a tin cup; and they let the silence become the resolution they could not achieve by homely reason. Web thinking: Maybe I didn't see her at all. Stinking Indian. If she was upwind we could smell her.

"Never," Dawe said. Announced like the clout and echo of a distant axe, out of his apparent indifference.

The others looked away from their trance-like concerns. Each was eating alone; Web and McBride at the sweeps, Grizzly seated on a wooden crate beside his stove.

15

Dawe picked up his tin coffee cup off the deck, put it down without drinking. He gestured across the water and up at the broken landscape. "There is no way any woman could walk through that country."

Web tipped the fishbones from his plate, into the river. "She was tough enough to dig her own grave and crawl into it."

"Wasn't a grave," McBride said. "Just a place to sleep."

"Won't catch me there before I'm hog-tied and hammered in." Web both ignoring and answering McBride. "Bone-on I'm developing now, it'll take them a week to get the lid down."

"Jesus Christ, Web," McBride said. "She was a *child*."

Above them, again, a hawk cried. Web, watching for the girl, seeing only the hawks. "Fuck a snake right now, if I could get somebody to hold it."

"I don't think you saw her yesterday afternoon," Dawe said. "I don't think you saw her this morning. And you sure as hell aren't going to see her tonight, no matter how horny you are." Dawe began the ritual of lighting his pipe, indicating by his actions that he intended to hear no answer, no further comment. "But I wouldn't call her a *child*, McBride," he said, more to himself than to his listeners.

The four of them waiting now. All of them at once weary from too much sun, their eyes sore, their lips burned, noses raw and peeling; all of them infused with and then exhausted by the double blaze, the naked sun, the blank glare of sun off water.

5. *Man Overboard*

By 10:30 even Dawe had run out of ways of appearing indifferent to their night's running; he no longer pretended, in the muted mauve light, to be studying his maps. Lulled, bemused, he watched his lame bow-man, McBride, hunch towards the downward slope of the river, the water turning to mirror, the mirror to smoked glass, to shadow. McBride in his forties was too old for this folly, and yet not old enough not to be tempted. And if there was a tempter on the boat, Dawe decided, it must be Web; Web in his twenties, standing theatrical at the stern sweep, not only the sunburn scalding his fair skin, but the innocence too, the secret violent innocence that overcame his fear of water. Grizzly alone wore a face of indifference; Grizzly looking older than the others put together, durable as a stump might appear, a lizard on a rock; Grizzly who could not be tempted at all because he merely distrusted the river that Web hated. And Dawe now, needing the light to read his maps of the water as McBride needed light to read the water itself—Dawe turned first from his crew, turned then from the vanishing shore. He rolled his scattered maps with the same care he had used to spread them on the stacked and tarpaulined sacks of plaster of paris; he inserted them into their leather tube.

Only then, after he'd snapped shut the top, did anyone hear the rapids ahead of the boat.

"I thought we were through the rapids," Web said.

And Dawe, defending not so much himself as the maps that were the emblem of his conviction and intent: "Well we aren't, you see."

"I don't see," Web said.

And the silence darkened, the valley darkened,

17

under the almost illumined sky. No birds sang at that hour. But the whisper of the rapids would not cease. The swallows that swung out all day from their holes in the vertical cutbanks had long since ceased their quick flights. But the sound came up the valley, soft, unrelenting, and Web at the stern sweep glanced back, saw the last glow of the far and barely set sun. And it was Web who, trying to see the wakeless water behind the boat, remarked softly: "Get braced, you unlucky bastards."

But when they believed they should be upon, into, the rapids, they were not; the unrelenting whisper of the water seemed hardly closer at all and McBride let go of his sweep, stepped to the squared-off bow.

"Would you do your pissing," Web said, "*after* Grizzly dips up our drinking water?"

Not the motion of the air but its quickened chill told them they were moving faster.

Dawe: "Should we light a lantern?"

"Couldn't see then," McBride said.

And Web: "Cripes, listen; this is one dirty stretch—"

They were into the rapids. The current took them, swept them down in a motion they could not see. Web braced his legs against the rising deck; then it was falling away, he was weightless in the air, his stomach going queasy; then the deck caught him again, the slow-motion bronco of the night's river lifting against his tensed thighs—

The sweep vanished from his hands.

The echoed thunder of boulder on wood came up from the boat's hull. Dawe pitched forward through the open tent flap, into Grizzly's embrace, carried himself and the cook and a stack of groceries onto the first cot while Web, a split second later, hurled against the tent by the same momentum that had snatched him away from the sweep, not only tore loose the lines that held the tent upright but carried it down on top of Grizzly and Dawe; the tent collapsing forward, entangled the forward sweep, covered the long wooden arm that might have given support to McBride.

Grizzly was first to free himself from the groceries and cots and bedding and the collapsed tent. He crawled out onto the open deck and, confusing the darkness of the tent with the darkness itself, very nearly crawled overboard. It was Grizzly who called, once:

"Dawe."

William Dawe, hearing his own name, stopped wrestling against the canvas that enwrapped him; he recognized in that moment's consolation he was struggling not to escape but to find the pipe that only he smelled.

It was Grizzly, also, who pulled at the tent lines so that Web might free his neck and stand up and grope in the black air. Web struck on the stern sweep; automatically he pulled it into position. The current tore the sweep out of his grip; the river, he realized, was moving past them; the boat was standing still.

Grizzly alone struggled with the heavy tent, pulled it open so that Dawe might emerge, might crawl head-first out into the air. Dawe started to warn them about his pipe, started to speak and found the pipe in his mouth. Knocked clean of ash, glowing, it made in the sun's absence their only light. In its presence Dawe himself, then Grizzly, then Web too, recognized that McBride had not responded.

"McBride!" Web shouted.

The water of the rapids tore loudly at the boat, ripped into, through, the attention of the listening men.

"McBride," Dawe commanded "McBride, answer me."

Grizzly was crawling about on his hands and knees on the bow of the boat. "Bow-man not here now, Mr. Dawe," Grizzly said.

Web, groping down the tilted deck, plunged one arm into the water that boiled up over the starboard gunwale of the boat. He lurched away and shouted a warning.

It was that that made Dawe laugh. Then he could tell them—command Web and Grizzly—to lie flat and not move: and the three men lay together on the collapsed tent, holding and not holding each other, resisting each other, stiffly resisting the boat itself, the river itself; they lay side by side, Dawe in the middle, all of them staring at the deep sky above them, the sky they could see when they could not see the river a yard away; each of them trying not to think of McBride, gone, trying not to think they might slide after him, cracked against the rocks, trapped under the splintering boat, shrouded in the canvas tent in which they should have been sleeping; Web, looking up at the huge and almost-lit sky, could see on the sky itself, on the lids of his closed eyes, the hawks he had seen all day.

And Web thinking: They'll get you, Billy Dawe.

Those hawks, swinging up there, crossing back and forth. Web seeing the skyline, the hawks riding the updrafts at the edge of the cliffs. Out over the river, they swung, out and back again, to the leaning cliffs, to the sandstone cap on the sliding clay. To the tops of the storm-broken spruce. Web forcing open his eyes: and one nesting pair of hawks had hardly disappeared behind the boat, was hardly out of sight, when the next pair cried down upon the boat, cried high in the sunlit air above the shadowed valley. Web flinching at the scream that wasn't a scream, the one and piercing and raptorial note that was older by millions of years than any human call. Web, in the night, in his mind, curing his mind of the night's memory: Hanging up there on the sky they wait, swinging up there, riding back and forth; they'll tear the hide off that hump of yours, Billy Dawe; they'll find you sticking out of the mud like those bones you dragged us into this mess to find; like your own damned dinosaurs, floating bloated and belly up and then drifting into the slack water, into the shallows, the bones picked clean, the bones sinking into the mud, into the hardening clay, the darkness—

The sun.

They would not believe they had dared to sleep. Forcing open their eyes.

They were into the Badlands.

The stiff blade of light came over the rimrock; the light grew from purple to a blue veil, from blue to red to orange; the tall and starkly outlined buttes emerged from the darkness. The buttes came as pyramids against the light; they came as mounds, as beehives, as cones. They had those forms of the past, and yet they were not any landscape that Dawe had known, that Web had imagined.

The three men, stiff from the cold, stiff from the biting cold of the summer night, at first did not dare to move, as if one gesture might upset their precarious hold on that coming day. They were into the Badlands and high on the buttes the light poured extravagant and yellow on top of the red, on top of the orange; the buttes became layered, layered in brown and grey, then in green and purple, the colour going out of the sky and into the land itself.

The three men, warmed like three insects, stirred and sat up into the new sun.

"A man could get hurt here," Web said. "Where are we, Dawe?"

Grizzly, with a grunt of surprise, bounced off the collapsed tent. He did not seem to see the water or the sky. He must perform his assigned task, must find them something to eat.

The boat was stuck fast on a glacial boulder. Web looked at the dark, dizzying water he had listened to all night. Only a yard beyond his boots the waves leapt and leapt, and yet he saw now they never moved, were never gone. The rapids seemed all motion, and yet their sound did not vary; each wave, for all its rush and motion, was always where it was, and Web stared and felt his stomach rise towards his mouth, and still he stared, he himself seeming to move on the rush of water, motionless.

Dawe watched, beheld, the gaunt buttes, the raw and exciting exposure of clay and rock, the pure and sensual exposure of the clay that might, that must, contain the skeletons he was looking for. He sat up to find his maps. Big Valley Creek. This must be it, the first major bonebed. He burst alive, scrambled like a spider over the tent. The maps were not to be found and he cursed, ordered the two men to help him search.

"McBride—" Web said.

"Ashore," Dawe said. "We must get *ashore*."

Web staring at the violence of the surrounding rapids: Right here on this marooned boat we could build a boat, sail away then, leave everything, rescue ourselves. Web turning feebly to search for the maps and planning the escape, the reckless, brave plunge out of this catastrophe, towards dry land.

Grizzly would neither hear nor help. Grizzly went on moving the sacks of plaster of paris that had toppled onto his flung stove.

Then Web was not helping either; Web, beginning to feel seasick, closed his eyes against the rush of water. Then he felt beneath him the boat's motion, the snake-like motion, the boat weaving, insinuating itself up and down and not moving; he struggled against the slant of deck, hauled himself up the deck towards the sky, hung his head out over the swish of water.

Web, tears flooding his eyes, thought at first she was the stump of a balsam poplar, an animal come to drink.

The girl was standing on the shore.

The girl, the woman, on the shore, slender, silent, watched the three men, the boat itself. She might have been there all night long, waiting, watching, motionless, the woman standing, while the three men lay in a row.

She was standing by a black birch, her hair and

her shoulders wrapped in a bright, patterned blanket, her feet lost in silver-green wolf willow. The slope of clay behind her was clumped with cinquefoil and sage. For an instant Web saw her so clearly he might have recognized the grass, the prairie needles, caught in her long and shapeless dress. She was raising her right hand towards the boat.

And then he could not see because the veins of his eyes seemed to explode, bloom redder than the red of the woman's flowered cotton dress, and he knew far back in the quiet of his mind, knew and was so sick he did not care, that he was retching.

Anna Dawe

When I found her, last summer, out there on the dry and wind-burned, wind-scoured prairies of Alberta, on that awful landscape of sorrow and denial, she was an old woman getting drunk on bottled beer – in the Queen's Hotel in Gleichen: that fading and sun-smashed and awful town on the edge of the Blackfoot Reserve. At first she pretended never to have heard of my father.

I suppose I was tempted by her ignorance. Perhaps by pretending I too might deny his ever having existed.

"He was head of an expedition," I explained. "If three or four men on a flatboat floating down the Red Deer River with nothing more than two sweeps to guide them can be called an expedition."

She glanced disdainfully at my white dress, at my white hat – and she said nothing.

I was standing at her side, almost over her; she was seated at a table.

"They were hunting dinosaur skeletons," I said.

Again that Anna did not respond.

I wished I might dare sit down at her table, at her side, facing not only her but also the two men who might have been her lovers, her husbands—even her sons – who had fallen silent at that small, round, black-topped, beer-wet table.

"He came out here from the east," I said. "William Dawe. He was thirty-five years old that spring. Old enough to have some sense, along with his obsessions and his passions. He had a black beard, with eyes to match, and a heart to match the beard and the eyes."

25

She would say nothing in reply to the speeches I had been rehearsing for so long. I had no choice but to play my trump card.

"He was a hunchback," I said.

The Indian woman straightened. She stretched her legs, moved them apart, as if even the memory of that man was enough She was sitting not so much at the table as beside it, parallel to it, her left hand resting on an empty glass. I saw she was wearing worn canvas shoes on her bare feet; her dress was almost but not quite long enough to cover her rather handsome ankles; a dirty blue sweater only accentuated her breasts.

She was much larger than I had expected from those abrupt and guarded conversations I'd had with my father, when he too was aging. And then the simple and shocking truth bore in upon me: Anna Yellowbird, when those men commenced the inversion of their souls, was fifteen years of age. She had in those few years been wife and widow, a feat I have not accomplished in a lifetime. But she was also what my mother would have called, had she known of the outrage, a growing girl.

"He did what he did," Anna said. That other Anna.

"He did what he wanted," I corrected her.

"Then he is not the man I knew," Anna said.

Even after fifty-six years she would defend the man—her recollection of the man—who in her days of grief found her: and ignored her, and used her grief, and then let her vanish again.

"He did as he pleased," I corrected her.

"I did not know that man," she said.

But then she signalled the waiter to bring four bottles of beer; she signalled me to take an empty chair from the next table and pull it up to hers and to sit down.

And yes, I obeyed.

And I assumed the occasion would demand of her a formal telling, would sponsor the curious little narrative tricks of a male adventure: the lies that enable the lovers to meet, the mystery of who did the killing, the suspense before victory. As if we didn't know all the answers long before they asked their absurd questions. . . . They have their open spaces, and translate them into a fabled hunting. We have only time to survive in, time, without either lies or mystery or suspense; we live and then die in time.

That Anna watched me drink a glass of beer. I suppose it was the one test I knew how to pass. For a while she said nothing. Then she said only:

"I will go with you."

The boat moved.

It was then that Dawe, looking for Web, looking instead to where Web was looking, saw the girl he had refused to expect to see. Saw Anna Yellowbird. Saw the fossil in her hand.

The boat moved; Web went on vomiting.

Grizzly, in shifting the sacks of plaster out of his way, off his stove, had loaded them onto the lower and starboard side. The starboard corner of the rectangular stern went down further; the boat's flat hull lifted off the boulder.

They careened on into the rapids. Web, choking on his own vomit, ran to get hold of a sweep. They hit more rocks; the sacks of plaster of paris tumbled overboard; half of them, more, were gone—the powder that, mixed with water, was supposed to be used to encase and protect for shipment the precious skeletons. The boat was righting itself, even while slamming against the rocks.

Without McBride as bow-man the boat swung, turned end for end; they were floating backwards, the men absurdly staring out from the advancing stern, Web, without McBride to signal orders, piloting the boat stern-first down the river. But they were into deep water, moving now in the deep and fast but steady current. The rapids lay like spilled treasure in the light behind them, the water ahead of them, dark.

The girl was gone from the shore.

A coyote looked up from where it was drinking at the water's edge, saw the approaching boat, turned, trotted carefully into the bush.

They needed McBride, watched for him. A hawk circled overhead and Web could not look up at the calling hawk but rather watched the shore, saw a flock of Canada geese waddle up the bank and into tall grass. The three men, caged and almost helpless on the open flatboat, moving from side to side of the deck, stumbling around and then over the collapsed tent and needing McBride and helplessly drifting while they watched the shore, the gravel bars, the mud, the tell-tale ripping point of a snag on the water's apparently still surface.

They were watching for a corpse, on the absurdly still water, on the pond-like calm of the deep, moving water, and a pintail swimming ahead of the boat began to fake an injury; she fluttered clumsily to draw the danger away from her three ducklings; the brown, instinctual mother faked a broken wing, walked up onto the water's surface and would not go into the air; she dove, came up and faked again: and now, behind the drifting boat, the three ducklings surfaced, waiting for the female to fly, finally, to rise up into the light and circle back and join them.

The hawk called, over the layered buttes.

They drifted six miles, eight miles, staring at the sunlit morning calm, listening to the birds. And then the badlands on either side of the river were more than William Dawe could resist. He signalled Web to move the sweep, to ease the boat against the shore.

Their voices drifted ghost-like up onto the high buttes.

"You see something?" Web said. His voice across the water like a voice dreamed.

"Look at those hoodoos." Dawe's hand pointed up at the crest of a butte, to where a capstone of harder rock had resisted while the clay beneath it weathered away. The looming forehead of rock was supported by columns of clay, each column layered brown and black and grey-green and rust; and where the capstone had finally broken, begun to fragment, solitary pillars of clay stood alone, supporting great plates of stone.

"You see her?" Web said.

Dawe pretended not to hear. "Good place to prospect. Along the base of those hoodoos."

And Web: "But what about—"

"By now, Web, he's either safe ashore or gone under. But if you like, put me ashore and you go on looking and then wait—"

Web moved the sweep.

Web landed, and went ashore himself to set the sternline, and found a reason why he could not return to the boat. But now Grizzly would comprehend no English. Dawe asked him to come ashore and prospect for bones, then commanded him; Grizzly, in silence, went on cleaning the freshly caught fish that would be their next meal. Dawe explained more slowly: they were short of time, they must all work together. Grizzly might have been deaf. For McBride's sake, Dawe explained. For the memory of McBride, in honour of his sacrifice, if not for their own personal gain. And Grizzly not hearing. And Dawe, embarrassed at his own plea, or believing it; Dawe turning away to where Web stood in a foot of water, unwilling to return to the deck. Dawe raising his small, hard fists in helpless anger.

They leapt the mud, the two men, flailed into the

tall and weed-thick willows. Hardly had they moved ten yards from the boat when the mosquitoes came up in whining waves. But they would not notice the mosquitoes, Dawe and Web. They scrambled through the bushes, found a gravel-bottomed creek bed. They walked knee-deep in the water, scrambled up onto a beaver dam. Together they crossed out along the wet and whispering dam, crossed over, into the spruce and the aspen. Into and through the grove of trees.

Then Dawe paused. He touched the sweat away from his forehead, wiped inside his black hat with a red handkerchief. He indicated, with affection, the gullied and rilled and layered face of a coulee wall; with a shy, unlikely flash of smile, revealing his milk-white teeth, he motioned Web up into the rasping sun.

They moved apart and yet together, up onto the buttes that paralleled the river for as far, north and south, as the eye could see. They scrambled up from the last grass, the last few flowers, onto the flaking clay. Eagerly they climbed; they leapt to a pinnacle, they crawled, almost flat against the almost vertical slope of clay, they slid and clambered again, as if their eagerness itself must plant the bones and sprout them, out of the barren clay and rock. From seventy million years deep in the black matrix of the past, the bones must leap to light. Must loose themselves from the bentonite. Must make their finders rich and famous. The bones that must satisfy their finders.

Noontime came and Dawe did not signal a stop for dinner. They were dizzy, the two searching men, riveting their eyes on each brown knob or fragment, then looking up again to move, beholding far along the river below them the buttes and coulees multiplying themselves towards the faint horizon. And the gaze again brought back from the valley, from the naked sun, from the cumulus clouds that drifted white in the windless sky; the searching gaze brought back and sliding away through grey gullies and rills to the next outcrop, the next fragment that might be a fragment of bone; sliding away over the clumped sage and into a shadowed hole in the earth or onto a cracked rock where a grasshopper, basking in the heat, clacked into the air of a sudden, leapt down the cliffside.

And a hawk above them, calling, watching the two men.

And Grizzly, on the deck of the boat, watching the hawk that was watching the men.

Grizzly saw Dawe signal; he saw both men straighten, turn, commence the precipitous and jarring descent to the valley floor.

It was then the chinaman acted. Grizzly, who hated the wilderness, who had found in his tent one day in the mountains a bear eating the pies he had baked, the bear like a grotesque and oversized human, shaggy, stinking, unknowable, hunched over a table and eating the pies— Grizzly, who raced the bear to the wooden frame of the tent's doorway, who met in the doorway with the bear, smashed the frame, brought down the tent, and in the process both embraced and was embraced by the grizzly: a stifling, hot and terrible eternity of a moment, before they raced, neck and neck, jowl to jowl, into the dark timber.

Grizzly, who yesterday, the day before, would follow Dawe up into the coulees, rather than stay alone. When he might have been back at the river fishing for goldeyes. Grizzly, who in one day had learned a fear of the leaning, sliding cliffs above his head, the sudden and unpredictable flash of hundreds and more hundreds of bank swallows, darting and looping around his head, as if to snap the mosquitoes away from the very lids of his eyes.

Grizzly saw Dawe signal: at that moment he pushed out the two-by-ten that served as a gangplank. He dared delay no longer. He picked up the tin can containing bread and a slab of bacon, dried apples, sugar, tea, matches. He watched intently the willows, and, on the bank behind them, the saskatoon bushes, the chokecherries in blossom.

The heat of the June day brought down an aromatic and lulling odour from the balsam poplars. Grizzly went like a memory through the first bushes, away from the creek, into the wolf willows higher on shore, then into the long row of towering poplars.

The dark grey bark of the trees was furrowed, the thick ridges of bark webbing each trunk. The webbed trunks, the almost sweet odour, the patterns of shadow, seemed to hold Grizzly silent.

And then he heard the sound he had been waiting to hear. He heard a quickened hush where a bird had been chirping.

Grizzly set down the tin can and disappeared back to the river.

7. *Skunked*

Dawe sat down on a folding canvas stool not to

33

rest but to bring his field notes up to date. He wrote, to exacerbate himself with his own doubt: *Didn't find, in all those tons of debris, one fragment of fossil that was worth collecting, after a mere slip of an Indian girl, walking ignorantly along, reaching down with her eyes shut, picked up a piece of the dental battery of a hadrosaur.* And then, rereading what he had written, he was surprised at his own generosity. And then, holding the field book on his knee like a baby, a child, he recognized, understood, admitted that this, finally, might be his way of communicating with his unborn descendants, with the wife to whom he could not speak but upon whom he intended to father those descendants of the renowned if momentarily unknown Dawe dynasty. He might, it struck him, as the boat had struck the boulder, speak to her, to them, to himself, not only of the day's activities but also of the ambitions that drove him, the anxieties that obsessed his barren nights, the immaterial thoughts that shaped themselves against his headlong hurry. *I despise words*, he wrote; he stared at the sentence, enjoying it. Writing it down had freed him, in some way he did not fully comprehend. *Had a dream last night*, he wrote. Not intending to add what the dream had been, that in the night with death a mere accident, as much a whim of rock and water as was life itself, he had dozed into a wakeful sleep; a fantasy had assaulted him while he lay helpless on his back on the deck of the flatboat. And he added: *You and a lover met at your cottage on Georgian Bay. He invited you in swimming. You saw a snake in the water and panicked and drowned.* Dawe thinking: I'm losing hold

34

of myself, too much time in the sun today, running in the dark last night when I should have ordered the boat ashore. And he wrote, carefully, deliberately to conclude the paragraph with a mere statement of fact and reason: *No sign of my bow-man or my maps.*

Web, eating while he worked, had set the boat in motion; he refused to clear the deck, to set up the tent, as if to prove by the disarray that he had hastened to seek the missing man. And yet for all his, Web's, haste and deliberation, it was Dawe who glanced up, the boat rounding a bend hardly 200 yards below the spot where they had stopped, and saw Claude McBride.

Dawe turned his head to attract Web's attention.

"Godall fuckingmighty," Web said.

"There is no God," Dawe said.

Claude McBride was downriver a half mile or more, seated in what they took to be a rowboat. Dawe, holding his right knee steady, scribbled: *McBride. Found. In a rowboat. In Range 22, Township 33, I would guess, not having my maps immediately available.*

McBride was sitting in what appeared to be a boat, sitting stock still as if he might have been fishing, except that he had neither oars nor a fishing pole. He had somehow got himself onto a gravel bar, in the middle of the river, and he was sitting alone, not lifting a hand, not making a sound, the water swirling past him as if he might himself have been an island, a boulder deposited there twelve thousand years earlier by the advancing and retreating ice.

Now it was Web who said: "Look."

"I see," Dawe said.

They drifted slowly; they had something like twenty minutes in which to contemplate the object and goal of their accidental quest. But even then, granted the preposterous sluggishness of time, they were slow to recognize McBride's condition.

Dawe thinking: How much more of this? Ninety days, if all goes without a hitch and I'm lucky as well. If a miracle occurs. Ninety days and nights to the end of the season. Time enough in which to drift another 150 miles, in which to hike through thousands of acres of coulees, and over buttes, and up dry creek beds. Looking and looking . . . *Daweosaurus magnicristatus* . . . the lost bones . . . the dead creatures immortalizing the mortal man. The bones as crazy and obscure as my own . . .

"Kee-rist on a crutch," Web said, "the goddamn thing is a pig trough."

Slowly Dawe recognized, realized, why he had felt uneasy at the sight of the rowboat; McBride was sitting in what looked like a long wooden box.

McBride put one leg over the side of the trough and gave a push, his leg flashing white, out of the water. That easily, he was afloat: his trough began to swing out into the current, in front of the flatboat, into deeper water where the two might move together. Except that now the current was carrying the trough as fast as it carried the boat: and McBride, awkwardly, hastily, began to paddle with one hand, trying to control the small craft that might have been a comic imitation of the larger one. His hand came out of the water, suddenly and indecently white.

And Dawe, watching, noticing the white hand,

the white leg, went forward to lean on the two short posts that were intended to contain the forward sweep. "What in hell are you *wearing*?" he shouted.

McBride tried to stand up without overturning his craft.

He was naked, except that he was not naked but dabbed and smeared from head to foot with mud.

It was Web who shouted now, calling from the stern sweep to the bow to tell Dawe: "The asshole is naked as a jaybird."

"Could you avoid hitting that gravel bar?" Dawe said. "Even if it spoils your record."

Dawe in momentary resignation thinking: This is what I come upon, discover, when I should be unearthing skeletons to grace the museums of the civilized world. Mudman. Madmen. Claude McBride is worse than Weber, and Weber is as bad as they come. There must be some factor in my life that makes me seek out only those disasters that will be total. Commencing with a task that is guaranteed to be impossible, I hire one crew member who gets sick at the sight of water, another who cannot keep his balance when the deck is motionless. The originating specimen— And he wrote quickly, staving off the words that swarmed into his mind, *He is safe and sound*; and he shoved the pencil and field book into his pockets.

"How did you get here?" Web yelled.

The mouth formed the word, the sound followed: "Swam."

"Seven miles? Eight miles?"

"Guess so." McBride grinning now, gingerly sitting down.

"Bullshit," Web said.

"Couldn't see to land," McBride said. Almost softly, across the water. "Couldn't seem to hit anything but rocks or mudbanks. Rocks were too slippery. Everytime I caught at something along a mudbank, the mud came down on top of me. So I swam."

McBride paddled with both hands, the trough not seeming to respond at all. But then Web recognized that he, McBride, was not paddling to bring the trough closer, but rather to stay away, to stay ahead.

"Hang on," Web shouted. "In a minute or two I can throw you a line—"

And then McBride was into a windward position and the first faint odour hit the men on the flatboat. The stink hit them.

Dawe reeled away from the forward posts, caught at his nose.

"Holy—" Web said. "Skunk piss."

"I *know*," Dawe yelled. And then: "Skunks don't stink by pissing, Web." And then again: "How—" Towards McBride. Dawe unable to choke out the words: That total incompetent, that stubble-jumper that fool—The one damned thing he can do is find the current, the channel in a river, as if he sniffs it out, smells it—no, not that—hears it, by God; outside of that he can't tie his shoes, or if he is able to do so has never done it, he can't comb his hair, or if he can, won't, he can't feed himself, for if he did our deck would be cleaner for his marksmanship and his hunger. And now, grief and woe, we can't possibly bring him on board—

"What *happened*?" Dawe shouted, gasped.

"I got pissed on. By a skunk."

"Did it steal your clothes, McBride?"

"No sir."

"Well where *are* your clothes, McBride? God forbid that anyone in this ragtail outfit should own two pairs of anything—"

And McBride, not even surprised at the question, the tone: "Pulling me down, sir. Had to get out of them or drown."

Dawe, who could not swim, was silent; Web, who could not swim.

"After just about drowning," McBride said. His voice so matter of fact, so unconcerned, the others hated him. "There in the mud--skunk hit me. Couldn't breathe; simply couldn't breathe the air. Then the mosquitoes. Then the sun."

And Dawe, hating both the man's incompetence and his survival: "How *did* you get *pissed on*, McBride?"

"The skunk was under the trough, sir. I was just about all in. I was done for. I thought to myself, it's all over but the crying. I have a family, sir." McBride going on now, repeating himself because he sensed that Dawe did not understand what it was he was trying to say: "Wife and family. Kids to support. . . . I hit the whirlpool, just before I saw the trough. Don't know how I made it, sir. Total mystery to me. . . . I saw the trough, thought it was a rowboat, went to crawl under. To get warm, maybe. . . . Don't know how I made it, Mr. Dawe. Just started in under, on my belly, hauling myself over the mud."

McBride paddling automatically now, his long, awkward arms strangely white to the elbows, his face and hair hardly more than a blob of mud.

"And the skunk, with its kittens, was under there

ahead of me. Lucky I can see now, sir. Heard of a boy who went blind. . . . For the first while I just lay there in the mud by the trough, wondering if I could see. Felt the sun coming up. Couldn't see it. Felt the mosquitoes. . . , I'm a married man. . . . "

Dawe not wanting to listen. Dawe thinking: This should be the cataclysm and the end and instead it's the mere beginning. Whirlpools and rocks and drowned men talking of home and no bones in the vast, empty grave we've contrived to enter.

And Web, his usual, godawful attempt at humour as usual failing: "A man could get hurt here."

And Grizzly coming out of the tent with a tin plate of cold, greasy chunks of fried fish.

8. *"You got till sun-up."*

McBride drifting: McBride, floating beside, behind, ahead of the flatboat, could smell nothing but skunk. He put on the shirt that Web found for him, the trousers that were Web's only extra pair, the too large boots that were Web's only extra pair. But soon he dabbed mud over the shirt and trousers; he could taste skunk on his tongue, feel it on his vaguely burning and mudplastered, cool, warm, skin. The sun soaked into the caking mud and warmed him and then, warm, relaxing, he caught again the first and terrifying odour. The smell began to usurp his sense of hearing; for him there were no birds singing on the shore, rocks gave no sound to the water; and he the guide.

Let the trough drift too close to the flatboat and he was motioned away; let it drift too far away and Web was shouting, Dawe signalling. And he, Mc-

Bride, indulged them, using the small paddle Web had sawn from a plank. But they would not be assured, ever: even Grizzly looked uneasy for those few minutes while the trough bumped against a cutbank, McBride replenishing his supply of mud. But he pushed off again, sat hunched, dabbing the mud onto his arms and shoulders, onto his face, onto his knees and thighs and testicles. He glanced up long enough to indicate a ripple that to him betrayed a rock. He motioned Web to avoid a snag, to commence a crossing. And he slouched again, bent, dabbing into the flow of mud that buried his borrowed boots in the trough's bottom.

It was after nine o'clock when they stopped. They pulled in at the first house they'd seen since leaving the sawmill where the boat was built.

The unexpected house was of stone: set well back from the shore on a patch of bald prairie, it was both of this world and alien; the stone was as brown as ironstone, like a layer chipped out of a nearby butte; and yet the clothes hanging on a line, the curtains in the small windows, bespoke a domesticity of women rather than a camp of men. Dawe wrote, nostalgic for a moment: *There is a wife here. How can she endure the silence?* And he closed the field book, slipped it into a pocket of his dusty flannel trousers.

The rancher's wife had seen or heard them land; she came down to the shore carrying an empty pail, pretending to come to fetch water; but her hair was newly combed. Hardly had they exchanged greetings when she was asking if they'd had supper, the loneliness rising in her voice, the eagerness to talk: and Grizzly understood this time, a table set with chinaware and glass, food prepared in a kitchen, served on a table; and not just remarks passed, oaths idly sworn, orders given and received, but the grace of conversation; and children, wondering, silent in the presence of visitors; and a woman's hands in their midst. And Dawe not saying it: she is as lonesome as my wife must be.

The woman called a name up the low bank. She called inland to her husband.

Then, accidentally, while speaking, the lone woman turned from the hunchbacked figure who seemed to speak for the group. Pleased by the travellers who had come to her shore, she was smiling; softly, kindly, she smiled, her work-worn face, it too, remembering ease and the quiet of an evening's talk, a last cup of coffee, and voices eased into laughter; and she turned her head, for no reason, or to show her trust, or to let them see the profile that was younger than her sun-worn face: and she saw the man coming out of the mud.

McBride, the one among all those travellers who dreamed insistently of home. Who did not want his name on a crate of bones, or the kick of adventure in the pit of his stomach. . . . Or those nights when footsteps whispered in the dark and lifted his head from his cot, set his heart pounding. . . . He wanted his children and his wife.

He was a farmer, and maybe did not think of the mud on his body any more than he thought of his skin and considered it something other than himself. But the lone woman, facing the three odd men, saw the man behind her, the man caked in mud from his feet into his hair, his body like an alligator's; she saw him step from his trough and into the willows. And it was not the smell that came with him that made her hesitate; she knew the smell of skunk. It was the man himself, coming formless out of the mud. Onto the land. The mud, the grey mud, cold, reptilian, come sliding into the yellow-green flame of the shore's willows.

The mud, sloughing from his body like skin from bones, even while he emerged.

She went towards him.

The woman, after her moment's hesitation, went towards McBride, reaching, speaking —

And the voice behind her: "Mary."

She stopped.

"Mary," the voice repeated.

She was calm. She was gracious. One hand, she discovered, held a pail; ridiculously she was holding an empty pail in an outstretched hand.

Her husband was a huge man, stout, black-bearded; he'd come down off the patch of dry prairie wearing rubber boots. He took the pail from his wife's hand. He glowered at McBride:

"You keep your goddamned hands to yourself."

McBride silent.

The rancher's wife looking again at the man caked in mud, starting to speak: she turned and walked, began to run, up the path towards the stone house. She went up the path and was gone.

"Guess you boys are hungry," the rancher said.

"Guess so," Web said.

"Guess you better eat then—before you shove off."

"Boat's leaking," Web said. "Got to pump it out."

"You boys better mosey on down your river."

The rancher combed his fingers through his black beard, stared not at Web or McBride but at Dawe now; at Dawe's black beard, the small, misshapen body.

"You got till sun-up."

Anna Dawe

It was not *Web* I appreciated at first, but *Claude McBride*. In the western yarn those men were trying to tell each other, he was the only one with the ability to become a hero, the wisdom not to. Home was a word he understood, and heroes cannot afford that understanding. Which meant he must become the fool among those fools.

Or so I would assume, from reading the field notes: and I allow, generously, for my father's weariness at the end of a long day, for his sinking ambitions. . . . Action and voice: how strange they should have so little connection. Or is there any at all, any familiar knock at the closed door, between the occurrence and the most exact telling? That I should have left home, determined to set straight the record — fifty-six years after the event — is part of my folly.

The woman in the ranch house on that riverbank

I was like that woman. Except that my fortress, my prison, was on the shore of Georgian Bay, and ships not flatboats came by in the night, ore carriers, grain boats, freighters with crews as unknown to me as were those four men to that woman with the preposterous name, Mary. And the man who protected my honour from human decency was not a husband but a father. An absent father. And when the stranger came to my shore, he, my father, was that stranger. There are no truths, only correspondences.

45

9. McBride Builds an Ark

McBride slept in the roll of burlap that was to be used, along with the plaster of paris they no longer had in adequate supply, to wrap the skeletons of dinosaurs. He did not bother to take the mud out of the bottom of the trough; he piled the burlap in on top and slept somewhere in the burlap, on or in the mud, hardly knowing his own body from the soft and comforting earth. In his sleeping, in the reverie that came with his not being quite able to sleep, he began to see in the skunk a sign. As he had in the sight of the child lying in the earth at Tail Creek. As he did in the woman, now, too, who had tried to tell him something.

The sign's import came to him slowly, forced itself against his denial. And he slept then, to deny the reverie, the prodigy, the omen; and he dreamed that he crawled willingly in under the overturned trough with the mother skunk and her smell was no longer acrid, ammoniacal, but rather burning sweet to his burning nose, sweetly overpowering.

McBride awakened the others in the morning, before even Grizzly was up and cooking. He called them out of their warm bedrolls, Dawe shivering, disappearing in his black hat and long underwear into the willows, returning sullen, indicating with a toss of his hat and head the stone house: Dawe indicating a man in a window of the towered house, a black-bearded man holding a double-barrelled shotgun down towards the river and the boat, protecting not only the woman inside but the house, the garden, the land itself. It was not Dawe but McBride who got them onto the river; the tent, ballooning in

46

a morning breeze, passed ephemeral and small beneath the guarded stone house, the guarded woman.

Web tried both to steer and to work the pump, for now it was Dawe's notion they must float as far as the mouth of Ghostpine Creek before pulling the boat to make repairs. The pig trough, swept out of a farmer's yard by the spring flood, lost by children trying to use it as a canoe, danced a slow, mimicking dance around what seemed a sinking boat. A lone deer, a whitetail, drinking, dared watch the spectacle, watched the two objects approach, begin to slide away, before it turned and leapt up what seemed an unscalable slope, vanished inland behind a ridge.

They came to a ferry crossing. If the ferryman was in his small white house on shore, he was either asleep or chose not to show himself. The empty ferry, a white shape riding on its own ghostly reflection—square-decked, painted and scrubbed, lines neatly coiled—was the perfected river craft of which the flatboat was an unpainted and leaking imitation. Web and Grizzly, whispering, lifted the ferry's cable over their tent while the boat slipped under. McBride too passed by the ferry without speaking; McBride aware that here a road or trail came down from the flatlands above, found a way into and through the coulees and out the other side.

Little more than an hour later they were approaching the mouth of the Ghostpine; the creek's long valley, deep, grotesque, beautiful, swung and then locked into view. It penetrated the buttes and walls of the Red Deer, led back towards the north and west from which the men had come; and they'd hardly found a place where McBride might work when Dawe and Web, eating as they walked, struck out to prospect for a few miles up into the creek's valley.

McBride, with Grizzly helping, set to work as if he must in ten hours of declining sunlight create against the night not merely a watertight hull but some strange ark with which to venture out onto the dry prairies. Together the two men shifted the cargo to one end of the deck, then, with a line and the small capstan, winched the other onto the mud, then onto rollers made of poplar logs. McBride, with his farmer's ingenuity and the help of the silent Grizzly, not only moved the bow ashore but with the aid of more logs, used as blocks and levers, raised it up as if he would make the boat not only float but fly.

Grizzly, bent over a campfire, heated a pot of tar. The smell of the melting tar commingled with the stink of the skunk, the odour of burlap and oakum. And McBride, wading to his knees in the mud with oakum and a chisel and a wooden mallet, began to calk the weakened and leaking seams. Eager to finish the job, he asked Grizzly to begin tarring the calked seams; but Grizzly hated the mud as much as he hated the flies and mosquitoes that came to his sweating body, the tar and oakum that burned his face and eyes, and he would not squat down on his knees beside, under, the raised hull.

All afternoon McBride worked in the cooling, stinking mud around and under the boat, limping, kneeling in silt and muddied water, his torso and arms and face burning in the sun and the fumes of the tar; he would make the boat more absolutely watertight than the carpenters at the sawmill had ever made it: he strove, pounding and bracing and tarring in the heat and the stench, the sun a furnace in the blank prairie sky.

Grizzly threw down planks on the mud and walked out to carry to McBride a drink of water, more oakum, another bucket of tar. But he would not touch the boat itself, as if to touch it would be to violate the mystery upon which his life depended. McBride knew, sensed, Grizzly's quiet hatred of the mosquitoes and the mud; and he knew also that no temptation he could offer would make Grizzly abandon the boat; and McBride then, helped by his silent helper, wrapped himself in burlap against the sun, splattered tar onto the burlap and the caked mud that covered his body, and onto his body itself, seeming to seal and preserve himself into a watertight conviction that he would never again travel at the mercy of water; and he sealed the boat, the boat raised up on its crib, as if it too must be saved, forever delivered ashore.

At suppertime it was the turn of the others—Dawe and Web as well as Grizzly—to stay away from the boat. Dawe and Web came back dusty and weary from the coulees; they had once again found tons of fragments, and once again they had found nothing that might be worth wrapping and carrying and shipping by boat and wagon and train another two thousand miles to the civilized world. McBride warned them off from the flatboat, ordered them away when they approached, and they sat useless and spent on the shore while Grizzly prepared, over a new campfire, a meal of bacon and beans and tea; Grizzly took a tin cup and tin plate out onto the plank walkway he had made, and McBride, humming to himself of a sudden, did not so much as glance away from his oakum and his mallet long enough to nod a thank you.

Grizzly too had made his choice, and McBride was totally alone; and yet he was as free as his own hands could make him, his feet in the mud working their way towards dry land. He would build those others a boat that even they, in their incompetence and ignorance, could not sink. But he would never again touch anything that looked like a sweep or an oar.

And the night towards which he had worked all day came down. Big Web, timidly, climbed aboard the tilted and marooned boat and took three bedrolls and three mosquito bars out of the comically tilted tent. He and Dawe and Grizzly went downriver and slept in the darkness under a huge, twisted poplar, avoiding the bonfire that gave McBride enough light so that he might go on calking and patching.

Singing now, singing as he worked, his face and hands blackened with tar, his burlap clothing dirtied black, McBride was hardly to be distinguished from his shadow as he moved back and forth in the mud, around and under the hull. Singing to himself, he secured the ark for whatever it was that Dawe proposed to rescue from that dry oblivion. The black and glossy seams made a coffer of the spruce planks, a fools' ark against whatever calamity Dawe's ambition prophesied for all of them. Let them do whatever they would, in their insistent folly, the boat would not betray them. Not if he, McBride, had pronounced it ready; he had kept his part of the bargain, he would abandon no one. And when Grizzly fell asleep, and then Web too, and then even Dawe, Claude McBride went on limping, sweating, working, burning, singing, between the bonfire on the dry shore and the boat suspended on its delicate web of logs and driftwood over the mud, away from the pushing river. And only McBride was dreaming: and he dreamed his sleeping children, his quarter-section of rich black dirt, his greening wheat, his stabled horses, his Saturday drive to town, his Sunday rest, his garden behind his house, his peas in blossom in the morning sun, his potatoes swelling in the dark earth, his set table, his blessed food; he dreamed his wife's surprise at the figure returned from the water's edge, her cry of joy and her quick embrace—

10. *Graverobbers Beware*

"McBride isn't here," Web repeated.

"I heard you," Dawe said. "Go find him."

"He's not on the boat," Web explained, still not persuaded that Dawe had grasped the import of what was being said. "He's not on shore where the fire was. He rolled up a lot of that stinking burlap we intend to wrap dinosaurs in, but he isn't inside."

"Go *find* him," Dawe said.

"I'm asking you where I'm supposed to find him."

"He went back upriver."

"Why would he do that?" Web said. "He probably went downstream to Drumheller to get himself drunk."

"But he didn't take his trough," Dawe said. "He

51

burned the damned thing—you can see the parts that wouldn't burn over there where the fire was."

"He's faking," Web said.

"McBride got scared, the poor son of a bitch. He walked back upstream to that ferry we came by. He'll cross over and head for the ranch to get himself a horse. Or at least a nod of recognition. Go up there and tell him I'll double his wages."

"What if I don't come back myself?" Web said.

Dawe was sitting in his bedroll on the ground under the poplar: he burst into his short and unamused laugh. "You will." Dawe, who did not laugh easily. "I wouldn't let it worry me if I were you, Web."

And Web, even while he struck out, yelling back over his shoulder: "Forward my mail, Dawe—" Web tripping over a rock-like piece of petrified wood, picking himself up. Wrong way, but what's the difference, we do everything else the wrong way in this haywire outfit. Web stumbling through the willows, through the mosquitoes, into and through a drying creek bed, balancing on a fallen tree trunk, then hanging onto sage and thistle on the sudden bare slopes that threatened to launch him into the swirling water. No wonder that squaw gave up; she'd have to be crazier than Dawe himself, Dawe sticking to a coulee wall like a fly on a ceiling. Web murderous in his own mind: I'm a free man, fuck off, Dawe. Out into the open, running across an iron-hard flat. Sure I'll find McBride. Without him I'm captain and crew of the *S.S. Titanic*; with him I can borrow a crowbait myself, the two of us ride on back to wherever we made the mistake of coming from.

Web stumbling, stopping.

The ferryboat was standing still in the middle of the river. Riding on its own reflection, it was hung on its cable, standing still.

Web, hardly able to find his breath, tried to shout. He did not hear his own voice, but a figure straightened from amidships on the ferry:

"You just keep going."

Web trying to catch his breath, trying to speak.

"You cross this river, you going to cross it by swimming."

Web strode into the water; he signalled with his right hand for the ferry to come in to shore. The water touched his knees, reached his crotch.

"I might be shack-happy," the ferryman said, his voice high-pitched. "But I ain't that damned shack-happy."

"You see a man," Web said, "dressed in burlap ... covered in tar...limping ... smeared in mud—"

"You damned tootin' I saw him. Talked to him too."

"I got to catch him," Web said.

"He crossed the river. You ain't going to cross the river."

"I'll break your fucking skull into about thirteen pieces."

"You keep talking," the ferryman said, his voice high, old.

"I'll kick your ass right up between your eyebrows, I got to find that man, catch up to him, hold on to him, or I'm dead."

"Didn't that squaw tell you what I told her to tell you?"

Web tried to step backwards.

"Well let *me* tell you." The old man stooped forward, moved across the deck towards the water that separated him from Web. "Dead is dead. We don't need none of you damned graverobbers down here."

Web, in trying to step backwards, felt himself sinking into the mud, felt the current pushing him off balance."

"Dead is dead," the old ferryman shouted.

Web struck out with both arms, trying to stay afloat. He went down, into the green and brown of the sun-streaked water, then he fought his way up, kicking against the mud and the gravel. He burst out of the water, he put out his arms to catch himself, to hold himself away from the depth; then his hands melted back into the planed surface, he was gagging on water, his boots lifting up from under him, walking into the air; in four feet of water he was driving his head against the mud, his constricting fingers finding some weeds, holding on; he was holding on to the weeds and the current that had pushed him under lifted against the rooted figure, raised the head, Web's face, out of the water. His boots struck gravel and he was scrambling ashore, dripping, cold, in the morning sun.

"You ain't going to fool me," the ferryman said.

Web, coughing the water out of his lungs, dropping the weeds onto the dry prairie grass.

"And you tell that damned squaw—when I tell her to deliver a message I want it delivered."

Web turned away from the old man with the woman's voice. That was what had made him angry, reckless: the voice that wasn't the voice of a man with whom he could argue, bargain, reason. He turned onto and then away from the prairie trail, the dusty and rutted trail that served as and was a road; and then he was walking in the mauve blooms of bergamot, the radiant yellow of buffalo beans; he was loping through patches of wolf willow that rustled against his wet and dusty boots, the odour of sage rich and curative in his living nostrils. Downriver he ran, rehearsing: the ferryman wouldn't allow me to cross, demand my rights, you go talk to the bastard, Dawe, tell him who you are, what we're doing here; in daylight the trip is free, as decreed and provided by the Province of Alberta; the old highpockets skin-flint wouldn't take me over, I begged him, explained, goddamn laws posted right there on the wheelhouse or whatever you call the wheelhouse on a boat that can't go anywhere but back and forth across 100 yards of river; we need McBride or we're done for, dead and gone, lost, kiboshed and kaput; need my boots too; need to get that Indian woman hog-tied and corralled into leaving us alone or give her McBride's job and stop pretending; need to by Jesus get into those dinosaur beds, yes sir, into bed with a dinosaur, where the corpses rolled in the spring floods, drifted into lagoons, swelled and busted in the same sun and settled into the shelving sand: open the goddamn graves and rob them and get us on out the other end of this calamity—

He staggered up beside the boat at Ghostpine Creek.

Dawe and Grizzly, with a sledge hammer and an axe, were knocking at the blocks and cribbing under the flatboat's bow.

"Where is he?" Dawe said.

And Web saw then: they couldn't get the boat to

slide back into the water. He wanted to smile but his anger wouldn't let him. "Where is that dead-assed stubble-jumper?" Dawe said, puffing, swinging: "Couldn't even do *this* right." And Web looked at the boat marooned on shore, Grizzly pounding with the sledge hammer as if to fix the boat to the earth, Dawe swinging the axe as if he intended most of all to cut off one of his own legs. And then he, Web, softly:

"I found no sign of McBride."

The speech that was in his throat, caught in his throat.

And Dawe went on, shamelessly unskilled, aiming the back of the axe's head at something caught somewhere between the boat's hull and the mud beneath it.

"Hide nor hair," Web said; elaborating his lie, delighting in the ambiguity of his discovery, the skeleton that was not the beast, not even the bones of the sought beast but the chemical replacement of what had been the bones: "Didn't find hide nor hair—"

And Dawe was stooped over, swinging the axe backwards, and Web saw then, saw through and beyond the anger in his own mind and smiled: for the hump on his, Dawe's, back was like a butte, the land itself stirred into destruction, come hunching down to the shore to destroy the boat. Dawe stooping there by the water, remote, dry, sculptured down to naked clay, a landscape unto himself, different from and indifferent to all the real and natural world. Web remembering: Touch the hump of a hunchback and you'll have a lifetime of good luck.

Dawe, sweating, puffing: "You didn't goddamn look, did you, Web?"

"Oh yuh." Web turning to Grizzly, jerking the sledge hammer out of the chinaman's hands. "Gone is gone."

Web raised up the sledge over his right shoulder, up into the sun, the raised hammer raising him; he felt the sweet spasm of his belly's recoiling muscles, his tightening arms, his whole tall weight transferred off the earth and into the falling hammer. He swung again. He swung again.

Not with Web's violence but with a gentle and even unnoticed start the boat was moving; Web was beginning to strike again, trying to stop the raised hammer on nothing but air as the boat went sliding back into the river, the stern end pushing out a square wave against the current; and the boat was suddenly free of the shore, escaping, leaving the three men on the shore.

And Web was plunging into the water, leaping and splashing into the water up to his armpits, catching a line that was fastened to the capstan.

And Dawe, wiping the sweat from his brow, straightening his wide-brimmed black hat over his black hair: "Let's get this boat *moving*, Web. We'll pick up a new man in Drumheller." And adding: "You sure as fuck took your time."

11. *Field Notes*

Dawe writing: *Departed Ghostpine late morning, the valley a mile wide here, the Badlands 400 feet deep, ridged, pinnacled, some of the buttes cut down to tables, the tableland cut down to sugarloaves and knolls. And up above us on the high plains, open prairie now, the wind blowing. A dry prairie wind comes scorching down into the valley. The Edmonton beds soon to run out, and I have not yet got a full crew, let alone any fossils:*

And then he had not only to tell his field book what he was not telling his remaining crew but must torture himself, punish himself as well, with the recollected details from the flat, bland, exhilarating government reports he had read while seated in front of the west-facing windows in the splendid comfort of the cottage that was not a cottage but a mansion, the mansion that was not his own but his wife's, the visiting friends not his either but his wife's and they not driven to go out into obscurity to seek fame or into the desolation of sand and clay to answer impossible questions with a carload lot of bones:

While Barnum Brown, in these Edmonton deposits, found the skull of a horned dinosaur unknown to science; while Charles Sternberg, here above Drumheller, found loose saurian bones piled up like driftwood:

Dawe writing those flat, bland, exhilarating statements because he did not envy, at that hour at least, at that moment, his wife's friends or even the man, the lover, he imagined for her as the excuse for his own not being her lover:

He was jealous rather of a found armful of bones of *Ornithomimus*, fragments of turtle shells, the teeth of Upper Cretaceous fish: and he wrote, in a fit of love and jealousy that should have been a poet's, scrawled in a quiet prose that hardly contained his only enduring passion, his furious need to dispossess and recover:

On Michichi Creek, the mouth of which we shall shortly approach and pass, he, Sternberg—carefully counting that man's obscene conquests against his own fine impotence—found on August 13, 1912, the exposed tibia (itself measuring three feet in length) of what proved to be the complete skeleton of Trachodon, *a duck-billed, herbivorous dinosaur, a specimen measuring nine feet ten inches in height at the hips, thirty-two feet in length; the entire and magnificent specimen excavated and packed and loaded in six weeks: and found another and larger if less complete specimen above the ferry which we passed in silence and humiliation, the skull alone four feet in length: found a third specimen larger than either of the preceding, the head, however, not present, the femur or thighbone of the hind limb of that headless individual measuring four feet six inches—And I have not yet scratched the pencilled price off my new shovels.*

12. *Fugitive at the Landing*

Web leaned into the stern sweep. Grizzly, on the starboard side with a long pole, was helping Web to make the landing. They had seen, in the distance, downstream, the riverflat, the row of small miners' homes along the shore. They had stood motionless, drifting down upon the log cabins, the tarpaper shacks, the tents, the few frame houses—they had been puzzled at seeing no people and, now, as they approached the riverbank, even the dwellings, the roofs of the dwellings of those unseen people, disappeared from view, seemed to sink into the ground.

Web eased the craft towards the steep bank, into the underbrush that leaned out rank and summer-green over the water. Grizzly raised up the pole to slow their approach. Web touched a thumb and forefinger to his new blond mustache, Web thinking: This is the last town. The last town we see before the end of the season and payday. He was too close now to stop from their stopping, close to whatever he thought of as the world he had abandoned: bars, pool halls, beds with clean linen, restaurants where meals were selected from a menu and served by waitresses who might be teased, admired, propositioned even. Yes, a woman: Web thinking: The last town, and this by God a good one, the toughest, wildest boom town east of the Great Divide: women to be sought out and found not in back streets or flea-bag hotels but in the comfort of whorehouses—*hoo*-er house, he thought, letting his mouth hold the first syllable like a swoon.

Dawe went to the bow and took a line in his hands. Even he would try to help. He intended to leap ashore and tie up, would have: he was crouched, poised, ready to make his awkward jump, to uncoil and pounce.

And then a figure hurtled out of the bushes, onto the deck of the flatboat. Leapt and struck Dawe down, as if his own intended action had been reversed and had come from the shore and down onto his crouched self.

The man was wearing bedroom slippers on his bare feet. Dawe saw that. The stranger reached down his pale, delicate fingers, helped Dawe to stand, then looked up to the top of the high cutbank.

Above the boat, on the breaking edge of the bank, three men appeared, one of them carrying a pickaxe.

Three coalminers, their faces smeared black with coal-dust and yet pale; they were wearing their caps and their lamps as if it must be dark night instead of mid-afternoon; as if they must be figures escaped from the far underground, from the bowels of the earth itself.

One of the miners yelled down to the boat: "Hold him."

Web had picked up a coil of line; he broke it into two halves, swung one half over his head, tossed the long line up towards the top of the bank: "You hold us," he said.

The fugitive spoke to Dawe: "Where're you guys headed?"

Dawe whispering: "Downriver."

The fugitive insistent, demanding: "Downriver *where*?"

And Dawe hesitating. Dawe with his new man aboard, the new man located, shanghaied, kidnapped; and all he needed was a few words, the necessary lure, the irresistible temptation. Dawe himself tempted by his own vision of himself, of his new life: "The prairie. The Badlands. The bonebeds."

The stranger, the fugitive, again and simply: "*Where*?"

Dawe with the man he had stopped to find already on board; Dawe eager to signal Web to push off, drift on: and the necessary word failing him—

Above them the leader of the miners raised the pickaxe.

The fugitive, looking away from Dawe, saw the arm, the raised weapon that should have been the persuasive sign for which Dawe could find no word.

He looked again at Dawe, looked at the black beard, the eyes black under the broad-brimmed hat, the humped back.

"Thank you," he said.

And he leapt.

The fugitive flung his body into the underbrush and was gone; and above him the leader of the miners saw the motion, hurled the pickaxe. Then the three miners, drunk, shouting, together plunged over the edge of the bank, themselves disappeared into the underbrush.

Grizzly came out of the tent. He had taken off his apron in the middle of the day, and that too seemed unlikely to Web; Web leading the way now, leaping, flailing his way into the blur of branches and leaves. They were not prepared; they had not intended so quickly to go ashore, unwashed, wearing dirty clothes. Web had not wanted to shave, in order to set his new-sprouted mustache into sharp juxtaposition against his burnt face; Dawe and Grizzly had had no time even to change socks. They pushed their way into the dark underbrush, searching. "Hey," Web shouted, at a loss to give a name to the man he sought.

They climbed the almost vertical mudbank. They pushed their way, almost fell, out of the underbrush; and they were on a gravel street, the street thronged with women and children.

At that moment a band struck up a march.

Anna Dawe

They had, in spite of themselves, those three men, the chinaman, Web, Dawe, arrived at a version of civilization; even if that version found its rank and symmetry in a marching band made up of boys too young and men too old to be soldiers. In the anchorage of that town, the bosses sweetly advocating order, work, taxes, tradition, family, possession of house and wife, the gypsy men who dug the coal were in fact some of them gypsies, displaced citizens from the feudal corners of Europe, from dying empires elsewhere. Men as inured to violence as they were to the rules that shaped it.

My father, there, in that brand-new town, found the word fugitive, and lovingly underlined it in his notes. Good God, how men do love their symbols. Each of them, every man, symbolic of another. Fugitive. From all the women in the world, no doubt. Those men, expeditionary, running upon their own running, had found in error what McBride, presumably, in his running backwards, sought: a cluster of wives and children. Women as desperately alone, there together on that civilized street, as the woman in her stony ranch house. As sadly alone as the women who, as cloistered as nuns, ran the half-dozen whorehouses on the lower side of town: unless those women were happy.

13. *Woman in Green*

Web saw, guessed, that the straggling group of women and children were part of a rough column, lifting up banners. Between the marchers and the band were six men, dressed in black; they carried on their shoulders a black coffin that bore on its side in gold lettering, a period misplaced, the inscription: JOHN BARLEYCORN DEAD. AS A DINO-SAUR.

Web began to strut in time with the music. Dawe and Grizzly stayed with him; together, and yet not quite, they entered downtown Drumheller, Web leading, Dawe almost at his side, Grizzly following behind as if by some optical illusion he walked faster than the other two and yet could not keep up. They walked along one wooden sidewalk, then another and another, hearing their footsteps hollow beneath their boots, the false fronts of the wooden buildings rising higher, the raw and unpainted new lumber of the new buildings too bright, glaring in the after-noon sun.

Dawe thinking: this is the last town we have to look at before we get there. And a good riddance. Damn civilization. Web, silent, resolved in his strut-ting secrecy to have one last blowout, one final and absolute falling-in-the-streets fling. Grizzly, carrying in one hand a shopping list written in Chinese char-acters.

They had come to the wide veranda of the Wal-dorf Hotel. The members of the band marched past the wooden steps and stopped. Web saw the banners in column behind him: in red needlework, WOM-EN'S CHRISTIAN TEMPERANCE UNION.

Two small girls holding up to his eyes: TEMPER-ANCE AND MORAL REFORM SOCIETY: BAN THE BAR. Two old women: ANTI-TREATING LEAGUE: JULY 1: FOR GOD AND COUNTRY.

The pallbearers went up the steps and put down the coffin on the veranda. The marchers and the crowd formed into a half-circle around the band, around the steps, the coffin; someone was counting aloud, one, two, three:

"Onward, temp'rance soldiers,
Bravely onward go—"

And while the band played, while the trumpet's notes cut high into the cloudless day, two of the pall-bearers, with solemnity and deliberation, lifted off one half of the lid of the coffin, then the other half. People strained forward and then tried to back away when pushed from behind. Web could not resist: he forced his way into the open space at the foot of the steps. A clown had appeared, a clown with a huge red nose; he placed a large book in Web's hands and Web held the book and waited.

A woman sat up in the coffin.

Perhaps she moved slowly, but to Web her ap-pearance was sudden, totally new; only after she'd already appeared did she seem to move, as if awak-ening from a dream, new to the light, her dark jour-ney over: she was black-haired and pale, so pale she might never have known the sun, fish-pale as if she had drifted up from a depth so deep the light had not there penetrated down. And yet she was young, mysteriously young, in her long green dress and her earth-black hair.

Two pallbearers helped her to her feet. She stepped from the coffin, staring, staring out over the hushed crowd, her eyes fixed on a sight so far distant she might never be recalled to this gravel street, these wooden sidewalks.

She was at the top of the stairs when she raised her hands. Her voice when she spoke was unexpectedly strong, a deep and trembling voice that excited the gathering miners. And she said to them: "Wine is a mocker. Strong drink is raging. And whosoever is deceived thereby is not wise."

The miners were gathering from everywhere, from bars and pool halls and gambling dens, coming to hear her. And the tiny group of women and children clung to each other, clung to their banners, stared around them at the men whom they, with this secret figure, were calling out of unknown places.

"Temperance," the woman said. And still she had not looked at the crowd, at the men gathering below her, but stared at some knowledge beyond them that they might never possess. "Restraint. Restraint of the self in behaviour. Restraint of the self in ambition. Restraint of the self in desire and in anything that will inflame desire." Her gaze fell like a sword upon the watching men. "And strong drink is raging."

A great and tearing lump of drought worked in Web's throat. All the prairie winds of his growing up awakened in his mind, the dust so dry in his nostrils it stung like alkali, the dust pinching shut his eyes, binding his throat. A lifetime of trying to grow free on these open prairies. And yet he must be closer to that woman; he eased his way between two listeners, stepped across the open space.

"Denial," the woman said. Her green eyes raging. "Hunger teaches the perfection of appetite. Separation teaches the perfection of union. Absence teaches the perfection of love. If you cannot *deny* yourself--"

She moved now, she was moving, lithe as a dancer, moving from side to side on the veranda, talking and talking. Web did not so much listen as let his eyes possess her. "Temperance," she said. "Yes," he answered. Not hearing himself speak. And he was thinking of the madness of Dawe, the fanatical silence of Grizzly. The wisdom of McBride, gone back out of folly to abstention and home. And he let his eyes go into the dancing form, surrendered to the deep and trembling voice.

"The pledge." Only distantly did he hear the tolling voice, the sought and finally found words. "The pledge."

Behind him the crowd was stirring, awakened; a blurred sound of assent, at once inarticulate and growing, gave itself back to the dark melody of her harangue. The tall woman in green, her green eyes caressing, burning, talked now of lost families, lost homes. Talked of dissembling pleasures. Summonsed before the hushed men their wicked nights and secret longings, the stumbling body, the abused and abusing flesh.

"Prohibition, nearly one year ago, was passed by the plebiscite vote of the vast majority of the voters of this fair province. And yet in this one town, time stands still. In this one town the boozing goes on." She was speaking to the gathered miners, those hundreds of men from all the pits of Europe, come here to endure the bitter winter cold, the extreme heat of summer; believing all the while they would, by their underground venturing, recover, redeem, save from the nightmare past their almost forgotten children, their dreamed women. She paraded out of their secret recollections the squandered money that might have bought the unbought ticket, recalled the wasted days, the forsaken children, the abandoned wives. "And yet in this one town, here, *time stands still*. The gamblers take your money. The sickness of the bawdyhouse destroys your limbs. The stink of liquor eats your lives. *Because you will not take the pledge*—"

And now the drunk clown was sober; he took the book from Web's hands, carried it to the veranda steps. He held the opened book in one hand, pointed with the other:

"You can be first to sign."

"Who?" Web said.

"You. There. The tall man with his hands in his pockets."

Someone snickered.

Web wouldn't move; he took his hands out of his pockets, put them back in.

The young woman in green, moving across the veranda, stopped behind the open coffin. "Let him be first," she said. And she too pointed at Web.

Web might have resisted. He planned to resist; he wanted her to come down the stairs, to single him out, to lead him away.

But the woman in green bent down over the coffin, reached in.

They strained forward; all the waiting men

strained forward to see. And Web thinking: It's the fugitive she has in there. He surrendered to her. She's gone and saved the lucky bastard. Saved him from us, from the boat, from Deadlodge Canyon. He's stolen all.

And then she lifted out of the coffin a skeleton. She raised up a cardboard, life-sized, Halloween skeleton; but it might have been her lover. She raised it and held it before the crowd, touched with one hand the hips to slow the swinging legs.

She looked to Web.

And she had been there in that coffin with him, that vital and caring woman with her voice of love and pain; with her dead lover she had lain, beyond the intemperate living; and betrayed even there, betrayed by a lover who could not be worthy of her love, she had come back from death to deceive them into wisdom.

They surged forward, the gathered men. They left the women and children standing ignored, together, banners raised into place; they surged towards that lone woman's fiery wish, her call.

Web held the lead; he was first to the blank book's ceremony; pushing, elbowing for the privilege, he signed; he made of his name an outcry, a promise, a moment, a fate; he took oath that he would ever and always practise denial of the self, the necessary restraint, the absolute of temperance; he would make of his thirst a first virtue, parched as the desert and pure; he would embrace chastity, faith, love, fatherhood, wife, family.

He turned away to be praised.

He saw they were gone, Dawe and Grizzly; they had slipped away without either signing or waiting, had fled into the See-Saw Bar while the crowd of men made ample room.

And Web went in to rescue them.

14. *The See-Saw Bar: A Prophecy*

The woman, America, without looking up from Dawe's hand: "Did you hurt him, Fekete?" Her voice at once reprimanding, affectionate.

"Wouldn't hurt him for the world."

"Where'd you find him, Fekete?" America, while she spoke, letting her knee, her hip, touch Dawe.

Fekete alone at the next table: "Cornered him down there by that raft some assholes are using to run the river with."

The woman, more aggressive, her voice deeper: "What did you do to him, you son of a bitch, Fekete?"

"All I did was haul him back onto that raft. But Toth and Bobo held him flat on the deck with his arms stretched out." Fekete trying to excuse himself even while he boasted: "Had to search him. . . . Took this here pickaxe. . . . another one. . . . pinned that goddamned crooked dealer's hands to that deck."

Fekete's audience appreciative, amused.

Web feeling himself begin to get sick: "Did you hurt him?"

Everyone near Fekete's table burst into laughter. Someone offered Web a glass of whisky. "Looks like you need a snort there, Slim."

Web's eyes adjusting. Now he could make out not

only the shadows of Dawe and Grizzly but the woman tracing with the first finger of her right hand the fate in Dawe's right palm. She was blonde, he saw; her blonde hair was arranged to look like a turban and at first he'd been deceived.

Web accepting the glass, emptying it.

"Like a bad seam of coal." Fekete turning to acknowledge his audience, the lamp on his miner's cap catching a ray of light. "Kept hitting a lot of bone."

Web bending down over Dawe's back, touching it: "You hear that, Dawe? Those bastards crippled—"

Dawe lifting his glass of whisky in his left hand. "He'll just have to live with being crippled, won't he, Web?" And then, without waiting for a response: "This, madame, is still another member of my illustrious crew."

The fortune teller, ignoring Web, bent again to Dawe's hand, touched it again: "You are a man who gambles everything."

And Fekete again: "And loses."

Dawe swelling with irritation, with pride: "Of course I gamble everything. But do I win?"

"You will have a disaster."

"But do I *win*, damnit."

The woman was silent. She traced the lines, the mounts, of Dawe's outstretched hand:

"If you hold back nothing . . . "

"If I——"

" . . . hold back nothing," she repeated.

"That's easy enough."

She glanced at him in surprise.

And Web, noticing: "What's in store for his illustrious crew?"

71

The fortune teller staring for a moment at Web's belt buckle, glancing up from his embossed silver buckle to his new mustache: she smiled at Web.

Web in his mind: You need two men now, Dawe.

And America: "I'll be right with you."

"What's this?" Dawe said. Dawe pointing into the palm of his own hand. He pinched the flesh at the base of his thumb.

"The mount of Venus. Strangely strong for a man of such reckless ambition." She touched the callus at the base of his first finger.

"I use a pickaxe," Dawe explained.

Fekete, interrupting again: "Hey. You sure as hell ain't a *miner*, are you?"

"No," Dawe said. "But I sure as hell need to hire one."

"I'll drink to that," Web said.

Dawe glancing up suddenly: "I only want you to know this expedition departs tomorrow morning at six, with or *without* you, Web." And then, across the room to the bartender: "Bring us another round."

"I'll get this," Web said. "Make it doubles."

America signalled to Fekete and Fekete stood up, picked up his glass of beer and his pickaxe and joined Dawe's table.

Dawe explaining that he needed a man, beginning to explain, and Fekete interrupting:

"Grimlich."

America shook her head of heaped hair. Web saw the glitter of jewelry in her hair, the stars, the crescent moon.

"Grimlich can't go," America said.

Fekete banged down a fist on the table: "Perfect

for the job. Works with dynamite. Just bam and the job's done."

The bartender was setting drinks on the table.

And Dawe responding to Fekete's enthusiasm, the vision of the task completed in a single boom, a shower of dust and the bones exposed:

"Requires a special breed of man. A brave man. A fool. An adventurer who can endure the boredom of flies and heat. Searching all day in vain. Digging a grave to get the corpse *out*."

And he laughed, and Fekete laughed too.

"A man who knows water," Dawe went on. "Yes, he should know water, these two I've got with me can't tell water from land."

"Not a worry in the world." Fekete, laughing, still. "Where's this Grimlich on July first? Pumping water out of the ABC Mine. Drilling his holes. Tamping in the powder, sealing in the detonator, jumping his ass around the nearest corner."

"Fair enough and a blessing." Dawe finishing his glass. "And by God yes, on top of it all, beyond everything, it calls for an act of will: He's got to *want* to find the bones of a dinosaur."

Fekete beaming, his coal-blackened face beaming: he lifted the pickaxe and slammed it down, drove its point into the middle of the table: "There's one man in the whole damned valley who fits the bill. Tell him America—no, tell him *Fekete*—sent you."

Dawe no longer able to contain himself: "Grizzly, you go do your shopping. Web, you hold the fort here, in case this Grimlich fellow is on his way up while I'm heading down. And stay away from the women."

"What women?" Web said.

73

And America to Fekete: "Fekete, love; show him how to get there."

That suddenly, Dawe was gone. Grizzly and Fekete were gone.

Web sat down in Dawe's chair, bent his face to the stars and the crescent moon in America's hair. America, too, bending closer:

"What's your job on this immortal expedition?"

"You tell me," Web said.

"I might tell the truth," she said.

Web shrugging: "I run this show. I'm the brawn *and* the brains behind this thing. That guy Dawe couldn't find his own asshole with both hands—"

America nodding.

Web nodding: "Without me we'd be sitting on a rock some place upriver, waiting for the next spring runoff. I could sail that raft on the morning dew if I had to." And he added:

"What did you say is in store for me?"

America lifted his right hand off her thigh, turned it over and touched a finger delicately to the palm, delicately traced a pattern. She wore many rings; there were stars, moons, on her fingers:

"Jeee-*zuz*," Web said, "look at that."

"You don't like water," she said.

"Hate it," he said. "I hate water. Let's have another drink."

"But you can't leave it," she said.

"Leave any damned time I feel like it."

"And you've met a woman," America said.

"You bet your life I have."

"Yes," America said. "She's going to take you on a long trip."

74

Web, smiling, affecting a smile.

America, quiet for a moment, touching his hand, the palm worn shiny from his working with a sweep:

"Says here you've got the courage of a fool. And a fool's luck."

"Don't know what that means," Web said; Web laughing.

America, touching, running her finger down the palm of his hand:

"Says here you're a good dancer."

"Damned line is mistaken. I'm perfect."

"Let's you and me go dance."

"Let's have another drink."

"Let's do both," America said. "Before Fekete gets back."

Anna Dawe

And if the stories I heard fifty-six years later in Drumheller were true, then the two women were sisters, and the blonde was not really named America —nor for that matter was she blonde—and the dark-haired woman in green had a name I didn't bother to write down and so lost from memory. But they were sisters and made a good deal of money between them and lived together and never married; and when the penitentiary was built in their town, on the federal premise that hell should be constructed in hell, it was those two sisters who established inside the penitentiary a library and a lounge.

Web would divide his women into virgins and whores. And yet it was the virgin who seduced him into his fine mockery of virtue; and I suspect he never went to bed with his whore at all.

Total and absurd male that he was, he assumed, like a male author, an omniscience that was not ever his, a scheme that was not ever there. Holding the past in contempt, he dared foretell for himself not so much a future as an orgasm.

But we women take our time.

15. *In Which Web Goes Dancing*

The caller calling: "Swing like thunder."

The accordian player seemed to pull himself apart, explode; the man with the bones clacked them, the black ivory sticks disappearing into their own motion. And then everyone was dancing again: they were sweating, their eyes burning from sweat and smoke, and someone was opening windows and Web, pushing, turning, lifting, carried his whole square over in front of an opened window; he felt his old exuberant self, a self he remembered vaguely at first and then clearly as it was before he met Dawe; but Dawe was gone now, Grizzly was gone, he need never see either of them again; he had recognized his old self and the only nagging presence was Fekete, his back to the wall beside the window, his hands in pockets; Fekete watching either Web or America: "Ladies bow and gents bow under," the caller was calling, "Hug 'em up tight and swing like thunder"; and Web was swinging his partner, he and another man together swung their partners, the women's feet lifting up off the floor, their bodies lifting straight out and parallel with the cornstarch-sprinkled floor; and Web knew that Fekete was watching; Fekete watching either America's lifted skirt or Web himself; and then as they swung Web felt his hold slipping, felt his hands slide from the other man's wrists, the arms that were locked under the women's raised arms and around the women's backs letting to; and then people were shouting, screaming: Web spun around and then around again, alone, caught himself; he was standing at the open window without a partner.

America was gone. Web's partner was gone, had vanished. She had flown through the open window.

People crowded against the window frame, trying to see her. Web realized he couldn't get to the window because of the crowd. His partner gone, dreaming her lithe body, carefully now, vaguely proud of the logic that guided him, he went to the fire door, pushed at the bar and stepped outside.

It was dark. He could not remember, imagine, where the night had come from. And outside in the dark an enveloping stillness gave shape to the strange buildings. He could not guess where he was, could not imagine how he'd got to that place. He waited; he thought he was holding his breath and heard himself breathing.

"America," he whispered. No answer. "America," he whispered. Somewhere, almost beside him, someone was pissing on the ground. A woman stood up out of the shadows and brushed at her skirt, went into the hall. Web felt the night's chill on his sweating back, his sweating face. He called the name again and got no answer. He went carefully into the long, dark alley.

16. *The ABC Mine: Dawe's Descent*

It was the horses that gave Dawe his only assurance. He went down the shaft of the ABC Mine, rode down in the clanking iron cage pretending he was not astonished or afraid or ignorant, wondering what combination of luck and folly had brought him to this gut-wrenching fall. Descending from the arid plain to the lost sea he had expected the thick seams of coal. But not the pit ponies. They were alive. Buried deeper than the bones he had so far sought, destined never again to see the light of day, they were alive; they were eating, shitting, pissing, working, resting. And they might have been like horses of the sun, except that in the darkness they were each of them going blind. Which in itself was, for those horses, only a harmless way of becoming crippled, sight being deemed irrelevant to their simple and solitary chores.

The man who had been bedding them down led Dawe, Dawe himself almost blind in the small light of his miner's carbide lamp, along the tracks, deeper into the labyrinth; the pit props ticked off the distance; the rooms were cavities of darkness.

They found Grimlich, his face black as the coal, at a high face where coal was to be won; Grimlich signalled them to retreat. And they did so, running out into a crosscut; they were running when the powder, somewhere behind them, exploded. Coal dust came down onto their shoulders, came racing into their beamed light.

Grimlich, hunched into a reptilian stride, moving with the dust itself, came into the crosscut. He was oddly, muscularly, stout; Dawe did not see the small, silent chinaman who followed him until both men had sat down, eased themselves down against, seemingly into, the wall of coal.

Neither Grimlich nor the chinaman would speak. They sat in silence; they sat listening, and Dawe listened too, now, to the slightest hint of cracking in the coal around him. He had believed their own silence would be matched by the silence of the earth; he began to believe instead that the roof of coal must any moment crash down upon their heads.

The dim light on Grimlich's cap came up at Dawe's face.

"What do you want?"

Dawe had waited so long he burst out: "Fekete sent me."

Grimlich tilted his dust-covered face, the light on his cap cutting a dim arc across the roof of coal. He laughed, his laughter echoing down the black tunnel. Then he said: "What do you want me to blow up?"

And Dawe, knowing he had found the man he needed, began not just to talk but to argue, exhort, propound:

Time. They were losing time. The season was too short to begin with, and they'd spent too long building the boat. No luck in the Ghostpine coulees. They would have to head for Deadlodge Canyon and gamble all on finding what they wanted in the greatest bonebeds of all. Even if Brown and Sternberg had already been there and had raped them, had measured their take in boxcar loads. And then to unearth the inevitable finds in a hurry to get them wrapped and loaded onto the boat—

"Whatever your wages are," Dawe said, interrupting his own peroration, "I'll double them."

Grimlich turned to his partner. "How long has it been?"

"Twelve minutes."

Grimlich stood up and signalled Dawe and the hostler to follow. He led them into the room he had just blown. The face of sub-bituminous coal was tumbled into a heap of chunks that looked freshly washed in the light from the men's caps. Grimlich kicked his way into the heaped coal, bent, lifted up to Dawe's face a lump of coal and on it the imprint of a fragment of a leaf. He bent and found another, then another: the outlined leaves were delicate, symmetrical, daintily fine.

And Dawe only now realizing the truth of what he already knew: here, once, there were green branches of fig trees. Sycamores. Magnolias. A delta and a swamp. On this spot: *Ornithomimus* snapping fruit from the high branches, digging for the eggs of other dinosaurs. Carnivorous *Tyrannosaurus rex* stalking *Saurolophus*; dinosaur stalking dinosaur; the quiet, day-long hunt, the sudden murderous lunge, the huge and bone-cracking jaws finding at last the solid-crested skull, the long tails flailing the water a frothed red. The carcass-eaters, hunched and silent, awaiting their turn. Daring to move now.

Grimlich's protruding blue eyes swam into the pool of light in front of Dawe's face. The stout man's eyes opened, then narrowed slowly to slits in the coal-blackened head.

"You go tell Fekete," Grimlich said, "I want him to bring his goddamned pity here himself. I want to ram a stick of powder up his horny ass and seal it in with his own balls and use his prick as a fuse."

"Come and talk—"

"I don't come nowhere. I stay right here. The weather is fine here. I sleep right here. Wong Lee brings in some food. I eat right here. When something happens here, I make it happen—"

Dawe started to argue. Dawe might have persisted, might have tried once more to persuade him to return——

Grimlich interrupting, speaking softly his agony: "I killed my . . . trying to dynamite . . . a fishing hole . . . "

He, Grimlich, helpless, standing beside the heap of broken coal, pointing down: "You go—"

And Dawe not arguing. Dawe resigned. Grimlich, pointing not up but down, and Dawe realizing: He and his crew must float downriver, float down below this geological level to still an earlier age; somewhere to the south and east they would fall below this Edmonton level, onto a bed of fossils buried a few million years before this one came into being, or flourished, or itself perished, itself was buried into oblivion.

"And you're a greenhorn," Grimlick added. He signalled his partner to bring the breast auger. The little chinaman picked up the eight-foot auger by its double handle and followed after: Dawe watching the spot where the figure of Grimlich had turned into darkness.

The hostler shook his head, lifted up his right hand, tapped his own skull with his middle finger. Dawe didn't move. The hostler, to make a final and irrefutable argument to Dawe, pointed over his own shoulder at his own back: "Broke my spine in here."

Dawe himself rooted to the spot, the hostler turning to follow the iron tracks to his stabled horses, to the shaft—

"Wait."

Grimlich reappeared. Grimlich approaching not the departing hostler but Dawe. "Here." With one motion he ripped open the wooden box he was carrying under his left arm. "You'll have to get your own batteries. But take some detonators and a few sticks of black powder. . . . Do your own murdering."

17. *Scarlet Lady Sound Asleep*

And Web, in the dark, hearing the sound of a piano: in the night, somewhere, someone was playing a piano with one finger, Web hushed into listening. Clear on the bell-like silence of the night, the sound guided him. He had wandered through bars, a pool hall, through greasy spoons and gambling joints. He had spent his last cent. He had gone on wandering, searching for the missing woman, the frail and eloquent creature who slipped laughing from his arms in their moment of dancing; and long ago now he had wandered downriver from the town, beyond the last street lamp: in the dark, stopping, then walking again, he let the music guide him.

A river of stars flowed on the blue night, gave edge to the valley's walls. Against the outline of a heap of slack he saw a house, the square house oddly peaceful against the shadowed hump of coal. He had found it: The music, note by note, set free into the darkness, led him to the wedge of light, to the token light, the open door. He did not knock.

Fekete and Bobo and Toth, in their miners' clothes, were playing cards at a dining-room table. Beyond the table, a man and a woman were seated in easy chairs facing each other across a small Oriental rug, sipping drinks and chatting. The upright piano stood against the far wall of the large room;

on top of the piano were a half dozen framed photographs, a bouquet of buffalo beans and shooting stars.

The young man, the boy alone, seated on the piano stool, was picking out keys as if each was a discovery, precious, recovered from an immeasurable silence. Web, in the doorway, listened, then carefully let the screen door close onto his heel; he tiptoed in his boots across the room.

The boy at the piano was overweight, almost fat; sweat poured down his neck, staining the back of his new blue workshirt. His mop of brown hair was curly; Web, glancing down to find the hidden face, saw the boy's fat forearms. Only his fingers were thin; the pale, thin fingers moved in mimicry over the keys, sometimes touching one into sound.

Two men came through a door to the left of the piano. "Okay, Tune," one of them said. "It's paid for."

The boy not responding.

And then Web, enjoying the strange music of the dancing fingers, the simple sound: "Let him finish."

"We're going to make a miner out of him."

And Web, guessing, making a lucky guess, the ceremony and occasion revealed in an idle comment: "It's his cherry."

The boy glanced up, his instant's glance away from the keys meeting Web's; and Web saw the young face, pale enough to have come from underground. Web surprised:

"You a *coal*miner?"

The boy nodded.

The two men went to a second door to order

drinks. They turned their backs: and Web's good intention, in that space, began to corrupt itself into a scheme: the boy was a miner, knew how to dig, swing a pick, move earth and rock

Web saying: "Listen."

The boy playing, bending over the keys, sweating.

"You don't have to take that shit from nobody."

"It's not the work," the boy said. "I can stand the work. It's the dark down there. I can't get used to it."

A middle-aged woman came into the room with a tray of drinks. Smiling, motherly, she put down two glasses on the piano top: "Goddamnit, Tune, play something happy for a change." She laughed, winked at Web: "You're not a coalminer."

Web, watching the motion of her breasts as she mixed whisky and water on her tray:

"I'm in the reptile business."

"You're a snake in the grass."

"Is this the famous hospitality of Mary Roper's famous *hoo*-er house?"

"It ain't a church."

He tried to pinch her as she dodged away; then she was greeting the newcomers who were jostling in at the door; she went to bring in more drinks, to bring in more girls.

And Web yielded to the scheme that had now begun to compound itself into a growing enterprise, a devious plot. In the crowd, yes, he would take the boy's place. It was paid for, damnit. Never leave food on your plate; people are starving in China. He in the boy's place if not predicament, the boy, by the same gesture, acknowledging that one good turn de-

85

serves another. Any attempt to debate the point had already yielded to the impulse: yes, by his sacrificing himself, it was clear enough, the boy might be delivered. And paradoxically, he too: Web.

"It's a blue-eyed cinch of a job," Web said. "You sit on your ass on a boat in the sunshine, floating down the river."

Tune went on playing.

"Don't know how you stand these slave-drivers," Web said. "Fellow named Dawe is our boss. Comical little jigger, sniffs at every rock he sees like a dog looking for a place to pee."

The boy laughed.

"Damnedest guy, doesn't know up from down. Good money for watching the sun shine. Plenty to eat. Riding round on the water like you're on a holiday . . . with pay. Now and then just for fun you dodge through some bad water, catch a dinosaur by the tail. . . . " He let his voice trail off, almost persuaded by his own reckless argument. "It's not bad," he added.

He looked away at the three men inside the front door, quietly playing cards while around them a dozen people talked, joked, paired off and disappeared through the door beside the piano. Web thinking: domestic bliss. Right here with me in its midst; I'm a natural homebody. Web finding a chair and pulling it close to the piano: he sat down, a drink in his hand: he began to relax to the music.

But hardly had he dozed off when young Tune stopped playing. Web blinked. He tried to think where he was: he looked at the drawn blinds, remembered: he saw the sun was pressing in from outside, the light pushing in, the heat pushing in.

Tune stood up, awkwardly stretched his fat, young body, then of a sudden turned towards the mysterious door—

"Wait," Web said.

The boy stopped.

Web could find no adequate words. Then he said: "Well I mean — Denial, Tune. . . . Hunger teaches—"

Tune looked puzzled. Then he turned again, abruptly, went in through the door.

And Web could not resist: he moved onto the piano stool. He put out his brown hands over the keys, looking at the keys, his fingers. Then he risked it; he touched a key. The one note sounded flat, broken, against the realm of Tune's playing. He was looking again at his hands, at the black and white keys, when Tune came back through the door—

"Good Christ," Web said. "That's a new record."

Tune gestured back through the door. "Number seven. She's asleep. I can't wake her."

And then Web was on his feet, explaining: "Listen, Tune. I'll tell you. The sun is coming up. The flatboat leaves at six. Dawe. That's the guy. Little hunchback. You walk right up to him and say: 'A fellow named Web sent me.' The job will be yours. You'll have the summer of your life."

And then Web wheeled away from the piano, lumbered, charged at the closed door, swung it open and stepped through and closed it and was reading numbers in the coaldust- and semen-smelling hall: three, four, five . . .

He opened the door; he stood stock still.

He had found her, after all; unexpectedly he had found her when he had forgotten that he was searching: she lay on her right side, apparently naked under a single white sheet on the narrow bed, her left eye blackened, the left side of her face skinned and swollen and crusted. She lay in an oddly broken position, away from the light that pressed through the small and blind-drawn window behind her.

Awkwardly, not expecting to, he said: "America?"

Outside, beyond the hallway, beyond the closed door, Tune was playing again. Web wanted to rush out into the huge parlour and strangle him, push and shove and wrestle the piano onto the floor, kick it into silence.

"America," he said.

She stirred, groaned softly, in her sleep.

Web went to the one chair in the small room, sat down, began to unlace his boots. He kicked the first one across the floor and under the bed, sent the second one after it. He pulled off his socks, stood up to unbuckle his belt; and he dropped his pants and kicked them away too, stripped off his underwear with one motion of his right hand.

He looked down at his limp prick.

He sat down on the chair, flinched away from the chair's bottom, sat down again.

Again he tried: "America?"

The sleeping, broken figure did not stir.

And Web thinking: Goddamn, like those pictures on the piano. The fucking bride. The first night. That piano player keeps on like that, I'll go out there and club him over the head with a bone-on. If I get one. Opportunity of a lifetime. He bent towards the bed, touched the white sheet, then let it go. Ought to get old Mary in here for a tussle; goddamn, I couldn't slop the hogs without doing it wrong. Leave it to me. If I had it to do over again I'd just roll in the mud, wallow in the mud. Sleep. Stuffy hot in here; I could sleep myself right now. Studying the stars in America's messed-up hair. With his left hand brushing at his new mustache, with his right giving himself an encouraging tug. "Hey, America. Look what we got here." But the woman went on sleeping. Too many worries; they're turning me into a corpse. What's the word for fucking a corpse? Don't believe it. Unless it's warm. Had to do it over again I'd be a boar. He stood up, pulled his flesh free of the chair, unbuttoned his shirt and decided to keep it on. He noticed the long, narrow mirror on the back of the closed door. Like those pictures: those wedding pictures, the smiling brides, the proud husbands. He stood in front of the mirror: eighth wonder of the world, he told himself. After *Tyrannosaurus rex*—

And then he noticed: the music had stopped. He froze still, waited. Waited for the footsteps to come into the hall.

Silence. He could not resist; he opened the door to peek out. Only silence, in the long, narrow, hallway.

"Goddamn," he said, aloud. "He's going to do it."

"Do what?" America said.

Web, closing the door, slammed up against his own image.

"Ouch."

"When?"

America, sleepily, having seen the man standing

in his cap, in his shirt, seeing him slap himself
against the mirror, the image disappearing as he hit,
the prick vanishing into the prick; America, awakened, shouting:

"Help! Help! Help!"

18. *Tune Hires On*

The boy's first confusion, on coming out of the
tent where he'd gone to spread his bedroll on a canvas camp cot, was in seeing, ahead of them, the man
in a skiff trying to work his way out of the mouth of
the Rosebud River, flailing the water with two oars.

"What's he doing?" Tune said.

"That's my captain and my pilot," Dawe said.
"He's trying to row a boat."

"Maybe he wants his bedroll."

Tune had seen—smelled—the bedroll in the tent,
had noticed the almost empty dufflebag, the ragged
suitcoat.

"He can't bear the thought of the three of us floating down the river without him."

Tune unwilling to believe the flow of words erupt-
ing from the strange man who earlier greeted him
with stubborn silence. For he, Tune, had arrived
running at the high edge of the riverbank where the
boat was tied up, a bedroll under one arm, a pillow-
case in one hand containing all his belongings, and
the hunchback had wordlessly, aggressively, signalled
him aboard, had gone ashore himself to free the
headline, the sternline.

"Shouldn't we help him?"

"How would you recommend we direct this disaster at him?" Dawe said. "I see Web has gone and found me another veteran of the deep seas."

Young Tune, silenced, turning away, testing his weight against the motion of the river beneath his boots. He went to help Grizzly carry boxes and sacks of groceries from the open deck into the tent.

A number of miners, on their way to work a Sunday shift, were straggling down to the shore across the river from the tipple of the Old Star Mine. Six men stepped into a big rowboat; two of them began to pull slowly towards the opposite shore. They were entering the main current as the flatboat approached and all the men in the rowboat waved, smiled, were amused at the unlikely dawn spectacle gliding past them and down the river with the flow of water. Not one of them recognized Tune or spoke; as if the illusion they perceived and were amused by was not likely to give back an answer.

The second boatload was setting out as Web zigzagged the skiff up alongside the flatboat. Tune went secretly to the bow, crawling carefully under the lines that supported the tent. He was too heavy, awkward; he almost fell overboard as he lurched, attempted to reach out to take the line that Web was about to offer and then didn't, Web shouting instead:

"Gave that fortunate woman the screwing of her life." He gestured out at the water, the sky. "That wasn't enough for her, hell no. She starts yelling at the top of her lungs: 'More. More. More.' "

"Anybody hear her?" Tune said. Tune out in the open, taking the line now.

"Since that piano was quiet, they did. If you'd stuck around I'd have been all right. Hardly had time to get my boots out from under the bed when those three pimp card players were in the room and trying to jump me."

"Oh those—" Tune said. "Fekete and Bobo and Toth. They keep order."

"A good time to tell me."

"They'd kill you rather than look at you."

"They might kill some people, Tune." Web stopping to catch his breath, to master or fake his anger. "I knocked the first one so goddamned flat it'll take a ton of ice to bring him to. He'll be out stiff into the middle of next week. I was so goddamned mean and mad I was scared of myself."

Dawe, now, couldn't resist; he stepped from where he was watching the shore and bent down over Web in the skiff:

"How come you got all that shoe polish on your balls?"

"Huh? Oh. That." Web pretending to look surprised. "Sheer bad luck. Sheer absolute bad luck." He still had not quite caught his breath. "I was in the process of crawling through a small window. That goddamned woman of Tune's, she pulls the window down on top of me. I still had a cast-iron hard-on, so I couldn't wiggle through. Should have pole-vaulted, I suppose, but I thought of that too late. This bouncer bangs up a quart of stove blacking under me—and even then—if I hadn't stopped to fuck it I'd have been home free."

"Then he let you escape?" Tune said.

"I guess he let me escape. I kicked half his teeth

right down his throat. And you keep jabbering, Tune, I'll do the same for you."

"I thought maybe the third bouncer got hurt too," Dawe said.

"Couldn't tell you. He followed me down to the riverbank. Last I saw of him he was sticking head-first in the mud at the bottom of the river, his feet kicking in the air."

"Should have left your boots and stole his," Tune said.

"Too big for me. All those bouncers were huge men. And five or six more were coming to their rescue."

"And they were big men too," Dawe said. "But I'm still wondering how you're going to get clean."

"Don't plan to get clean. Stove blacking makes your prick grow. Ever look at a stovepipe?"

Web talking himself out of his anger, or his fear, beginning to laugh: "Here," he said. He tossed his boots and his pants onto the deck of the flatboat. "Sheee-*yit*," he added.

And young Tune: "Let me row that skiff ashore and leave it and I'll swim back."

"Do it myself," Web said. "But I guess I ought to take charge here."

Anna Dawe

*They had entered their last leisure. That it looked
for an hour, for a day, like paradise, was no one's
fault, I suppose. They were only men, and in that
paradisal drifting they invented their mythologies of
the flesh. Web, dreaming grandly, boasted his trivial
failure into magnificent success. He was the great
and raging beast of those wide prairies; he could
dream himself as irresistible and endless as the
wind; the disguised king; the world-long lover. . . ,
Young Tune, out of the coalmine and into the day's
sunlight, felt the white fat melting from his body.
Under Web's direction, or in the hearing of Web's
illusion, he could dare to become what Web, if not
my father, would have called a man. My father was
busy being as silent as Web was full of sound.*

*William Dawe dreamed more savagely. In that
paradisal ride he recalled my mother, her cottage,
the steel-blue reaches of Georgian Bay, the rising of
thunder from the mysterious west, the gathering of
visitors, polite, successful, polished, secure: the men
and women who carried into the mock-wilderness of
the lake for a weekend the mock-drama of their
mock lives. He thought of those others, back east —
down east, Web would have said — and when Tune,
timidly, asked my father how he liked Drumheller,
the ironic answer was: "It was like home."*

*He was satisfied with the mere sky, the fall of
water that was the river's flow, the edge of mud. And
he was more than satisfied; he was genuinely
pleased, when, below Willow Creek, he saw in the
riverbank a black, crumbling seam of coal.*

They had sailed under the Edmonton formation. My restless father then could lie down and surrender to a stretch of seventy miles of river where he would find no dinosaur skeletons, the Bearpaw shales intervening for a few million years between two bonebeds. He was permissibly at ease, able to listen to the birds or the creaking of the boat, able to dream his ferocious and secret dream.

And he wrote in his field book, after the date, after the hour of that sighting, not of why he had so far found nothing or of what he believed he would find: he wrote, both deceiving and not deceiving himself: We are sailing off the map. *And he added, oddly:* No sign of the woman.

19. *Crew Bathing*

South and east they drifted. On their port side long stretches of prairie sloped undulating and ocean-green, under the white and exploded puffs of cumulus cloud, sloped and fell from the horizon to the water's edge; on their starboard, under the blue outline of the Wintering Hills, the low buttes were humped far back from the water, across a flood plain where ranchers ran cattle. Sandbars replaced the gravel bars; the water was low enough, but no more, to make the channel easy to read; the wind, at last, was in the right quarter.

Web and Tune working together, the chinaman both watching and helping, managed to hoist a crude sail. They worked easily in the sun, Web showing his apprentice how to move the oar-like sweep, how to recognize the main channel, where to begin a crossing to avoid a snag, a shallows, a rapids. Grizzly helped and watched and listened, then split a few sticks of wood, working on the deck beside his stove, then once again got out his fishing rod, began again to fish for goldeyes.

They stopped early, in the bend where Crawling Valley joins the valley of the Red Deer. They tied up below the dry creek bed, above the shallows, a stand of trees providing shelter and firewood and a toilet. And Dawe, having landed, did not explore the valley for traces of fossilized oysters and ammonites of the Bearpaw Sea; instead, slowly, quietly, he tramped inland and up onto high ground; so that he might look for miles across the bald prairie.

He was back to the boat in time for a supper of fresh beef and garden peas and new potatoes. They spent the evening loafing, all of them relieved to be away from the town. Grizzly let young Tune use his fishing gear, something he had done for no one before. As the air cooled, Web, to the amusement of the others, suggested they go into the river and bathe: he stripped down, in the evening sunlight, found a bar of soap, leapt into the waist-deep water and waded out to where it was shallower still. He turned his back to the boat and began to scrub at his private parts.

"Don't know if you're getting clean," Tune called, "but the river is getting dirtier."

"Scrubbing up after is half the fun," Web said, rubbing with exaggerated vigour. "Watch me hit one of those geese."

A flock of twenty or so Canada geese, having waddled down from the tall grass on the shore, were daring to swim near the boat; they only abandoned their curiosity when Tune and Grizzly plunged into the water, shivering, shouting. Then, to the surprise of his crew, Dawe himself stripped down naked, for the first time exposing his crippled body: he too leapt into the water.

They swam or bathed or splashed for half an hour, joked, lay on the deck getting warm; and having warmed themselves they returned to the water, again scaring the geese away. Somewhere in the trees an owl hooted and Tune, reminded that he would have to be up at five-thirty, suggested they call it a day. He was first into bed, luxuriating in the camp cot, the tent overhead, the whisper of water that gently rocked the boat - only to discover, as darkness came slowly down upon them, that he could not sleep on his first night out. Expecting silence he heard through the night the owls hooting, the coyotes howling. Strange and unknown creatures splashed into the river; birds that sounded monstrously huge dared to land on the deserted deck.

Web awakened first in the morning, saw how late it was and sang out:

> "Hands off your cocks
> and on with your socks,
> it's daylight in the swamp."

"Shut up and sleep," Dawe answered; and Web was astonished into silence, into dozing again.

They ate a leisurely breakfast of pancakes and bacon and fresh eggs and coffee, then while Grizzly did the dishes the others cast off; and Dawe, for all his long night's rest, lay in the unnaturally hot morning sun and let himself drowse, apparently free of his compulsion to seek fossils. He seemed infinitely at ease; the long hills sloped gently down, became the valley; shortgrass and tumbleweed and wolf willow gave up to his occasional fretfulness their quick bird-song, bird flight: the larks, the sparrows, the buntings, the longspurs. Daisies and brown-eyed susans bloomed down to the layered and drying mud that marked the river's steady fall. And though the water was falling the boat moved easily past Homestead Creek, past Dip Creek: until, a few miles above Bullpound, Dawe sat up from his cot abruptly, ordered Web to put him ashore on the starboard bank.

Surprised out of his own lassitude, Web lowered the sail; there was almost no wind now, except when a dust devil came out over the water and rattled the canvas.

They touched into shore. But this time Dawe did not make his awkward, unlikely leap. He hesitated. He was about to say something—perhaps to explain the impulse that had startled him awake. Instead, he leapt; hesitating even while he did so.

He picked himself up before the others could rush to his assistance. Embarrassed, testy, he said across the water: "You'll see a creek on the other side of the river. Just stop on this side and wait."

The boat was drifting away, leaving him on shore.

"Jesus," Web said to Tune and Grizzly. "About as much chance of finding a dinosaur in this stretch as there is of finding a cold beer."

Even in the middle of the river they felt the heat now. The smell of sage came across the water from land. The men on the boat, surrendering to the heat, lost interest in Dawe. While they slumped, shading their eyes against the glare of the water, the cumulus clouds in the west became one towering cloud, gathered and lifted, bloomed white and turbulent from a darkening base.

Tune was first to recognize what must be Bullpound Creek, and it too was dry. Web pointed to a green island on the facing shore; they tied up under a row of tall cottonwoods, hoping to cool off in the shade of the trees. Tune went ashore to set the sternline; he stopped to marvel at the bark of the cottonwoods, the deeply grooved trunk of each tree like the limb of an extinct reptile. The leaves of the trees were wilted, motionless. Only a pair of birds, mourning doves, moved pale brown and slate blue in the heat-laden silence of the island, their wings squeaking oddly, dryly, when they took flight.

It was near suppertime when Dawe, carrying no specimens, caught up with the boat. He had worn himself out, walking too fast in the heat; he was irritated when he came to the shore and found no place where he might easily cross the narrow channel; he continued to walk downstream, forcing his way through berry bushes, his boots scaring up butterflies from the dusty grass. He noticed a small bullsnake and, distracted for a moment from his irritation, followed, attempted to follow, its secret, reptilian way.

Almost at once he lost the snake from view. It was too quick for his eye. Distracted, he bumped into Grizzly, stooped over in a saskatoon patch. Dawe was vaguely surprised to find his cook picking berries so near mealtime.

Together they turned to go to the boat, to wade through the shallow water.

"You forgot your pail," Dawe said.

Grizzly went back to the berry patch, picked up the tin pail, while Dawe, impatient, waited.

20. *Web, Unwilling, Goes Ashore*

Web thinking: Getting blackballed wasn't enough, hell no, some mosquito'll swipe my pecker, use it as a sting. He swatted at his own bare ass, his hand coming up bloody. He cursed the swarming, singing insects and cast about him to find the catalogue. A small gust of wind brought the leaves of the cottonwoods to life, set them to whispering, rustled them. Web hoisted and buttoned his pants, picked up the Eaton's catalogue, hurried back toward the boat.

On deck he could see, through the trees, huge

clouds swelling and rising out of the west, mounting each other, clouds that were almost black but not quite, retaining an electric whiteness against their shadowing of the sun. He returned to where Grizzly and Tune were playing gin rummy on Dawe's steamer trunk. He was about to tell them to move into the tent when Dawe motioned with his right hand, then with a tilting of his head.

Web went across the deck to where Dawe was seated on his camp cot, his field book on his lap; Dawe raising his chin now, his beard, his black eyes, to indicate the moving clouds: "It's going to come down."

Web watched the looming and tumbling clouds, the roiling motion, the seething, torn edges of the rising and descending darkness. "Rain pitchforks," he said. "And hail to boot."

"Maybe just rain. At least it'll raise the water."

Web shook his head. "Hail cloud. We're right in its path." He lifted one hand, indicated the grey-white underbelly of the moving cloud, the storm within the cloud, the electric intensity.

"Go get her," Dawe said.

Web stood with his arm raised, his fingers, his hand, closing into a fist, his arm like the broken limb of a cottonwood. "Go get *who*?"

"You know damned well who."

"Jesus, Dawe—"

"That woman. That squaw of ours. You know she's out there—some place."

"Shit almighty, you don't think she's still *following* us?"

"What do you think, Web?"

"No woman can walk—"

And Web bringing his closed fist down like a club, trying to clout the air itself. Web recognizing, understanding; then not able either to recognize or to understand or to believe that William Dawe would save anyone or anything—not even himself. From himself.

Bones. Bones were more to Dawe's way of thinking about life. The carcass out on the open prairies, then the coyotes, the hawks, stripping the carcass down to bones, then the rain and the wind and the sun stripping the bones down to art and glory, the fossilized beauty that was the sole object and intent of Dawe's enduring passion. The unflushed remainder.

"You've lost your fucking mind," Web said. And then, more out of apology for what he'd said than from any shared recognition or belief—or passion— he turned to obey, to act out the requested folly:

"My slicker is in the tent," Dawe said. And added as if Web might not comprehend: "Wear it."

21. *Thunder, Lightning, and Hail*

Lightning broke in and from the sky, lacing the clouds, the clouds like precious china for an instant fractured and broken, the perfection of dark blue laced with the lesions of light. The thunder came distant, ominous. It rolled and faded. Web was gone into the rustling trees, disappeared; and at that instant a chill hit the boat; the first cool air came like a wave, washed over them; the air was transformed from hot, from stuffy and dank to something that was mysteriously, lasciviously, cool.

102

Grizzly stood up from the rummy game and went to put away his dish towels.

The first few drops of rain, large, cold, were upon them before Tune had dragged the trunk into the tent. The large drops hit hard on the deck, spat, hit dully on the tent's roof. The forked lightning, far in the west, webbed and patterned the sky, mapped the blue sky black and white; and then, in final counterpoint, struck almost on top of them, broke down onto the island, near the boat, and even while the tent was an appalling white bloated creature on the black water, on the black boat, thunder crashed; lightning burned again, out of the rising and descending clouds; and they saw the white wall moving down the low slant of the hills from the west; then it tumbled onto the trees, thrashed into the trees; then the first hailstones bounced off the deck of the boat, hit and bounced high; the lacing white hail smacked into the river and the three men turned their faces away from the kniving stones; they ducked into the tent; it was dark, of a sudden, the roar of the hailstorm caught them, the hailstones drummed themselves into a hiss on the roof of the tent, shook it; the flash of lightning showed the three men to each other; they sat now each on a cot, each of them oddly, helplessly, watching the roof of the tent:

And Tune, the labyrinth of his memory come into the air to find him, remembering the coalmine: the hole in the earth, the tunnelled dark, the smell of blasting powder. Tune on the cot's edge remembering the whorehouse: his pale, fat body contradicting the quick beauty of his hands; and the miners, seeing his rare hands, had led him, taken him and his unwillingness, to the only piano they knew. The hailstones like piano keys on his strung nerves. And remembering too the still figure in the bed, the sleeping figure, the broken face. The light of the lightning came again. Bone-white, almost to blue. But the crack of thunder came after. Came from the east, not building but fading. . . . The storm had swept over them. *We suffered no significant damage.* Was letting up. And Tune heard again the madam's delight at the song he made, after: and she had asked him to stay, had asked him, dreaming what his dream of manhood must be, to find there his living:

Dawe and Grizzly and Tune ventured beyond the flaps of the tent. The deck of the boat was covered in hail. On the shore the trees, the tall cottonwoods that had protected them from the full force of the wind, were stripped of leaves. As if summer in those few minutes had come and gone. The leaves lay on the ground, buried in hail that was melting now, beginning to look like drifted snow: the trees stood gaunt and broken against the heavy sky.

Young Tune found a pintail afloat by the boat's hull, two ducklings following the dead mother. He said he would go ashore to find the mourning doves he'd seen on the island.

"Stay here," Dawe said.

"Why?" Tune said.

"Stay right here."

"What about Web?"

"He's big enough to take care of himself."

"Then why doesn't he come back?"

He, Dawe, had been out for hours, seeking the girl, hunting her, determined to prove to himself that she was still following. And with every failure to find a trace of a fire, a camp, a footprint, he had become more certain that she was nearby, close to them. And then, in a perverse moment, he believed that Web would know how to find a woman in a thousand square miles of prairie with nothing but his prick to guide him.

"Shouldn't we go look?" Tune said.

"Where would we begin?"

"I'll try," Tune said, eager to go ashore, to continue his adventuring.

"It's too late now." Dawe was trying to peer into, through, the darkening island. "We'd be hunting for you too— out there."

Grizzly had lit a lantern and now he hung it on an upraised sweep on the stern of the boat. The deck only held them the more, compacted them unbearably. Tune went to where the gangplank led down into the darkness, cupped his hands and shouted:

"Web!"

Somewhere on the hail-covered island, raising its green head, its protruding eyes, a frog croaked: amphibian, back beyond any human sound, a frog, croaking.

"Web!"

Tune silent, listening.

Then the frog too, getting no reply to its croaked signal, fell silent. A light rain was beginning to fall, a cold drizzle that misted the air. The overcast sky brought down the darkness so close that the lantern on the sweep seemed smothered, about to be extinguished, its light turned back upon itself.

"The path of a hailstorm is narrow," Dawe said. "Maybe it missed him."

Tune cupped his hands, called again towards land: "Web!"

No voice answered. And Tune, then:

"What's up there? What's up above the valley?"

"Nothing." Dawe gestured out at the darkness. "This is ranching country. Nothing but—Once you get away from the river—" He went to the boy, put his arm around the boy's shoulders. "Are you really as young—"

"Going on sixteen." The boy, proudly. Defensively. And Dawe, then, holding him. The hunchbacked man, the boy too fat for the small embrace:

"Sixteen?" Dawe said.

"In September." And Tune, adding: "I'll be big enough then to join the army. . . . Have to work hard. Out in the sun. . . . So I look older."

"You'll be older." Dawe moved his arm. "Your voice is changing."

They waited on the stern, the man and the boy, silent, together. Grizzly came out on deck, looked at the fine rain for a few minutes, pulled the corner of a tarpaulin over his stove, then went into the tent to go to bed. Dawe wiped at a wooden crate with his handkerchief and he and Tune sat down as if they would wait all night for Web's return.

No sounds came out from the underbrush on the island. No owls. No rabbits moving. No mourning doves. No whining mosquitoes.

"Wish he'd come back," the boy said.

"Be here any minute," Dawe assured him.

They turned from the river to look towards the gangplank, listening for sounds in the empty night. Listening.

"You hear something?" Tune said.

"No."

Only the gentle touching of the rain onto the canvas tent; Grizzly, on his cot inside, shifting against the drone of the voices.

The silence came at them, out of the dark. Tune glanced from the darkness into the small light of the lantern. They were under the raised lantern and in the shadowed light Dawe's bearded face was a black hole.

"You got any kids?" Tune's voice not changed yet, a boy's voice; almost, in the night there, the voice of a girl.

"Me? No."

"You going to?"

Dawe not listening to the words. "Going to what?"

"Have kids."

"Maybe. . . . Guess it's natural to want a son."

"What's your wife's name?"

Dawe had to think for an instant: a frightening instant that made him flinch. "Elisabeth."

"I'm never going to get married," Tune said.

"Why not?"

"I like to bum around too much. They tie you down. . . . Women."

Dawe smiled, his teeth white in the dark hole that was his face.

"Look at Web," Tune said. Defensively. "He doesn't even have to come back to the boat if he doesn't want to."

"Web will have a story to tell. He'll need someone to hear his story."

"I'll stay up," Tune said.

"He'll wait for the morning light," Dawe said And added: "Web."

Tune, unwilling to enter the dark tent: "I'm wide awake. I'll stand watch for a while."

And Dawe, in that moment, seeing for himself a son, seeing the boy's need to dare the night, nodding: "If you hear him up there—" Dawe gesturing at the shoreline, up at the invisible hills. "Sing out."

My father slept soundly, no doubt. He could leave the wounded and the dead and the missing behind him as an officer in battle will leave his beloved and unfortunate men. I know, because if McBride was once left for dead and Web listed with the missing, it was I who carried the wound. I was born woman when he expected —had decided his surname must deserve— a son. Not that to be his son was any good fortune, as Tune should have guessed. As it was no fortune at all to be his wife, his daughter. But a son, born of his flesh and blood and blind obsession, might at least have grown up to kill him.

He would accept and endure destiny, my father. It was chance he could not abide. And the sexual act as he provoked it, in his diabolical and maliciously meditated and organized and executed fashion, was intended to foreclose on randomness itself.

The unintended nature of Web's existence drove my father beyond the decencies he would have expected of a fish. But at the same time he could not endure in McBride the surrender, the willingness to be the agent of orderly existence. Perhaps it was in the old man, in Grizzly, that he could imagine a balance; as he was able, at least at that time, to imagine that Grizzly had grown beyond the illogicalities of desire. As he could believe Tune not yet to have entertained those stormy reckonings of impulse, opportunity and regret.

He assumed that I, his daughter, in error not born a son, must by virtue of that error be free of the folly he found in men. And, having made that assumption

—in order to assure its validity—he locked me up in the house I had inherited. Or was inheriting . . . . He locked me up in an education I might as well have inherited, it was so much mine before I realized it was given me; he locked me up in the money I did not know until years later, too late, was not even his to give.

Who could I learn to love, but him? And how, but in his manner? Loving loss as he loved it, finding no live world that was absolute enough to be worth the gaining, he would seek only the absolute of what was gone. His was a heaven of darkness. And if something was not gone far enough into that obscure necessity, that boneyard of the soul, he would send it on its way.

22. *Vanishing Man Makes First Appearance*

Grizzly was first to realize they were adrift. Young Tune had set the lines as he had been taught by Web to set them, in the slack and calm of a falling river. Now, with the water risen two feet and rising still, the lines had torn loose from the willow clumps; it was Grizzly, getting up to start breakfast, who realized the boat was moving and who returned to the tent, stuck his head in and did not ask or even plead:

"Dawe," he whispered.

William Dawe, bursting out onto deck in the longjohn cotton underwear he wore all summer on the theory that it kept him cool, intended first to cry his wrath at Tune for not tying up correctly, then at himself for not doing it himself, or checking after. But first he was silenced by the immense and deceptive emptiness, the unthundering hollowness of the clean sky, second by the realization that Web had not returned in the night nor at the first crack of dawn, had not come back injured and therefore useless to Dawe's intent, a mere burden. Had not come back with the child, the woman, he had been sent out to find and to save.

Tune was asleep on the stern of the boat, partially covered by the tarpaulin that was supposed to cover the cast-iron cookstove. Dawe nudged him with a bare foot—kicked him. The boy sat up straight, looked to where the gangplank and the island were supposed to be. He looked out across the open water and then he asked, in his voice that was sometimes a child's:

"What's that car doing there?"

Dawe went to the bow of the drifting boat: the river was up and rolling brown, lumber and up-rooted trees accompanied them in their swift descent. *Let everything float or snag or sink like so much driftwood, I told myself. And then, resigned, beheld the spectacle that contradicted my senses.* Dawe trying to focus his eyes on the mirage-like point where there must be a road, a ferry, a bridge, an island— And couldn't be. And wasn't.

Half asleep and at the same time fully awake he looked at and did not look at what appeared to be an automobile, at a standstill in the middle of the river. He looked away, at the driftwood, at what proved to be a drowned cow, afloat in the water. He thought in that instant of a dinosaur, dead upstream, floating downriver through the everglades or the delta swamps or the bayous, the stomach bloating, the dinosaur turning onto its back, floating legs up, the neck going soft and slack, letting the head fall backwards into the position in which the head of— the skull of—a dinosaur so often was found. And then he looked again towards what he had at one time and again now recognized to be an automobile: a tin lizzie, a remodelled Model-T, motionless in the middle of the river.

More exactly, it looked as if the driver had learned by some miraculous gift to drive on top of the water, only his engine had quit on him. The car was even then sunk only to its axles, its running boards, in water; the driver had waded downriver and was standing in that same water up to his knees. He was stooped behind a tripod and camera; his head was invisible under the black focussing cloth.

Apparently, in focussing, in preparing to take a picture of his car in the water, the photographer, or driver, or both, noticed in the background the unlikely spectre of a raft or boat bearing down upon him, two or three men aboard and doing nothing. He swung the camera, aimed at the approaching boat. And yet his head did not appear from under the cloth.

The name MICHAEL SINNOTT was emblazoned in gilt letters on the side of the Model-T; and the Model-T itself had obviously been converted into a portable dark-room. As if a pocket of darkness must carefully be locked up, captured, preserved, to console Michael Sinnott through the day. For under his name was the inscription:

Travelling Emporium of the Vanished World
We Specialize in Everything

As if he had been deposited there by the storm; as if the land itself had slipped out from under him and left him marooned in the original water, the storm that might have taken all else away having left him there in all else's stead.

Dawe, at last, had found some cargo for his ark. He would, must, save the automobile, as if it might be some remnant of a prehistoric existence. And he would save, accidentally, in the process, the man who was driver of the vehicle, itinerant and rude photographer, as well.

"Can we take you on board?" Dawe shouted.

Michael Sinnott's head came out from under the cloth. It was a huge head, as white-bearded as Dawe's was black. Sinnott stood bare-headed, blinking at the sun. He seemed, physically, double

Dawe's size. He wore a black patch over his right eye. He wore a shirt and tie and jacket.

"Can we take you aboard?" Dawe called.

"Vanishing," Sinnott said. More to himself than to Dawe. "Everything is vanishing."

"Can we—" Dawe began again.

"If it pleases you," Sinnott said.

That bothered Dawe: the supreme indifference. The ingratitude bordering on arrogance, when the man should have fallen on his knees.

"We can leave you if you like," Dawe called.

Sinnott raised his large hands in a gesture of indifference.

Daw signalled Tune to take the boat towards the marooned automobile. Tune obeyed; then he did not raise his sweep in time, it caught in the sand; before he could work it free it had cracked. The boat hit the invisible sand, rose slightly, rode forward on a wave.

"We're grounded," Tune said, despairingly.

Sinnott waded over to the bow of the boat. "Don't worry. The floodwaters rise by the minute."

"Come aboard," Dawe said.

"Vanishing," Sinnott said.

He waded back to his camera and tripod, picked up both and moved to a new location.

And Dawe, gruffly, hesitantly: "We could use a little help." He turned with a brisk, aggressive motion and ordered Grizzly and Tune to bring ropes, to take down the forward end of the tent, to find a second gangplank.

"Wish Web was here," Tune said.

114

"Never mind Web," Dawe said.

"Need him," Tune insisted.

"If we can't load that damned little car without him, then we can't load chunks of rock and fossil."

Sinnott disappeared under his focussing cloth. While the three men worked, he was busy taking pictures. He moved in a broad circle around them, taking photographs when they set two gangplanks into the water, when they ran a line from the bumper of his car to the small hand-capstan on the bow of the boat. Tune and Grizzly were pushing at capstan bars, Dawe holding the line tight on the drum of the small capstan, the automobile moving slowly, inch by inch, up the parallel gangplanks, up out of the water towards the deck of the boat: Sinnott's face came out from under the black cloth, his black eyepatch curiously blinding in the sun:

"Where're you headed?"

Dawe answered uneasily: "You've probably never heard of it. Deadlodge Canyon."

"I've been there," Sinnott said.

He disappeared again, under the focussing cloth. Without reappearing he picked up both camera and tripod, moved them: he caught with a squeeze of the rubber bulb, a click of the shutter, the moment when the Model-T rolled onto the deck: Tune seized the handle on the rear door of the vehicle to stop it from rolling across the deck and back into the water.

Sinnott called from under his cloth: "Don't let the dark out."

Tune let go of the handle with a start. "The dog?"

"The dark," Sinnott said. He reappeared, smiled.

115

"Got it all. Got everything. Even while it occurred, never to occur again. But I have it. Right here." He held up the plates in his right hand.

Dawe tried again: "You were—"

"I know," Sinnott interrupted. He stepped up onto the deck of the boat, went to the Model-T with the plates. "I was there. Taking pictures of some asshole outfit that was digging up dinosaur skeletons."

"Come with us," Dawe said. "We need a man."

"Not on your life. I was there—two summers ago I think it was. Three. Yes. Three summers ago. One of those outfits looking for bones. They were all of them cracked right out of their heads in the end. Took some beautiful pictures. Chap from the government wanted them, trying to figure out what happened to the men he sent in there—perfectly sensible people, decent men. Wanted pictures before. After. Worth a fortune to all parties concerned." He interrupted himself. "Ah. Look at this. We're about to move." He was transfixed on the spot, wanting to capture the moment, the boat moving south, a crow overhead flying north. He spoke to Dawe without turning his head: "Fetch my camera up here. Quick."

Dawe wouldn't budge. He too heard the sand grating on the boat's hull. The camera would be left behind. He stepped down off the deck, waded towards the camera, the boat beginning to move past him.

"Hurry," Tune shouted, Tune manning, trying to man, the broken forward sweep.

Dawe stumbled, went down on his knees, holding

the camera over his head, out of the water. He struggled up as Grizzly bent on the stern of the deck: Grizzly managed to catch hold of the camera: Dawe hung on, was dragged along in the deepening water. Then Grizzly had him by the shirt on his humped back, pulled him aboard: together they rushed the camera and tripod to where Sinnott waited.

Dawe, gasping for breath: "We——"

"I know," Sinnott said. "I could tell. The minute I laid eyes on your rickety little scow, coming down the river. I said to myself, 'Sinnott, my good man, seize your good fortune, get some pictures of these chaps. They're a vanishing form of life.'"

"Wouldn't——"

"No," Sinnott said. "Not for anything on earth — but I'll take a few pictures. As you go into the canyon." He carried his camera around to the other side of the boat; a second crow had appeared, behind the first, the boat moving easily now, south and east, the crow flapping into the north. "Everything is vanishing here. Every form of life. The Indians. I have photographed the Blackfoot, at great personal risk. The homesteaders who replaced them. The homesteaders who showed up here ten years ago are all gone. Dried out and hailed out and frozen out and eaten out by the grasshoppers and starved out by their own greed. Gone off to their European wars, like so much powder and shot. And the bone-hunters too——"

Daw broke out in anger: "Nothing vanishes. Everything goes on. Life goes on." He raised his arm——

"Ha," Sinnott said. "Wait. Hold it."

117

"Never." Dawe turned away from the camera, would not stand in front of the lens. "Look at the dinosaurs. Seventy million years later. The bones are still here. Right here in the rock and the earth."

"Where once they lived and then vanished from life," Sinnott said. "Precisely. The most splendid creatures in creation. I took pictures of the finest specimens ever hauled out of your precious Dead-lodge Canyon. Sternberg's greatest discoveries, bound for the museums of England—the ship by accident torpedoed and sunk. Vanished. As the island vanished whereupon I chose to camp last night. As the ford vanished where I would cross the river. We pass along this little conundrum of the soul's pathway, only my photographs remaining."

"We've got to fix this sweep," Tune said. To Dawe. "Or we'll lose it."

Dawe raised a finger to silence the boy. "There is nothing that does not leave its effect. We study the accumulated remains."

"Because of me," Sinnott said. He stepped up onto the running board of his Model-T, peered about him; huge, white-bearded, his head bare, he looked out over the river, out at the long hills.

Only then did Dawe notice: Sinnott was without shoes. His wet socks, the toes filled with sand, gave him huge, webbed feet.

"Gentlemen," Sinnott said. "I will make you an offer. A decent and reasonable offer. You will no doubt wish that a record might survive, a tribute to your own brief and foolish travail. I need a few additional photographs for my season's presentation." He looked down at Dawe from where he was perched. "We are both peddlers, you and I."

Dawe, icily quiet.

"The best yet. The best ever." Sinnott raised up his voice, to no one, a barker's voice, shrill, intrusive: "Grave Robbers in the Badlands of the West. See the Monsters Returning to Life. We *Dare* You to Look."

"Charlatan," Dawe said. "Come with us."

"We are both charlatans." And then Sinnott raised up his faked voice again: "Michael Sinnott, Artist, presents his one and only Travelling Emporium of the Vanished World. For the first hour only, adults a mere twenty-five cents, children—" He stopped. "Ho," he said.

He stepped down from the running board of the Model-T, knocked Dawe out of the way and rushed in his stockinged feet to the camera:

"Who the fuck is this guy?"

23. *The Tree of Hawks*

On shore, emerging out of a small stand of cottonwoods, a man running, shouting: Web, galloping full tilt along the top of the cutbank, waving his arms: "Hey, you sons of bitches. Wait!" Dawe seeing that Web did not have, could not have, the girl with him: Dawe in his mind leaving the man on the shore, Goddamnit Web, can't you do anything right, anything. Well. We did our duty. Tried. Maybe she wasn't there to begin with. Maybe he did find her.

Web running. In Dawe's slicker, running.

Web following after the boat that was not coming any closer to land, their two courses aimed parallel towards an infinitely regressing horizon: the boat making something like four miles an hour in the high water; Web, in order to keep up on the rough

119

ground, plunging headlong through underbrush, birds flying up in fright and terror, Web skating wildly over slippery wet clay, splashing through standing water, side-stepping gopher holes. Dawe thinking: If he breaks a leg we'll have to shoot him.

Then Sinnott was busy, or as busy as Sinnott was likely to appear. He was moving his camera, then standing still, his head under the focussing cloth; and he was trying to get a good picture of the figure that was galloping and yet standing still too, in relation to the boat. Calmly Sinnott worked, patient as the boat swinging in the current took him out of focus, as the figure on shore stumbled, rose up again and continued to run. And then Dawe could not endure Sinnott's calm indifference to the plight of the running man. "Take her into shore," he said to Tune: Tune ready and waiting: the cutbank ten or twelve or even twenty feet above the surface of the water.

Web would, almost did, leap, plunge, almost straight down and onto the deck: but Tune hit the bank too soon and too hard, a slide of mud came down, rattled and thumped down onto the deck: Grizzly disappeared into, under, the cloud of dust, the mud.

"Sorry," Tune said.

Sinnott turned his camera onto the heaped mud and dirt.

Grizzly seemed to be buried, there on the buried deck. Then a chunk of the earth itself stood up, shook itself, became Grizzly, the old chinaman, straightening his pigtail, brushing absurdly at his apron: Grizzly stooped into the partially lowered tent and reappeared with a brand-new shovel, the price clearly marked on the bright blade: he set to work, pitching the mud and dirt into the river while Tune tried to manipulate their one working sweep, then, instead, snagged the roof of the Model-T on a leaning bush. The boat began to turn end for end and Sinnott, calmly, turned his camera on its tripod.

Web in his wild, enduring chase chasing that which was not ahead of him but beside him, behind him, glancing back to see if he could catch up. And Dawe: Dawe recognizing the agility, the grace, of the running man: the pure animal force and energy; the mad animal dimension of the shouting, cursing man. And his own envy. And the realization of how absolutely he needed that man whom he would willingly, might by an act of God be forced to, leave behind.

The chase in full thunder: Tune trying to stop the boat when it might have been just as easy, and safer, to stop the river; Grizzly shovelling mud into the river as if engaged in a solitary conspiracy to dam it shut, working industriously, deliberately, while they were almost swamped in a tangle of jammed driftwood, almost stove in on a snag; Sinnott under his black cloth, silent and motionless, then his one good eye, then his eyepatch, appearing again, his stockinged, webbed feet going into a quick dance, his head disappearing again, become a cloth, a camera, a lens; Dawe, getting his black hat, his hump, into the pictures, shouting directions at the river, at the unmoving hills.

Web disappeared.

He was, apparently, attempting a shortcut, going overland while the boat followed an oxbow.

First Dawe saw a hawk soaring above, ahead of them, circling in the clear and quiet sky; he recognized the hawk's cry, then the hawk: the Swainson's hawk; Dawe thinking, goddamn, now Sinnott will want a picture of this as well, after the empty nests they had seen on the clay cliffs behind them, the heaped twigs and sticks, ten feet high, empty; and now the hawk itself, sky-soaring beyond their folly and watching the gophers below, the mice, the rabbits, Web running like a scared gopher unable to find its hole; and then he, Dawe, saw the tree: he saw it and named it, in his mind, a framed photograph in the Travelling Emporium of the Vanished World: yes, The Tree of Hawks: thirty birds, forty, perched on the dead branches of the huge, dead cottonwood, the great, spidered tree, black lightning on the pale sky; those hawks in the tree of hawks, another half dozen looped in the sky: and goddamn yes, Sinnott would want a picture: *never*, Dawe thought, *never*, I won't let him have *this*:

And Web appeared. Web, in the slicker, in the sun, looking comically like Dawe.

Web, this side of the dead tree, loomed up onto the bank, out of nothing, teetered, caught himself, held himself from falling. Then he began to teeter again, the earth giving beneath his boots and he flailed, flapped his arms in the air and still almost fell and the men on the boat laughed; Dawe: "Jump." Tune: "Hold on." Web shouting, absurdly: "I couldn't find her."

The current taking the boat in under the bank. Young Tune swung the stern sweep, held it too long, was caught in a mudslide: The sweep broke with a loud crack.

The hawks burst into the air, exploded out of the branches.

At that instant Web charged at the dead tree, charged into the feathered bloom of the hungering, crying hawks, the web of wings, went to the tree's base, swung himself like a slingshot with one hand on the polished dead trunk, stepped three paces beyond, to the edge of the cutbank, was taking a fourth step when the earth became air, commenced to fall as he commenced to holler, fell, caught himself or was caught on the exposed roots of the tree, fell again towards the water. As the hawks flamed upward he tumbled, slid, dropped down; he hit the approaching deck like a jumping frog in a shower of falling earth and gravel and clay.

Sinnott swiftly tilted his camera, had his picture.

24. *The Steveville Ferry*

"Perfect," Sinnott said. "Hold it." He squeezed the rubber bulb and the camera clicked again.

Web lay on his stomach in the mud on the deck, catching his breath; he touched at his mustache, raised his face into the lens. "What is this—going to be—in the newspapers?"

Dawe answering: "The Grave Robbers of the Badlands of the West."

"Holy shit." Web sat up, shook himself out of the dirt and the clay, straightened his cap on his head.

"Lucky you saw us," Tune said.

"Didn't—didn't see you—saw that damned lantern—all by itself in the air—moving through the air —broad daylight—before that—I was a goner—"

"You okay?" Tune said.

"Getting my wind." Web touched at the top of his head. "Thought I was a goner."

Sinnott picked up his camera, turned his good eye on Tune and Grizzly and Web. "Well my assembled *goners*. You will soon be in the land of your fatal little ambitions." He put the camera down. "Don't touch that sweep, Tune."

"Soon be there?" Tune looked around him; nothing had changed. "Deadlodge?"

"Not on your sweet life." Sinnott ducked under the focussing cloth. "The Steveville ferry. Where I shall depart your calamitous intention." He stuck his head out from under the cloth, looked at Dawe. "The artist must survive the calamity. And I will thank you, gentlemen, meanwhile, for a mite of silence."

Grizzly was shovelling the dirt from around their feet. The deck he had almost cleaned was buried again; now he compelled even Web to get out of the way. The boat was moving in the main current, turning easily, slowly, as it drifted; swallows came out over the deck, darting, skimming the water, returning to their holes in the bank; now Tune, with Dawe's assistance, went to lift the bow sweep onto deck. Web went to get some of the lumber that was meant for packing cases for bones.

Sinnott took great pains to compose the picture in his mind, then adjusted the camera, then snapped. He muttered to himself: "Men Repairing a Sweep." And added to no one: "Vanishing."

He set up his camera to take a picture of the

shore, as if that too must vanish. He waited, watched the shifting pattern of water, mud, grass, hills, sky: he snapped the picture, he said to himself: "Retreating Shoreline." Again he moved the camera, again he announced his title: "Chinese Cook and Cookstove on Open Deck." He had them, held them prisoners in his Travelling Emporium; actors and audience they must hear him out in his stubborn and impassioned and concentrated silence: Tune for a moment's rest took up a comb and piece of paper, hummed a sad song: and Sinnott aloud: "Runaway Boy Dreaming of Home." He picked up his camera, left the boy and went to where Web, leaning on the repaired stern sweep, in profile watched the water: "Pilot Looking for Trouble," he said; then took a picture of a tangle of driftwood, a part of a roof of a house caught in a windrow of bone-grey tree limbs: "Future Memory," Sinnott said. And turned his camera against the sky itself, the cumulus clouds incongruously ranked and ordered, drifting white and heedless across the blue of the sky: a turkey vulture, as if for Sinnott's convenience, a ham actor, a stage prop, an accomplice, sailed wide-winged and slow against a white cloud, Sinnott under his black hood aiming, announcing: "Waiting Bird."

And they could not resist watching him, the four men, listening. They were fascinated, transfixed, as he hauled them through the vanished world of his, of their, creation, the emporium of their sought descent. And Dawe quietly furious, offended by an obsession, a drive, a compulsion as extravagant as his own: Dawe, quietly, watching each mile of river slip under them, taking them closer to the depths of the Badlands, joy beginning to leap in his heart—he let himself imagine Sinnott on the submerged island again, the water rising, no help in sight.

"Pretty soon—"

"I know," Sinnott said. He began to study Dawe himself, stared at the man openly, curiously. "Leader Awaiting His Calling," he tried. He waited, letting the title balance in his mind. He saw the first rough butte swing into position, into sight, behind the unsuspecting man. And he picked up his camera and tripod—

Dawe moved away.

Then he too, Dawe, saw ahead of them the cable tower on the south shore, the second tower concealed by a small butte. They must be rid of their passenger here. Dawe went to the bow of the boat; Sinnott, deliberate, unconcerned, went to the stern: Grizzly was pulling a goldeye out of the turbulent waters: Sinnott insisted that Grizzly hold it up. And he focussed close in on the steel blue of the back, the silver belly, the gold of the iris of the eye; the fish was a foot long at least; Grizzly held it at arm's length, so he himself would not be in the picture, only his fingers in the gills:

"Descendant of the Depths," Sinnott said. "Pity it's black and white," he added.

The ferryman had walked upstream to meet them; he was shouting something from shore. Sinnott straightened away from the camera: he and the ferryman recognized each other and waved.

"What did he say?" Dawe said.

The ferryman's dogs, at his heels, set up such a din that his voice was not to be heard.

"What did he say?" Dawe repeated.

Sinnott had turned to young Tune. "Get your bedroll."

"Why?" Tune said.

"Better for all parties concerned."

Sinnott was moving his camera again. He placed it in position so that he might get a shot of the man at the stern sweep, making the landing. He turned to Dawe:

"Let me take a picture before I go."

Dawe looked from the ferryman, following along on shore, to Sinnott.

"Just one," Sinnott added. "One only."

It was that last refinement that made Dawe yield, the temptation of the one, the only, the unique. The vanity about his appearance that made him avoid the camera made him, finally, want to appear before its shutter and lens. He, William Dawe, had come to the supreme moment, the time and place to which all the expeditions sailed: the Steveville ferry. The point from which they went into the deepest and widest section of the Alberta Badlands, survival place of the last of the dinosaurs, one of the greatest bonebeds in the history of paleontology. He thought the word and kept it secretly from Sinnott. Sinnott would want that word for his emporium. But Dawe would give him instead one picture: he would let himself be photographed at the stern sweep, guiding his craft, his men, his expedition, the one and only and unique Dawe Expedition; into the Alberta Badlands and immortality.

Web, more from disbelief than by any act of will, gave over the sweep, stood aside to watch, was joined in turn in his surprise by Tune, then by

127

Grizzly. And Dawe, imperious for a moment, trying to look as alert and indifferent as Sinnott himself might look, smoothed his beard down onto his chest, took up his position. He had not once, ever, handled the stern sweep. Now he tried a posture of weary and yet accurate surveillance that must indicate a long journey, a desperate and calculated casting into the unknown.

Sinnott brushed at his own white beard, adjusted the black patch over his right eye; as if he must now save himself from vanishing. He had already, using Web as his model, adjusted the square bellows camera, set the flap shutter. Taking the rubber bulb in his right hand, he determined that his subject would not only pose but would smile as well. Sinnott announcing: "We are two of a kind, Mr. Dawe, you and I. Birds of a feather. You with your bones that are sometimes only mineral replacements of what the living bones were. Me, rescuing positive prints out of the smell of the darkroom."

"I recover the past," Dawe said. Unsmiling. Adjusting his grip on the sweep. "You reduce it."

"I know," Sinnott said. "And yet we are both peddlers."

"You make the world stand still," Dawe said. "I try to make it live again."

"Then let me save you from your inevitable failure," Sinnott said. "Tell me where you might possibly be reached and I'll send you the consolation of my masterpiece: The Charlatan Being Himself."

Dawe smiled.

Just as the camera clicked they heard the ferryman call out again.

Then Web, the others, saw what he had been trying to tell them. The sudden rise of water, the flood, had taken away the landing platform. The ferryman could not get to his ferry.

They were losing precious time. Quickly now they must decide how to attempt a landing, on which side of the river. Dawe, asserting himself, hesitating: "Tune can't leave."

"What's your pleasure?" Web shouted. Web at the forward sweep.

And Dawe, hesitating, heard the man on the shore, the ferryman, calling. He turned to listen.

"The cable!" the ferryman shouted.

Web, on the bow of the boat, hardly had time to see the danger: the floodwaters had raised them up to where the Model-T on the deck would snag on the cable, be torn apart; and he let go of the sweep, stepped to the bow's edge: Tune recklessly rushing forward to help: and they seized the steel cable, Web and Tune, leapt and stumbled to hold on, to lift it clear of the automobile: they held it clear of the painted sign on the side of the car, of the roof, and swept on under:

"Now you've goddamn gone and done it," Sinnott said.

25. *The Heronry*

They missed their landing. Downstream from the Steveville ferry is an island that stretches for a mile and a half along the eastern bank of the river. The boat, in making the turn above the ferry, had moved to the outer edge of the bend. High water pushes a current into the channel behind the island; the high water, now, carried the boat towards that narrow channel.

Dawe, at the sweep, held steady, frozen out of any motion and into a fixed course. They went in under the branches that touched their heads: the branches of cottonwoods, the bending willows. Sinnott was hurrying to get his camera and its tripod into the Model-T. Web had the forward sweep again; Tune was left standing beside the automobile.

Sinnott busy, talking while he worked, rehearsing the lechery of names: "Hare and Meagher field camera . . . hand me those dark slides . . . Watkins Standard with these dry plates . . . ." The boy only watching, then listening, then helping. " . . . folding tailboard . . . the lens barrel . . . Zeiss lens . . . pull this out, squeeze, the bulb raises the flap shutter, so . . . ." Sinnott lifting up an old battery, examining it. "Dead," he said. "Take it . . . careful . . . I was trying to make something that would light magnesium powder . . . night pictures . . . . damned near blew my head off."

Tune laughing: the warm intimate laughter at danger confronted and survived.

Sinnott carefully lifting, shifting boxes, chemicals, Tune getting the hang of it. Tune trying to help.

"My winter show," Sinnott said. "Greatest ever in the cities of this nation. I'll need an assistant."

Young Tune asking abruptly: "Where are your shoes?"

Sinnott, surprised, looking down at his stockinged feet. "Mystery to me. Floated away I guess."

They were rushing through the long channel behind the island. Ahead of them a tangle of brush, a part of a broken beaver dam, it seemed, had caught in the channel; driftwood was piling up against the dam, old logs, whole trees that had been torn from the banks upriver. The boat was riding down towards the dam; there was no way to stop, to change direction—

Then it hit, jarred into the debris, began to lose momentum. Web saw the danger. The water would back up over the banks, carrying the boat along; then the dam would give and they'd be left stranded. High and dry on the shore, on the island, stove in and shipwrecked and marooned when they might in twenty minutes have seen their goal. He snatched up a pike pole, tried to hold the rising boat in the channel.

"Quick!" Sinnott yelled. To young Tune. "Come along." Sinnott himself stooping, humped down in front of the radiator of the Model-T. He pulled the crank. "Jump in!" he shouted.

The engine started and Web looked back from the bow: he saw Sinnott slide in behind the steering wheel, saw Tune hesitating.

"Get!" Web shouted. "Go with him."

The Model-T moved forward, then lurched: the front wheels hit the driftwood. The logs, caught between the boat and the cutbank, held: the shore was almost level with the rising deck. Then the front wheels were on dry land, one back wheel, spinning, was off the deck; Tune went either to jump onto the bumper or to push, the car threatening to tip over; then the spinning wheel caught on the driftwood; the car leapt into the underbrush, into the tangle of wolf willow and saskatoon bushes and cottonwood branches.

The boat was visibly rising, going straight up instead of forward, into the trees, into the first branches, the water spilling out over the bank behind the vanished car, the willows on the island on the far side of the boat seeming to sink, vanish, into the seething water—

The pressure of the boat against the dam broke the dam's bellied rim.

Logs tipped as if into a flume, the water sucked loud away from beneath the tangled driftwood: the boat was pulled down, tilted headlong down into the shit-coloured foam: the stumps, the broken trees, the fallen nests of magpies and crows, a dead and floating porcupine, the silt and clay from the eroded hills, half the carcass of a skunk, the dung and piss of cattle, the stinking corpse of a drowned calf, the flatboat itself surged down the long and narrow channel on the rising and falling crest, Web shouting: "Save the sweeps!" And then he and Tune were lifting the forward sweep out of its wooden socket, onto deck; Dawe and Grizzly were struggling on the stern; the branch of a cottonwood swept low across the deck, caught Web in the middle of the back and hurled him against the part of the tent that was still standing. "Get down," he was shouting, lying on the tent, under the tearing boughs: the boat jarred against the trunks of trees, the thick trunks scarred by the floating ice of spring break-up; the boat snagged on a stump left by beavers, tore free with a gut-deep rumble; water and twigs and foam came up over the deck, over the hands and knees of the bowed and kneeling men, the branches whipping their heads, the torn leaves hiding the deck to which they attempted to cling: a fallen tree ahead of them, in the ripping and blinding shift of shadows, a chopping hand, the blunt edge of an axe: "Stay down!" Dawe was shouting.

They were lying on their bellies, all of them, heads down, all of them soaking wet and covered in bark and leaves and green slime and brown foam.

Dawe sat up, out of the tangle of fallen branches. Tune and Grizzly sat up beside him.

They were on a broad and peaceful river. Twilight had come.

Web disentangled himself from the dirty, wet tent. He was first to get to his feet. "Holy shit," he said.

They were encompassed, totally, by the Badlands. All around them, in the changed light, in the muted light, the high buttes were gold, all gold in the broken sun; the muted and failed sky let down across them, across the water, a silence they could see.

They stood, the four of them together; they were into a backwater under the island; the boat did not seem to move.

It was the great blue herons that held their attention. The four men saw the only motion on that landscape, the only possibility of motion; recognized in the distant shallows the heronry, the standing birds. The boat was hardly moving. It held to the edge of a lost channel, only hardly moved. The birds themselves, at first, would not be disturbed. The great blue herons stood watching, stood motionless and waiting; then a head, a neck, snake-like moved down to the water, found whatever it was the beak sought, came up again and was motionless. Another head found out its frog, its minnow, moved down, moved up and was motionless.

133

The boat was drifting. The boat moved towards the first of the birds; four herons, reluctant, raised their wings.

Silent, slow, the four birds did not move into the air but moved out of the water. They lifted across the water, their wings too slow ever to make them fly, their long necks folding back, reluctant to lead those slate-blue bodies into the air. They moved across the far reaches of the river, over the water's darkening sheen; and then when they must smash, vanish, into the sides of the golden buttes, they had somehow succeeded, were in the sun, their long legs spindled out and frail and seemingly forgotten. They sailed in a wide circle, moved in a circle away from the boat, returning, Tune watching in wonder, signalling to the others: the huge birds did not land in the water but, awkwardly, their forgotten legs remembered only just in time, came down on the tops of three crooked trees on the tip of the island.

"They can have it," Web said. "Fair trade."

A guttural croak came loud on their ears. Cracked the silence. Again it came, echoing or repeated: a hard, hoarse squawk, rasping, primordial. And again it came, Web trying to speak, and again——

Three herons rose up from under, from in front of the boat, lifted away in a sudden and eerie silence, their stretching wing tips touching down into the darkness that spread like a mist, now, over the surface of the river.

Grizzly and Dawe together took hold of the tent, began to set it up.

Web and Tune went to the bow of the boat, unable to resist the strange birds; together they spotted another pair, a lone bird, a pair: the silent, poised, long-beaked birds where at first they had seen nothing. They had expected something else, something other, not this silence, these unknown birds. They stayed together, lifting the bow sweep back into position, Tune caught in curiosity and awe, Web abruptly asking:

"Why didn't you go with him?"

Tune shrugging. "Uh."

"Why not?"

Tune looking out, counting the herons he could see. "Because you ran like a raving maniac to get back on . . . Why didn't *you* go when *you* had a chance?"

And Web then, eager to demolish the appalling silence:

"I *was* going."

"Going where?"

"*Going.* Making tracks. Skinning out . . . Then I got hit on the goddamned head. That's why I stopped."

"Hope it wasn't an idea that hit you."

"Good God Almighty himself, as far as I can see. Hailstones coming down as big as goddamned apples. McIntoshes."

"It was dark."

"Wasn't dark enough so I couldn't see." Web tilted his head so Tune could touch the top of his skull. Tune, touching the cap, felt beneath it a lump the size of an egg.

"Cripes," Tune said.

"Right in the middle of my common sense. Anywhere else I might have been hurt. Damned thing bounced a hundred yards after it hit me."

"Must have knocked you cold."

"Knocked me sillier than"—he signalled back over his shoulder—"you know who. I was travelling full gallop when I got hit, streaking across those bald-headed prairies, spraining both ankles in gopher holes. Ground was half covered with lumps of ice the size of softballs, more coming down, the wind blowing, the sky roaring. Then clonk. Nothing can knock me over, Tune. But somehow I got it into my head that all those big white round things on the ground were dinosaur eggs."

Grizzly was walking around the tent, killing spiders.

Tune was silent.

"I suppose you think I'm bullshitting?" Web said.

"I didn't say anything."

"Never told a lie in my life."

"I didn't say a word," Tune said.

"The eggs business was okay. Nothing wrong with a bunch of dinosaur eggs. Had half a notion to candle a few of them. But then they started hatching."

"Like baby chicks," Tune said.

"Chicks nothing. Those dinosaurs came out of those shells about a foot long and hopping hungry. And there wasn't one damned thing out there to eat except me."

"I'm glad I stayed aboard," Tune said.

"Thousands," Web said. "Thousands of hungry baby dinosaurs, roaring and snapping. I was doing the Highland fling out there. The schottische and the fandango all at once."

"Lucky they're extinct," Tune said.

"Extinct?" Web shook his head in disgust. "You

ever look at birds? You ever see birds' eggs? You ever look at a bird's beak? Where do you think birds come from, Tune?"

"Birds are warm-blooded," Tune said.

"So what? How about snakes? And lizards? And reptiles?"

"Lizards are reptiles," Tune said.

"Maybe that's what *you* think," Web said. "If you ask me they're stunted dinosaurs. You ever *touch* a lizard?"

"You're a true bullshitter, Web." But young Tune glanced around, at the waiting herons, at the darkening buttes, his world turned saurian and old. They had come to a valley of miniature mountains, mountains not in the sky but sunk in the earth. "You're a natural-born bullshit artist."

Web went to the anchor he had made with a rock and a rope, the rope woven to contain the small glacial boulder. He rolled it overboard. It gave back only a small splash; the anchored boat began to swing, hung in the sluggish current, bow upstream against the anchor line.

Just as my name was determined in that season eleven years before I was born, so were my character, my fate. For in that summer of his glory my father became not only what he had always implicitly been, but what he explicitly wanted to be. After that he was a man without a history, for in that season he became the man that twenty-six more seasons, in the bonebeds of the world, would only confirm. Failure might have ruined him back into history; but failure was never to be his good fortune. It is true that success never made him wealthy. But my mother's sense of guilt, or pride, or perhaps her need to keep him in the field, provided him with the means to live beyond his income. And beyond us as well.

It was in my fate to dream a father, in my character to wait. And I waited for ten years after his death, as if he must bring himself back from his own bonebed.

Surely, yes, I worked at the waiting; as he had worked at his starting out. I studied the documents. I read of the bitter feuds of Marsh and Cope, those first great collectors of dinosaur bones; and from that lesson I learned mostly that my father had been born one generation too late. But he was not to be deterred by a mere error in chronology. My mother and I read his field notes, and then I read them alone. And we---I---read of his ventures into deserts and jungles, into Africa and Texas and Patagonia, into the Arctic islands. I read of his brave and absurd and (needless to say) successful expeditions into Mongolia---in search of dinosaur eggs. But while he went on, annually if not endlessly, collecting evidence of Cretaceous and then Jurassic and then Triassic life; while he persisted as if he must one happy morning get back to the source itself, the root moment when the glory of reptiles, destined to dominate the world magnificently for one hundred million years, was focussed in one bony creature, one Adam-seed burrowing in the green slime—

But I was left always with the mystery of his own first season. For in his summer of 1916, in the Badlands of the Red Deer River, discovering the Mesozoic era, with all of Europe filling its earth with the bones of its own young—he removed himself from time.

Whatever the desperate reason that had taken him into that far place, he came back delivered of most of the impulses we like to think of as human. He could survive any weather, any diet, any deprivation. And that was necessary to a man whose back bore on it a hump larger than any of us could see. But somewhere in the course of that first journey that was his own—somewhere, somehow, he shook himself free of any need to share even his sufferings with another human being. His field notes, after that summer, were less and less concerned with his crew, his dangers, his days of futile prospecting, his moments of discovery, his weariness, his ambitions, his frustrations. They became scientific descriptions of the size and location of bones, of the composition of the matrix, of the methods of extraction and preservation . . .

And I had to visit those badlands where his success began. Because, there, in that beautiful and nightmare season—he ceased to dare to love.

26. Deadlodge Canyon at Last

Dawe writing: *Wednesday, July 5. Into Oldman formation. Moved downriver at dawn. Hot by 9 a.m. Herons wading in the shallows. A mule deer watching from a cliff. The landscape dusty and dry and brown beyond the green at the river's edge. Making shore-camp now, below the mouth of Little Sandhill Creek. Eight miles from rimrock to farthest rimrock, the canyon itself extending downriver, how many miles I won't guess. Web, as we landed, looking up at the endless buttes and coulees: "Where did you say you dropped that needle?"*

"Where's the pickaxe?" Tune said.

"Woops," Web said. "Knew we forgot something."

They were setting up a second tent, for the cook; Grizzly insisted that the cook's tent be well up on dry land, on the sagebrush flat above the cutbank, with cottonwoods and poplars nearby, a huge patch of thorny buffalo berries outside the tent flaps. They would leave the main tent on the boat, where they might sleep at night in a breeze, free from mosquitoes and the heat.

"What should I do?" Tune said. "Can't drive a stake in this ground."

I could have hit Web with an axe. But he's right. Now that we're here: where do I begin—

And Dawe, then, telling his crew: "Unload the lumber and the plaster of paris. Get a decent table built. Lay in a supply of firewood for Grizzly." And Dawe himself bent over his open steamer trunk, locating a specimen bag, a small pick, a brush, a compass. Dawe striking out: alone, hurrying, he walked

140

out across the flat, finding a path through the sage-brush, the blue-grey hairs of the sage, the twisted, upthrust branches blurring his figure, only his strange back, his black hat, clearly in motion. He turned off the flat, away from the river and up onto a ridge, went over and down, into a dry creek bed where not the slightest breeze stirred; and moving up the wall of a butte he found no relief, the sun glaring off the layered clay, off the rust-colored ironstone, the grey bentonite.

He was breathing too hard and he sat down on a boulder to rest; he must learn to move more slowly in the heat. Must. Wrong time to commence. Dizzy from hunger and heat and thirst. Precipitous. High noon the wrong time.

He started back towards the boat—towards camp: Grizzly's stove should be ashore, the fire lit. Time for dinner. Eat a square meal. Look for that canteen and down to the river and fill it. Dehydration can kill a man. After too damned much water for too long.

He almost fell into a deserted quarry.

The hole in the side of the butte had been hacked out, gouged out, by men working in this heat. Dawe thinking, hazily, bitterly: Brown and his five skilled assistants. Sternberg and his three sons and their trained crew. Dawe, down over the crest of the butte, staring into the empty niche. Already the sudden, harsh rains of three seasons, four seasons, had softened the broken edges of clay. But the hole was there, gaping, huge, reminding Dawe that his was only the latest, not the first, expedition. And if nothing new, nothing of importance was to be found, then not only the latest but the last. Skunked. The booby prize.

He walked into camp and found Tune and Web wrestling the stove up the cutbank. Dawe trying the cook's tent and finding it stuffy hot, going down to the river, back to the flatboat from which he had thought himself freed. Dawe, pretending he was busy, pretending he wasn't afraid: *The hole is empty. Redundant. Be careful of the sun. Redundant. A hunchback will, easily, if exerting himself beyond the natural, suffer from anoxia.* He looked at what he had written. He felt safer. *Redundant*, he dared to add.

Web and Tune, sweating, came up the gangplank to begin to unload the lumber, the wood for the packing boxes. Dawe, putting away his stub of pencil:

"Where did Grizzly get to?"

Tune, mopping his forehead with the tail of his shirt. "Went somewhere with a fishing pole."

Web groaned aloud. "Can't be another goddamned goldeye in this river. I absolutely refuse to choke on, spit out or swallow another fishbone."

Grizzly, small, silent, hurrying, came out of the cottonwoods that bordered the water; he was carrying his fishing rod and three goldeyes.

27. *Looking for Fossils*

Next morning Dawe took Tune and Web with him into the coulees, showed Tune, showed Web again, how to recognize a fossil if there chanced to be a fossil to be recognized. Without a fragment to look at he tried to tell them of creatures no one had ever seen, explained how to watch for the brown concretion that wasn't quite brown, the texture that wasn't merely rock, the shape that couldn't be expected to have been bone but wasn't quite anything else. And on the morning of the day after that day he elaborated further, unwilling to believe they had learned their lesson, believing they had not learned, for if they had they would not have failed so miserably as had he; he who could (blindfolded, he explained to Tune) without fail recognize a gastrolith or a horn cone in the rubble at the base of a cliff, a vertebra in a concretion in a sandstone outcrop. And that day, too, they learned again how to move slowly, the thermometer in the tent's shade reading 105 degrees by 2 p.m., how to make a canteen of water last, how not to drink too much when they returned to camp and fell down flat on the bank and dipped their faces into the river. And on the evening of that (third) day Dawe wrote something on page 39, Book A, of his field notes for 1916, then tore off the bottom half of the page and, presumably, destroyed it: Dawe, at last, come to doubt.

28. *House of Bone*

Smoke, as they commenced the fourth day of their prospecting, billowed down into and filled the long canyon. Somewhere to the west a prairie fire burned unchecked, the drifting clouds of smoke blurring the buttes with a veil that in its diffusion of light produced a blue-grey glare. The three men, out prospecting, kept their eyes to the ground, learned quickly they could lose each other from sight, learned quickly to listen. And it was Dawe's intense

143

listening, not his sight, that led him to his first discovery.

He was little more than a mile below camp, returning from the day's vain search, when he heard a voice that he took to be Tune's. The voice lifting into song. He was so exhausted he had passed it by, had passed by the singing, before he understood it was in a language that neither he nor Tune might know.

Dawe turned off the sagebrush flat, turned back, entered a clump of old cottonwoods.

The singing resumed.

He took another thirty paces, forty paces, broke through the circle of trees and into a dry gulch.

The heap of dinosaur bones at first appeared to him to be just that: he recognized at a glance the fragments of ribs and vertebrae, of the shells of turtles, of skulls, of long bones. He believed for a moment he was losing his mind, in the aimless light, was fantasying the bones he had not been able to find in four days of searching. Without a pause he began to walk in a circle around the heaped and apparently singing bones, vaguely aware as he did so that the fragments were arranged in some sort of pattern.

Then, on the river side, he came to the opening, two five-foot femurs, crossed against each other, tied to make an inverted vee.

He did not have to step inside.

Anna Yellowbird came to the low doorway, stooped from her dugout, her cabin of bones, her fossil tipi.

"Come in," she said.

She was as tall as the silent man who confronted her. It was his speechlessness, his absolute loss for words, that made him obey. He stooped after her into the tipi, straightened in the small and conical room. Saw, in looking about him in the subdued light, an axe that was from his boat, a blanket that was from his boat, a tarpaulin from his boat, food from his boat.

He might have reached up, had he been able, might have brought the bones crashing down upon their heads. And even as he confronted the futility of that proposal, he recognized that the girl, the child, the woman, had had help in building her strange house: from one or more or all of the men who were supposedly helping him seek these rare and precious specimens.

Dawe did not speak. It was the sheer domesticity of the scene that broke him away and back to the doorway. It was not the heaped and mysterious bones themselves, not the grotesque doorway of the joined thighbones of a hadrosaur nor the stacked and interlocked fragments of fish and turtles and petrified wood; not the broken and fragmented limbs and hips, the bony shields, the huge pelvic bones, the teeth, the jaws, but the fire in the middle of the small room, the pot by the fire, the knife and fork by the pot.

"Soon," the woman said, Anna Yellowbird said, "we will find them."

Dawe stepped out of the tipi, out into the failing day, turned, found the path into the crooked trees and through them, stumbled out onto the sagebrush flat, followed what to him looked like a path, a new, worn path through the sagebrush and the buffalo-berry bushes.

He stepped into the cook's tent.

Grizzly and Tune were kneeling on the ground in front of Web; Web sat on a bench, the legs of his trousers pulled up above his dirty knees.

"Fucking cactus," Web said. "Thought I saw a genuine dinosaur sticking its ass out of the clay and I got so excited I knelt right down on my knees in some fucking cactus. Found more ironstone."

Tune was dabbing iodine onto Web's knees, painting them brown.

"So she's here," Dawe said.

Tune began to put the cap on the bottle of iodine, as if he recognized at that instant they were all of them, Dawe, Web, Grizzly, himself, all past all healing.

"Did you hear me?"

Not one of the three listening men stirred. They held him off, excluded Dawe, ignored him, denied him his confrontation and his moral outrage at whatever it was he felt a right to be outraged about, refused him even the invited deceit of surprise or feigned refutation. A housefly buzzed in the stuffy air in the tent; Grizzly picked up the fly swatter he'd made from a willow stick and a square of canvas.

"I want to tell you men something," Dawe said. He feigned his self-discipline, as well as the others feigned their not feigning anything, let himself back towards the flaps of the tent; then he stood hunched and hesitating, like a bear that had entered a tent for bacon and found instead the stench of men.

"One of you gentlemen goes near that squaw, I'll

146

fire you. Fire all of you. You can *walk* out of here,
you can goddamned *crawl* out of here, all the way
out in the stinking heat and the smoke and the
flies."

He stopped.

"Like she did to get here," Web said. "And beat
us on top of it."

Dawe, turning away, limping away; he went down
to the river to soak his swollen feet so they, again, in
the morning, would fit his boots.

Anna Dawe

It was another of the ironies of that season that the wars of Europe had sent the Indian girl into the canyon of my father's dreams. She was fourteen years old when she married, fifteen when she became a widow. At fifteen, newly a widow, having learned that her husband was vanished and gone, with an iron ship bound for something called England, for something called the World War, she had wandered blindly towards the east, knowing that England lay to the east, the war raged to the east; she had listened for the guns, watched for the strange ocean on which an iron ship might float; she wandered disconsolate, desolate, on those western prairies that were taken from her family before her husband too was taken: and vaguely, desperately, despite the Anglican if not Christian missionaries who taught her husband submission and love, she recalled a shaman whose whereabouts she did not know but whose sacred and recollected words she knew she must heed. And she found, was found by, three strange white men and a chinaman. And she knew, had known, watching the four of them leave Tail Creek in their hurry to be away from her necessary if imitation grave, it was the hunchbacked man, not the others, who could find the way to the place of the dead. Even as she vaguely knew, vaguely and yet vividly remembered, what the shaman had said: do not eat, lie in your grave, wait for the guide.

And she had followed her guide so bravely she had preceded him to his own goal.

29. Dead Pronghorn

The caves appalled Dawe, tempted him. In his confusion he saw them as crypts, their doors broken, their treasures gone. They might have been smashed open, robbed, by the earlier expeditions that seemed to have taken everything else, and he, Dawe, hated the secret dark mouths up high in the cliffs. But he was tempted too; and after seeing the burned antelope he went down a cliffside, picked his way past the gnarled junipers, down past the bright yellow blossoms of prickly-pear cactus, and into the sudden, cool shadow of a cave's entrance. He unhooked the canteen from his belt, opened his specimen bag to find his sandwich. He ate automatically, without appetite; then, because he could not bring himself to face the sun again, he pulled his field book out of his pocket. He wrote, pompously, not for himself but for his imagined wife in their remembered, imagined home: *Dawe in the desert. After the endless water, the endless walls of volcanic ash. I have only stared at these ribs of death for four days, and already I can remember nothing else.* Liar, he thought. Liar. Looking out at the light from the cave's dark mouth. *The river itself a mirage that runs through this dry canyon. The wind is more real. The wind that lifts up the dry grass in mockery. The grasshoppers sawing it down again, the sprung, hard grasshoppers crackling into the bright air. Night is relief from the sun. A cave is a pocket of night, cooling and dark, saved from the day. But a cave smells——*

He could not write it. Of death. A cave smelled, as he had not expected, of a denned coyote, a wintering snake. Of death.

He had found the pronghorn antelope above the valley, on the burned prairie. It was not quite dead. It was burned; it had been caught in the flames that stopped at the valley's edge, the hair of its body had burned, must have lit and flamed like a dry tumbleweed. But the pronghorn, blackened, swelling, its hoofs seemingly melted, was not quite dead: and Dawe could not do it. He could not hit the animal with his hammer, could not kick in its head.

He closed the field book. He went back into the sun: he drove himself all afternoon, measured himself against the sun. All afternoon he strode, climbed, crawled through the heat of the Badlands, determined by an act of pure will to find the perfect specimen he had come here seeking; Dawe, after his sleepless night, his morning's shock, not only accepting but anticipating, looking forward to, rejoicing in the onslaught of the sun.

Towards evening he went back, went up out of the valley again. He found the sun-stinking body.

The pronghorn was partly devoured. Coyotes had caught the scent, had come up out of the coulees. Or bobcats. Or a wolf, surviving alone in the Badlands, had come to eat. The carcass was ripped open, scattered red on the edge of the blackened prairie where the fire had stopped. The charred grass powdered Dawe's boots; the black soot, the ashes, cushioned his footsteps almost into silence. And there were no ready bones to be shellacked and polished and arranged, no unbloodied fossils to be mounted and displayed in a museum. Flies had found the carcass too, and had not gone away; they were crawling, the bluebottles, iridescent and coppery-blue, too heavy to rise up now, laying their eggs in the stretched and scattered entrails.

In the falling night, Dawe turned again to descend into the valley. The river, far down, distant, was a long pale slit in the dark. All the Badlands were become a cave, and the river, mirroring an invisible light, was the opening, and Dawe was inside the cave, Dawe was inside. And he started down, towards the far slit that would let him escape; he touched greasewood, juniper, feeling his way with his swelling feet; he touched a rock loose and heard it tumble, fade, tumble away. He listened.

Somewhere near him, an animal moved. He believed he smelled it. The rankness of an animal, a coyote or bobcat or wolf, not burned and dead, but alive. The living animal.

And he moved down towards the river, afraid that he might slip and fall.

30. *Squaw Wrestling*

Web found a horned lizard in his left boot one morning, the surprised reptile, in the process of trying to save its own life, rubbing its horns and scales through Web's left hand; and Web, once he'd calmed down, announcing he'd pay Dawe to fire him.

And somewhere in the course of the next evening he, Web, uncovered, in a blanket he'd thrown over some sagebrush so that it might be aired, a shiny black spider: and he asked Dawe about it and was informed that the bite of a black widow, while not always fatal, was certain to be incapacitating, especially if the bite was delivered in any pubic area, the black widow being one of those fine female spiders that devour their mates after sexual consummation.

Web spent more time looking for spiders than for dinosaurs, and two days after the day of his discovery of arachnids woke up in the middle of the afternoon, under a cottonwood, when he was supposed to be awake and prospecting, and realized he had been awakened by the curiosity of an eight-foot bullsnake: a snake which, Dawe explained again, kills its prey by constriction, that death being an unpleasant one for any creature that gets its oxygen by the contraction and expansion of the lungs.

And on the seventh day of Dawe's desert agony, eleven days after they had established camp, Web was looking for a safe place to sleep, away from lizards, snakes, spiders and Dawe, when he recognized the smell of mash. He was peeking into a cave in an eroded butte, the cave's entrance seemingly guarded by ten or a dozen hoodoos. He entered the cave, found no one tending the still, helped himself to a swig of the raw liquor.

By six o'clock in the afternoon he believed he was not afraid of anything. He stepped out of the cave; a grasshopper clacked away from his boots; he thought it must be a rattler; in the process of leaping clear he fell twenty feet down the side of the coulee.

A peal of laughter came out from behind one of the hoodoos. Then a coyote appeared from behind the sandstone pillar that was the hoodoo's base. Then, as if being led by the young coyote on a leash, a man appeared: a tall, thin, wiry man. And Web noticed immediately, the band on his cowboy hat was the skin of a garter snake, his belt a bullsnake's skin: the snake man asking:

"You some kind of Prohibition agent?"

Web, hanging onto the side of the cliff, watching the coyote. "You bet your ass I'm not."

"What're you after?"

"Right now I need a drink," Web said.

"You guys couldn't find water in a river." The snake man eased himself down towards the cave's mouth. "Come on up."

"How?" Web said.

"Like you got here in the first place. Crawling on your belly."

Web worked his way up the cliffside, stepping on a rock imbedded in the clay, a juniper root; getting hold of some greasewood. And then, entering the cave, he almost leapt out again: two men were seated by the still. He looked back; the coyote was in the entrance.

"Pass this fellow some of that moon," the snake man said. "He wants *more*."

Web nodded eagerly. "Take a lot of this to kill a man," he assured them. He took the tin cup, drank, the moonshine burning in his throat. "How'd you two birds get here?"

"Other entrance." The speaker not glancing up, fanning the small fire alive.

Web looked around at the blank clay walls.

"That reminds me," the snake man said. "Who owns that squaw you got with you?"

"Nobody," Web said.

'Well who's humping her then?"

Web looked back at the coyote. "That woman thinks fuck-ing is a city in China."

They took turns drinking from the tin cup. "That's pretty good," the snake man said. "Like the fellow says, 'How's she hanging?' 'Straight up,' this other fellow says." He waited for Web to return the cup. "You ever do any squaw wrestling?"

"Not if I can help it," Web said.

"Maybe you can't help it this time," the snake man said.

Web asked for, and received, another drink; the tin cup went around the fire, went around the cave, each man carefully drinking his allotted share, no more, no less, each sensing the ritual of sharing and division. Web thinking, maybe if I drink enough I'll see dinosaurs instead of elephants. Web hearing himself, realizing he was talking too much, and going on talking. Killing time; unnaturally, now and then, holding his breath.

It was nearly ten o'clock when they heard a halloo in the coulee below them. The snake man, at the first call, went out past his coyote, disappeared; ten minutes later he was back. He brought in Dawe and Tune with him.

"We've been looking high—" And then Dawe stopped.

Web was raising up the tin cup: "There once was a pimp named Dave, he kept two dead whores in a cave—"

The snake man, politely, interrupting: "Give these gentlemen some of that moon."

They might have been late but expected guests, Dawe and Tune; Dawe not able to be angry because of his curiosity and uneasiness; Tune trying to drink

154

with, talk with, the men. All of them drinking now. They told stories. They talked about bones. Dawe despairing of finding a specimen; the snake man saying the valley was nothing but a bone heap, he knew a rancher built a fence around his house with dinosaur bones.

"I'm not looking for fragments," Dawe said. He was drinking hard, helping himself to the moonshine. "I want a complete and total specimen."

"You bet your life," Web said. "Whole hog or none. We didn't come here for the scraps."

"Fair enough," the snake man said. "You whip me at squaw wrestling, I'll show you a skeleton the likes of which you never saw in your life."

"I'll turn you inside out," Web said.

"Take off your clothes," the snake man said.

"Now wait a minute," Web said.

They had another drink together, Dawe speaking of the old quarries he was finding, each and every one of them deserted, a reminder that he was the last, the end. "Used to be a treasure heap," he said.

The snake man was watching Web. "You're just a damned big talker, aren't you?"

"I'd wrestle a bear. And if it was female I'd screw it while I had it down."

"But you're scared of grasshoppers. Not to mention spiders, ticks, mites and scorpions."

"Scorpions?" Web said. "What scorpions?"

"Not to mention your own goddamned shadow," the snake man said.

"I don't give a shit where the skeleton is," Web said. "I'm going to wrestle you into a knot just to shut you up."

And then he jumped to his feet, he was pulling off

his clothes. The snake man took off his hat, took off his trousers, undressed. They were both naked, the two men, they lay down on the cold clay; Web moved some bones aside, the bones of a rabbit or a badger, and stretched out. They lay stretched out side by side on their backs, their feet pointing in opposite directions. Web's head was at the snake man's right hip, his own right hip was at the snake man's head. They hooked their right arms together. At a given signal each would raise his right leg, they would hook legs and each would attempt to force his leg down again, turning the other man through a back somersault, a spine-bending somersault that would either flip him onto his belly or wrench his back.

Dawe was to give the signal. Web asked for more time; he settled his shoulders on the cold ground, tried his right leg a few times. Then the snake man sat up and asked for another drink. His coyote, staked at the entrance to the cave, growled: "Shut up, Claw," the snake man said.

Then they were both lying flat and ready, motionless, the light from the fire playing shadowed and red over their pale bodies:

"Go!" Dawe shouted.

Two legs flashed up, smacked against each other with a bone-breaking thud: the two legs hooked together, the snake man grunting; then Web thrust straight out with his leg, raised up to put all his weight behind the motion: the snake man went straight up as if he would stand on his head; then he broke in two, knifed shut; Web's leg stiffened and the snake man flipped in the air, somersaulted, his lean body slapping belly-down on the floor of the cave.

'Just about wrecked the family jewels." The snake man, grunting. "You sons of bitches. Come on."

They were putting on their clothes, the two men, Web trying on the hat the snake man wore, then handing it back.

Then all six of them bent away from the fire, crawled out of the cave, slid out into the night. They carried with them pails and small bones, and they pounded now, on the pails, the drunken band, Tune trying to get the other men to sing. They staggered out into the badlands, into the moonlit and cooling night, the snake man with his coyote taking the lead, Dawe humped and walking fast, following, stumbling at his side, the others straggling in two pairs as if they must, all together, lift and carry some invisible burden. They pounded their makeshift drums; they hopped and jigged as they went, through the rocks, the sagebrush, the cacti; they came to a spike of clay, as high as a tipi, white in the light of the orange moon; they danced once around it, twice, again, the snake man passing back a jug of moonshine. They slipped through a crevice, walked on, laughing, stumbling, falling, shouting against their echoed voices, Tune wanting to guide their song; they stopped. The last man, raising the empty jug, blew across its mouth; against Tune's voice he blew, up at the tugging moon, a deep and seashore sound:

"Look," the snake man said.

They were quiet, the gathering men. They formed a circle, found their mooncast shadows.

White clay, washing down from the coulee wall, had made a miniature flood plain, a white floor as smooth and seemingly as hard as marble. Raised an inch, two inches, above the floor, where the coulee wall rose up again, was a rim of stone: it might have been the socket of an eye.

Dawe bent to the blank, stone eye, touched it.

"What's the verdict?" Web said. Web placed one foot inside the rim of stone, pulled back.

"Ceratopsian." Dawe's voice deepened on the sound, caressed it, his small body caught in the vibration of the sound's enormous magic: "Horned."

Tune bent down beside him.

"The frill," Dawe explained. Speaking to Tune now. "The shield." He gestured, touched his own neck, with an upward gesture suggesting a sweep of bone behind his head, a skirt of bone and muscle over his neck. "The horned dinosaur."

"How big?" Tune said.

"Depends on what it is, exactly. Skull itself could be the size of Web."

"Feel kind of horny myself," Web said.

But the others didn't respond now; they were all quiet, looking at the solitary clue, then looking at Web. A skull the size of Web.

"Ought to have a drink," Dawe said. "I guess."

But the spirit of the party had collapsed. The mood was spent. Now the snake man muttered something to his two cronies; the three of them said they had to leave, it was coming morning.

Dawe didn't straighten to say good-by. He was pointing, speaking to Tune: "Whole thing must be right here. The skeleton. Going back into that hillside." He glanced up, asking for support in his supposition, asking for approval. But the three moonshiners were gone. He turned to Web; Web, drunk, spent past his drunkenness, was stumbling down the coulee, into the first light.

Dawe and Tune began to gather broken stones in order to mark the prospect.

31. *Into the Pit*: Chasmosaurus

The cook did not wake the crew next morning; Dawe called even Grizzly awake. Web had a hangover that threatened to split his skull; he blamed it on the fusel oil in the moonshine. His muscles ached from the squaw wrestling, his right leg was strained and stiff. He lifted his leg out of the cot with both hands, complaining to young Tune as he did so. But Tune was gone out onto the deck of the flatboat to gather together the necessary tools, to lift more from the musty hold.

After sitting down to a huge breakfast that Web could not touch, they carried their shovels and picks and chisels and hammers, their awls and brushes and shellac, up into the coulee. Dawe explained: they would cut a trench around the skeleton; once they were down several feet they would cut under it as well. Then the bones, encased in their protective rock matrix, could be wrapped in burlap and plaster of paris, transported down to the riverside. They walked back to the camp for dinner, Tune singing, Web holding his head and explaining that earlier he'd been afraid he would die; now he was afraid he wouldn't.

The afternoon sun turned the site into an oven.

But even then Tune's high spirits didn't fail; he was catching something of Dawe's excitement. Quickly he learned to work close to the fossil with a chisel and hammer, brushing shellac onto the newly exposed bone before it could crumble. They were discovering the outlines of the huge skull. Tune, digging, found a horn cone, recognized it without having to ask Dawe what it was. Dawe saw it: "*Chasmosaurus*. We've found the *Chasmosaurus* type. Small nasal horn, the way it looks. Larger horns on the brows."

"*Brow* horns?" Tune said.

Dawe explaining. The horn itself not fossilized, gone. The core of bone suggesting a horn that was two feet long. He raised his hands. "For fighting off *Tyrannosaurus. Gorgosaurus*."

Web stopped listening when he heard those mysterious names. Towards sundown he said to Tune, confidentially, correctively: "Take it easy. We're digging our own goddamned grave."

And Web's second day was worse than his first. For now, as they created a quarry, they cut themselves off from the prairie wind. Working in the rock bowl, the three of them, they were assailed by horseflies, by mosquitoes. They went back to camp, their necks bleeding, swollen, burned.

And on the third day, working from noon until evening, Web chipped away the matrix from between two leg bones. Dawe, once again delighted, announced they had found a skeleton that was certain to measure in length at least sixteen feet; Tune paced off the distance on the marble-like surface, stared in wonder; Dawe in his mind hoarded words for his evening's field notes: *Horned. The horned beast. The butt of slander. And bête noire too, the horny beast.*

And Web, at dawn on the fourth day, looked at the small heap of clay he had chipped loose in five hours, looked at the outline that Dawe had etched with an awl in the hard clay. At noon he took his lunch and his canteen and went up over the butte.

When he returned, in the early afternoon, Tune and Dawe were quietly, diligently, working.

Dawe glanced up from where he was down on his knees, brushing shellac into the bones of the exposed jaw:

"Well? Were they waiting for you?"

"Fucking cave," Web said. "Empty. Everything gone. Vanished."

He picked up his chisel and hammer and knelt down into the sun-glare of the white bentonite matrix, the radiated heat of the exposed fossil.

The curious thing about Web is that he obeyed my father's arbitrary command: he stayed away from Anna Yellowbird. And I suppose the curious thing about all those men on our frontiers is the sexual lives they lead. Where the two most obvious answers to their presumed needs are to love each other or to share a woman, they will do neither. They avoid violent relations with each other by violence; the squaw wrestling of their pale bodies is meant to deny the wrestling of their spirits together. And the notion that a woman is not to be shared is one of their notions also.

We have the instinct of community, will share or be shared: the avoidance of Anna was no idea of Anna's. Grizzly, of course, ignored my father's command; he managed to do what he pleased, either because my father thought of the cook as another woman, or because he was too much the male my father pretended to be to be put off by my father's bluff. And Tune, working in the sun, losing his body's fat, finding his male muscles, had not yet found the male instinct that would fling him against my father's possessive will.

Web, in a fashion, was the sole contender against that force. His indifference was his secret weapon. For my father, years later, could fly into a rage, remembering Web's indifference about the past they were seeking together. Web, arriving at the site in the morning, might have to be taught a method or technique he had been taught twice, three times, four times before. "He didn't care," my father would shout, starting up from the easy chair where he sat, facing out over Georgian Bay.

And Web's innocence would light the room.

As it lit the dark that night, years before, when he burned his own father's shack to the ground. And used the light of that burning to make his way.

32. *Above the Canyon*

On August first, after fifteen consecutive days of digging, Dawe declared a holiday. "Must be his birthday," Web told Tune. Young Tune ignored the remark and went out into the sun to wash clothes and darn socks. Web returned to the tent to sleep until noon. And would have: except that before he had taken off his boots, Grizzly was in the tent, holding out a handful of ripe buffalo berries.

"Make jelly," Grizzly said.

"Go ahead," Web said.

"You help."

"Damnit, Grizzly, those bullberries will taste a lot better after the first frost." Web lay back into luxury on his cot.

Grizzly shook his head and repeated, "Make jelly."

"I told you—" And then Web added to his own surprise: "Those pancakes and biscuits of yours would damned near be edible with some bullberry jelly."

Grizzly nodded his head.

Web groaned. He sat up and began to lace his boots. "Just one condition," he added. "No goldeye today."

They went into the sprawling patch of buffalo berries and Grizzly spread a tarpaulin under some bushes. Web picked up a stick and used it to beat at the silvery leaves and branches, the small red berries cascading onto the tarpaulin. He found himself enjoying the commotion, the feigned violence, the quiet domesticity —he, beating the bushes, Grizzly scooping the berries together, moving the tarpaulin —and then he was asking Grizzly again about that

164

time in the mountains, at the headwaters of the river; and then Grizzly, grunting, picking leaves out of the heaped red berries, was muttering the syllables that might be words like ice, lake, river, forest: and Web, working cheerfully in the hot sun, began to daydream the headwaters of the river, the pristine lakes and the green spruce forest, the trout streams, the glaciers hanging white over the icy waters ... The flies, the mosquitoes, came up at his face, and he went on dreaming the sweetness of the forest, the cool of the glacial calm.

It was the returned and compelling dream that made him do it: he left Grizzly to boil the berries into jelly and walked away, alone, from the camp. He made his way through the now familiar sage-brush and buttes; once out of sight of the camp he walked faster, made his way up a long coulee, dreaming now of the bear's climb into a mountain retreat, high up at the foot of a melting glacier; he walked in the heat, climbed, crawled, the insects brazenly shrill against the silence of the wide canyon: he came to rimrock. Web lifted himself up over the edge of the valley, caught at the thin layer of soil on the clay; the matted roots of the grass held and he hoisted himself onto the sod, then got up from his hands and knees, stood up on the prairie.

A dozen godwits rose noisily away; the sudden wind touched the sweat from his face.

He had not once come out of the canyon; now, in the cloudless day, he could see straight out to the flat horizon. The far line wavered, thinned in the heat, rippled upwards and became air. But he need only walk.

He need only keep on walking: in three hours, in

four hours, walking straight out across the flat prairie, the shortgrass plains, he would come to a barbed-wire fence. To a windmill. To a ranchhouse. The blank space of the prairie would grow into a ranch, a trail, a road into town, would grow into warm meals and clean beds and Saturday night dances and a case of bootleg beer concealed in a ditch behind the hall and men not talking compulsively about bones, men chatting about their horses, their hay crops, ballgames on a Sunday afternoon, the price of wheat, the press and consolation of work and friends and family.

Web thinking: old McBride had the right idea. Skin out. Haul ass for shore. McBride, today, right now, playing with his kids, watching the crops ripen. Web thinking: I could find the railway, hop a freight. Go somewhere.

He looked down into the valley. He could not see the camp; it was hidden by a butte.

Somewhere, down in that canyon, they had almost succeeded: they would have it now, in a few days: the skeleton unearthed. The bones themselves, freed from the rock and back onto earth. Right out of the grave, those bones, and some horny old dinosaur booted in the ribs like a sick cow and told to stand up again. Seventy million years later. Whatever that meant. Seventy million, when he couldn't grasp the notion of seventy: damned lucky to get out of that canyon alive, let alone live to tell about it. And that would be okay too, come winter, sitting in the pool hall in a little town somewhere, listening to the blizzard, telling how you went with this hunchbacked greenhorn from down east and dug up bones

all summer; wouldn't give us a day off except to box
up the specimens we'd found, had to wipe our asses
with cactus—prefer button cactus, myself, to prickly
pear—drank nothing but moonshine, the water so
full of clay it made you spit dust; ate nothing but
horned lizards and goldeye, got to the point where I
was breathing through gills. And money? Hell, we
weren't paid, we were *paying* for the privilege of
being there; and mosquitoes—one good thing about
them, they drove the crows and magpies away; a
summer's wages wouldn't buy you a ticket back to
town, and as for tail, pulled myself off so many times
I had calluses on my calluses, a fellow I was working
with screwed a porcupine one night, best thing I ever
got into was a pronghorn; you ever see a pronghorn
doe flash her white ass and skip around—and one
more thing: this eastern fellow Dawe was defeated,
down for the count, throwing in the towel and
wringing his hands in total despair; the boat was
loaded with no end of dinosaurs; there were chunks
of ice the size of the boat, coming down from the
mountains; there were sandbars like the dunes of
Egypt, blinding sandstorm right there in the ice
floes: this poor damned fool Dawe turns to me and
he says, Web, my boy, either you get us out of this
fix or we might just as well crawl into one of them
holes you dug and pull it in on top of us—

33. *Rainy Day: An Accident Occurs*

Sometime before dawn they heard the first fine
patter of rain on the tent on the boat, then the drum-
ming that told Web he could sleep in, that told Tune
he could go fishing, as he had been hoping to do for

five weeks. The sound that told Grizzly he would have, all day, three men in the cook's tent.

Dawe: "Bloody weather."

And Tune, sleepily, to Web: "You going for one of your big hikes the way you did last week?"

"Hell no."

"You see anything up there worth looking at?"

"Hell no . . . And shut up and let me sleep, Tune."

They drank coffee and played cards. Then at eleven the rain turned to a mere drizzle for an hour, and Dawe ordered them out and they worked in the drizzle and the wet, dead grass, building a stoneboat.

Web cut down a cottonwood and shaped two skids. Dawe and Tune sawed two-by-fours into short lengths and built on top of the skids a platform; now, with the help of a rancher and a team of horses, they could haul the blocks of rock and fossil out of the coulee and down to the river. For they had almost completed the wrapping of the blocks that contained the specimen, Tune mixing the bags of plaster of paris with water, Dawe working quickly to cover the top of a block of rock and bone with a thin sheet of rice paper, then with strips of burlap soaked in the plaster of paris. Web working in the space they had dug beneath the three main blocks, reaching up overhead as he lay in the narrow passageway, plaster running down into his armpits, burning his eyes, the fast-setting mixture fixing his arms and hands and the burlap into rigidity before it would stick to the rock. But he succeeded, cursing, giving up, trying again, and the neat patterns of bone in rock were covered, poplar poles had been wrapped and plastered onto the plastered rocks, and the great white chunks of treasure could be levered, now, one by one, out of the quarry.

The stoneboat completed, the three men went back into the tent, ate dinner.

Grizzly was cross as a bear, Tune said, and was pleased with his joke. But the cook would not laugh; his routine broken, the mystery of how he spent his day violated, he was on the verge of chasing them out when Dawe himself said he was going.

"Into this rain?" Web said.

The slow, steady rainfall was maddening to Dawe; it could go on for days; the clouds sat like a lid, down on the canyon. He ignored Web.

"Go ahead," Web said. "I'm going to get some shut-eye. Try to sleep the lime off my eyeballs."

"I'm going out," Dawe said again, to Tune this time. "I'll stick to the grass and the flat ground."

And then Tune, as Dawe was betting he would— Dawe realizing even in his reckless impulse that it was foolhardy to go out alone—Tune saying, "Let me get my coat."

And Web to Grizzly, as they left the tent, the man and the boy: "You got to hate that son of a bitch. Only way to live with him. Hate him."

Grizzly went on cutting biscuits with a sealer lid, and Web, picking up his coffee cup, went outside too: he stood in the rain for a minute, watching the figures disappear, waiting for them to slip or slide.

The bentonite was like soap in the rain. Dawe and Tune headed across the sagebrush flat, Dawe, under his wide black hat, leading the way, moving his head from side to side not just to see but to sense, to probe; the boy following behind him, learning, resolved now in the acquired habit of ambition to find the specimen his teacher missed, the fragment that was not cherty or tuff, the subtle shaft of bone.

They stopped at the base of a cliff, stood helpless, staring up at the slick bentonite. The volcanic ash had drifted from growing mountains onto the dinosaur deltas to the north, had accumulated and mixed with sand and shale and mud and rock, had silted over the dinosaur dead that were rolled and carried like driftwood into the delta swamps. The ash had compacted and decomposed for millions of years, until now it was a film of clay that shrivelled and flaked in the sun, that swelled and shone in the rain, shutting out the eroding water from the secret bones inside the remaining bluffs and buttes.

And Tune asking: "Where are those three prospects you found?"

Dawe kicked at a stone. "All of them. Nothing. Isolated bones."

And Tune again, innocently: "Then what will we do?"

It was then, only then, that Dawe, wordless, signalled: they started up a small stream bed that had come alive to the rain; four inches of water moved through the margins of brown-eyed susans and gumweed and sunflowers. They made their way, carefully, up onto the flat, grass-matted top of the butte; Tune had expected to be able to touch the clouds, and still they were far out of reach, torn, moving now, one layer faster than another.

The sight of Anna Yellowbird's tipi, below them in the valley, her house of bones, made Dawe remember his own: and he told himself, this first expedition, this season in the field must be my last. He would stay at home with his wife, have children, raise a family. He said it to himself, in the rain, the season half over and he with only one skeleton to his credit: he would stay at home with his wife and family and work in the museums there in Toronto, in Ottawa, the careful scientist, the new Cope or Marsh or Lambe, identifying the specimens, restoring, categorizing, writing learned articles. And at night he would go home, not to a tent and the smell of socks and a mosquito smudge; he would go home to his wife and his library; he would have sons, perhaps he would have three sons, one of them a young man like Tune, almost morose at times, dreamy, given to singing in the midst of disaster; young Tune who had learned to worship—yes, that was hardly too strong a word—Tune worshipping the old master, Tune already dreaming of his conquests in the field; but Dawe would be at home, at home with his wife and family—

He turned away from the sight down in the gulch by the river, the pitiful heap of bones; he turned and led young Tune in the opposite direction, led him not towards but away, and across the butte, looking for a means of descent—

In the rain-wet clay, Dawe saw what looked as if it must be a bone.

The tabletop of the butte ended, trailed off as a ridge, a knife-back ridge of clay that angled downward, running like a dinosaur skeleton's vertebraed back out towards a cluster of hoodoos, far below them. Dawe at first believed it was the illusion that

171

compelled him, the ridge like a skeleton's back, the slick mud softly purple, gently green, in the rain, like the imagined hide of a living dinosaur.

But the brown protruberance, the stone that was not a stone, was hardly twenty feet out, down, on the naked ridge.

Dawe stepped off the grass. He went onto his knees. He straddled the hard, slippery ridge; with the ridge of clay between his legs he put his hands forward, lifted his body, thrust forward and down, moved his hands again. He proceeded out, downward, three feet, four feet, the naked, unscalable walls of the ridge falling off on either side.

"I could get a rope," Tune said, bent out and over from the edge of the butte's flat crown.

"I'll make it. Don't worry. We might have to dig out here—"

Slowly, carefully, Dawe worked his way down, his legs swinging free, his body thrusting; then his knees catching again at the slick clay, his hands moving forward, the raindrops pelting and sliding away, forming rivulets, below his boots, in the fluted sides of the ridge. But he had let himself out, down, twenty feet. He caught hold of some greasewood with his left hand, used his right to pull loose the pick from his belt, to strike at the bog-iron concretion at the base of the outcrop.

He knew the texture at the pick's sharp point. He turned to shout up to Tune: "It's a bone."

Tune, in his excitement, leaned forward over the crown of the butte.

"Stay there," Dawe called.

But Tune had almost reached too far; his hands

broke over the edge, a fine spray of glacial silt, of gravel, rattled from under his knees.

Dawe raised a hand to protect the boy. He let go of the pick handle. And then his grip did not hold on the wet greasewood.

Dawe felt himself going, had time to reach for the pick, had time to free it, to try again to drive it into the hard, wet clay. But the pick did not penetrate. Tune was shouting; Dawe was sliding, the colours of the layered ridge unravelling under his open eyes; the yellow-grey gravels and silts, the brown of ironstone, the black and grey and white of slate, the ash-grey of bentonite rain-washed into purple and green; and he was falling, down past, down into Cretaceous times; down he fell with the rain, tumbled; a creeping juniper caught his face, twisted him upright: except there was nothing beneath his boots:

The grey rain. Falling. Where he lay on the rock. He was not moving. He lay on the rock and the rain fell, the rain eroding his face. And he tried to move and the fire seared through his right knee. He closed his eyes. And already he had gauged it, guessed he was on the capstone of a hoodoo.

Balanced in the air, in the rain. The sandstone cap indurated and coloured rusty-red by the blend of oxides that enabled it to resist erosion. Yes. His face was eroding. He was seventy feet down from where the boy was calling. The boy: hoarsely: "Dawe." The boy's voice a man's voice. And Dawe, fallen, was still 100 feet above the gully at the slope's base.

In the wide and empty canyon. In the rain-blurred canyon; the rain, cold on his face. He liked the cold, eroding rain. He closed his eyes, his eyes were shut,

173

holding in the fire in his right knee, and he heard the sound. He must keep his eyes. The slow, quick hop of the shadow. Protect his eyes. Moving towards him. They were not. In the rain. Coming. The hawks. No . . . not hawks. It was raining. And he thought, calmly to himself: I am delirous with pain. I am injured. And then, calmly, insanely: seeing in his mind the bet and gamble he must not only make but win: I must not let them go for a doctor.

He knew that. If Tune went for a doctor, he, Dawe, would be carried out of this canyon. Would be hauled up onto the prairie, loaded into a wagon. His back was not injured. He knew that: lying on the iron-hardened sandstone: kyphosis only left you humped and deformed but harder than a snake to kill. Kyphosis. The mountain on his back. He might have smiled, pleased with the thought. Yes. He would be cyanosed, blue in the face, when they got to him. He must make Tune understand that: it was only a matter of oxygen, the hunchbacked man unable to breathe.

As long as he could move. Yes, he could move; he was certain the leg was not broken. He had known bones for so long that his own were as private and familiar to him as his thoughts. But he must escape the coyote. It was the den-smell of a coyote that he smelled. In the rain, his eyes closed, he knew that darkness was coming; not only the darkness of his mind but the darkness of a clouded afternoon on the steep slope of a nameless butte in this west to which he had journeyed against the advice of his contemptuous colleagues, his silent wife. He must escape the doctor. And already he had a scheme, was waiting like a bobcat, a coyote, when Tune spoke again:

"Dawe," the boy said. Pleading.

"Tune?"

'Yes sir."

"Tune . . . Go get Web . . . Tell him to mix a bucket of plaster."

"You okay, Mr. Dawe?"

"Tell him to bring some strips of burlap . . . Cut some willow sticks . . . Get back here before . . . it's too dark."

"Yes sir."

"And Tune?"

"Yes sir?"

"You see a coyote?"

"A coyote sir?"

"Coyote . . . You see a coyote?"

"No sir."

"And bring that chinaman."

"I can't leave—"

"Bring all the rope . . . the headline, Tune."

"I can't leave you—"

'I'm not going anywhere, Tune."

34. *To the Rescue*

The three men, Tune leading, hurried through the coulees carrying ropes and poles, carrying the canvas that had been their sail, as if they would not rescue Dawe but erect over his head a scarecrow. A gallows. Would wrap him in a winding sheet. The three men struggling up the slippery slopes, their failure to stand on their own feet a mockery of the rescue they proposed to effect.

Young Tune upset now, blaming himself, worried beyond all caution that his hero might be dead: Dawe, who should have been dead from the fall he took, who groaned aloud about a coyote, who had fallen silent, under the rain.

The fine, cold rain washed their faces fresh and awake, soaked their clothes. Tune now led the way, big Web carrying poles that might become a stretcher, the poles wrapped in the canvas sail; the chinaman, stooped even smaller against the rain, seemed wrapped and entangled in coils of rope, one arm protruding from the tangle of rope to lift and lug a bucket of plaster.

In the late afternoon, in the cloud-filtered light they found the top of the butte from which William Dawe had slipped and fallen. They stepped one by one, each in turn, Tune, then Web, then Grizzly, to where the grass stopped or was broken off at the knife-cut commencement of the ridge, gave way to gravel, to clay.

Dawe, below them, lay stretched out flat on the flat rock, the capstone of a hoodoo, that had stopped him from plummeting into the gully at the base of the precipitous slope.

The coyote, or bobcat—it was too dark now, the rain falling steady and hard—was crouched within twenty feet of the fallen man. Only Web could see the animal; he picked up a stone, threw it:

"Dawe!" he shouted.

"Don't hit him," Tune said.

Dawe did not open his eyes. The three men feared he could not hear, must be unconscious, might be dead. Web began to knot a rope around Tune's waist.

"Web," Dawe said.

176

"Huh?" Web, startled, looked down over the edge of the butte's cap. "What?" he called.

"Web ... Come down here ... Bring the plaster ... "

"He wants you," Tune said.

"He's totally out of his feeble mind."

"You heard him."

"I'll push the bastard off if I go down there."

Tune was untying the end of the rope from around his own waist; Web, while he argued, picked up the other end, wrapped the rope twice around his body, tied a triple knot and then knotted it once more.

"Sheee-yit" he said. "Sheeeee-*yit*!"

"Be careful," Tune said.

"Careful!" Web said. "Now don't you boys get your clothes dirty." He stepped to the darkening edge. "You two little sawed-off pricks couldn't lift me out of a cactus bed. You'll drop me like a basket of eggs."

Tune offered him the bucket of plaster, the burlap strips, the willow sticks, the knife.

"Knew a girl one time," Web said, "claimed I had four hands."

"Hurry up," Tune said.

And Web: "Use your thick head, Tune. Lower that stuff on another line—" And Web stepping out, as he spoke, off the grass, onto the bentonite, to prepare himself to grope and slither carefully down on the grease-like clay; and by the time Tune and Grizzly caught the rope, both of them diving, leaping to catch the leaping line, both of them pressing

177

the line down on their thighs, their rope-burned
hands pressing down as the rope itself whipped out
and disappeared—by then the fading voice of Web
was shouting, had shouted:

"You fucking assholes! You trying to kill me up
there?"

"Where are you?" Tune shouted.

"Where *am* I! Where the piss-complected Christ
do you think I am?"

"Are you on the rock?"

"I'm on the wrong end of this rope."

"You want to come back up?"

"I ain't got wings, goddamnit Tune."

"We can't hold—Are you there?"

"How can I tell—Oh, wait. Yuh. Hey. Get your
asses moving up there. Send me down that junk.
And slack up a little will you, so I can get this noose
off my neck."

And then Dawe spoke, from beside Web, on the
narrow capstone: Dawe in his mind holding onto the
scheme as if it was his life. He must escape the doctor:

"You bring a knife?"

"I got one coming special delivery."

"Slit my pants . . . Ligaments . . . Pulled a chip . . .
of kneecap . . . loose . . ."

The bucket hitting Web's head and Web straightening carefully, looking over his shoulder to where
the coyote, the bobcat, was, had been; Web guiding
the bucket, untying the burlap, the sticks, the knife.
Hunched close over Dawe on the narrow rock he
was slitting the trousers, then trying to slit the long
underwear and giving up; Web muttering, apologiz-

ing for causing pain: he had to lift the injured leg
and Dawe passed out then, was unconscious, and
Web worked quickly, roughly, cursing while he
dipped the burlap rags into the plaster of paris,
wrapping the strips around the underwear and the
leg, making a cast, setting the willow sticks in against
the leg on three sides, Dawe moaning now, Web
hurrying, cutting a piece off the line that dangled
down the slope and wrapping it over the sticks, into
the plaster, tying a knot; Web bent close over
Dawe's face to hear his breath; he looked up at the
slope, the cliff, and yelled: "He's blue in the face.
What does that mean, Tune?" And Tune: "What?
What do you need, Web?" "What do *I* need? I need
some tail feathers and a good strong beak. *Now*
what do I do?"

And Dawe spoke: "Let it set. Then make a
sling."

35. *Dawe's Plan*

In the dark, in the rain, Grizzly, alone, walked
back to the camp, found a crowbar and a sledge
hammer; in the dark he returned to the top of the
butte. By the time the first hint of dawn came
through the clouds, he and Tune had driven the
crowbar into the hard earth, had made a web of
rope, a sling, had run it down over the side of the
butte, using the crowbar as an anchor point.

"What're you doing down there?" Tune called.

"Fighting off the dinosaurs with my bare hands. I
was a hell of a lot better off when I couldn't see
where I am. There's a cliff here below me."

Carefully, Web cradled and tied Dawe into the

sling; then, not for a moment believing the device would work, he eased the silent man, the encased leg, off the edge of the rock slab and into space. And then Grizzly and Tune, working from the top of the butte, eased the rope around the crowbar, inch by inch, Web pushing the sling away from the rock ledge, Dawe himself holding himself away from the rock stem of the hoodoo; Dawe letting his head, his back, ride against the rock and the rilled clay walls; he rode down, slid down slowly, ponderously, regally, into the gully at the base of the butte. Then Web, too, was following, the two men on the crown of the butte steadying the line, Web sliding down the taut rope, like a spider that had lost its magical ability to resist gravity; down he went to Dawe's side, slipping and kicking and hollering.

Only after they were all together in the gully, the four of them, did Web realize that while they could make a stretcher of the canvas and the poles, there was almost no way in which three men might walk down the boulder-strewn gully carrying the stretcher and its load.

Grizzly threw up his hands in a gesture of resignation and turned and walked away. "Useless chinaman," Web said, "I'm going to put his ass in a sling too." And then the two of them, Web and Tune, wrestled the stretcher, the grotesque white leg that seemed its principal burden, from juniper to greasewood to cactus, from glacial boulder to fallen brown capstone to pools of yellow mud: the gully was become a stream and Web and Tune worked their way, waded, down the stream's course, like a funeral barge that tottered its way on stilts: the stream became a waterfall and Dawe saw it and looked away and waited: the two men spent their last energy, hoisting him downward, portaging their ship and cargo through a broken labyrinth of lichen-stained, lichen-blooming rocks.

Grizzly was waiting at the base of the falls with the stoneboat.

"Shee-yit," Web said. "Shit-a'mighty."

Silently they lowered Dawe onto the stoneboat; Grizzly produced a rope, arranged the canvas, tied him down.

The three men moved out across the long and grassy slope of land, the stoneboat gliding easily on the film of water that enveloped everything but Dawe himself. Then they came to the sagebrush flat and they moved in among the old and broken cottonwoods. A dozen, fifteen, pronghorn antelopes were grazing among the clumps of sagebrush. The three men moved so silently the animals were not, for a long time, frightened; the pronghorns raised their delicate heads, stood frozen.

Dawe moved only enough to turn his head. He saw through the shifting pattern of sagebrush, glimpsed only, the leg of an animal.

"A coyote?" he said.

Only Tune turned to look back. "What's that, Mr. Dawe?"

"A coyote?" Dawe said.

"No sir. Pronghorns. Whole bunch of them."

Then one big buck turned away, flashed his white rump to signal danger; the band at the signal leaping away; the slender animals gracefully leaping away from the three men who bent heavily away from the loaded stoneboat.

When they arrived in camp, stopped, Tune was

first to break the monotony of their laboured breathing:

"We got to go for help."

They stood in the rain, the three men, unwilling to lift their burden into the comfort of a tent, unable to sit down until they had done so.

"I've been thinking," Web said. "All we got to do is load him onto the boat and cut the sternline. The way that river is up, we'll be down to a ferry inside of three hours."

Dawe struggled to get into a sitting position, fell back again. Then, looking up at the tearing clouds, Dawe: "I've got a hunch. The one I just found. *Gorgosaurus.*"

And Web saying not to Dawe but to the tent, to the blind rain, to his own disbelief; Web as if to correct the fault and imprecision of his ears: "You're crazy, Dawe."

"We aren't going to leave with *one* specimen."

"That's right. We're leaving with none. Right now."

"I'm putting you in charge, Web."

"Strike that tent of yours, Grizzly," Web said.

"A flesh-eater. Hind limb alone measure ten feet."

Web allowing himself a flicker of interest: "One hind leg—"

"We can have him down here on shore inside of six weeks."

"You show me how, Dawe."

"By having Grizzly help you."

"The only thing that chinaman knows how to do is fry fish."

"He knew how to get me into camp."

"I suppose he also knows how to be two places at once."

"He doesn't have to be here in camp."

"Listen, Dawe." Web signalled the other two men; they would not bother to undo the lashings; they would haul the stoneboat, the man, the plaster cast right on up the gangplank, onto the deck of the flatboat. "Dawe, I want to tell you something. Getting killed is one thing. But if you think I'll hang around for six weeks holding a tin can under your arse while you shit in it—"

"Nobody asked you to," Dawe said.

And then he, Dawe, was ready to make his speech, ready to unveil the scheme he had struck upon, hatched, in the time of his falling; maybe because he did not himself believe he could do what he had set out to do, had never believed it, and had always been preparing alternate schemes, alternate announcements, alternate failures: and now he was ready to make his eloquent speech, his hair-raising and tear-stained eloquent plea for duty and science and honour and loyalty: yes, he would appeal to Web's misplaced male vanity, to Tune's misplaced affection, to Grizzly's dumb integrity:

And all he heard himself say was, "Go get that squaw, Web."

At first no one said anything. Then Web said, "Huh?"

Dawe again: "That squaw of Grizzly's. The one that's been eating our groceries all the goddamned summer."

And then, for a moment at least, even Tune could

183

hate the mean, miserable, selfish son of a bitch. Both Tune and Web hating the man, hating his persistence, his courage, his ambition, his twisted knee, his humped back, his black hat pulled faithfully down onto, over, his stubborn head, his clay-smeared black beard. Each of them feeling resentment, a touch of pity, an instant of terror.

Grizzly went into the tent.

"You go tell her yourself," Web said.

"Are you going?" Dawe said.

"No I ain't."

Dawe called out: "Tune?"

"Yes sir."

And then even Dawe could not abuse and exploit that one surviving relationship of trust and admiration, could not bear the misuse of the formal word that enabled Tune both to express his respect and avoid the necessity of speaking the respected man's name. Or maybe Dawe was able to believe, for a precious moment, that he was what the title might have implied: lord, master, knight.

He could not raise himself up off the stoneboat, partly because he was tied down onto it like a log, a fossil, partly because he no longer had the strength to raise his own head.

"Tune;" he said. "Go get Grizzly, will you please?"

Tune did not answer, did not move.

Dawe went on looking up, staring, at the dark and drifting clouds, the tearing clouds that might now, in their own asundering, must now shortly let through the stroke and hammer of light.

Grizzly, of his own, Grizzly who usually gave the

impression that he understood not one word of what was being said around him, stuck his head, like a puppet master announcing his show, from the tent's flaps:

"Mr. Dawe?"

The little chinaman who had met a bear in his cook tent in the mountains. Who stood still, when he first saw the bear, because he had been told a bear can't see the mountain it's crawling over and all you have to do is stand stock still: and he, the chinaman, the cook, did: for what seemed an hour. No, a day-long hour, a season's lost life. Stood motionless in the tent, the high, rank stink of the bear reeking over him: and then when he knew he must either bolt or perish from holding his own breath, he moved: the bear saw the motion if not the man and moved too, bolted too: the man and the bear meeting in the tent's two-by-four framed doorway, embracing: the man, embraced in the deep hair and the overpowering stench of the bear's belly, struggling or surrendering was, in his imagination if not in mere reality, very nearly cornholed before they broke free from the collapsing tent, raced side by side and in terror together up the forested mountain—

"Grizzly," Dawe said. In that canyon heaped full of treeless buttes, the layered canyon and its layered buttes set and sunk deep into the sun-savaged and rain-eroded earth. "You go to that tipi of bones you built—"

Grizzly's face a study in nothing.

"You tell that woman to come here and get to work."

Grizzly holding his breath.

"And while you're at it, Grizzly—" Dawe interrupting himself to groan, to make the effort at, the pretense of, lifting his useless leg: Dawe, in his moment of conquest, unable to resist a gesture of extravagance, a twinge of self-pity to accompany his eloquent adjudication of his own righteousness:

"Tell her," he added, "to bring back that axe of mine you gave her. I might need the damned thing."

*It was the one victory my father ever gained over
Grizzly. Grizzly was vulnerable just then; from
being too old, from having worked too hard. And in
that conquest my father violated not only the old
man's pity and trust but also his body, as surely as if
he'd taken him to bed and done what males do to
each other in bed. And Grizzly recovered his loss,
not by fighting back, but by submitting — with an
irony so blatant that even my father had difficulty
pretending he missed it.*

Grizzly, through the tent flaps, bowed.

*Perhaps, in that self-effacing gesture, if it was
that, he redeemed himself from the depths in the
instant he made his entrance. . . . In his not resisting. . . . In his letting be, perhaps . . . he already
knew what Anna was learning, what the others would
never learn —*

36. *Anna Yellowbird*

Anna Yellowbird brought Dawe water to drink fresh from the river. He lay in the hot sun until the heat seeped through his clothing into his flesh, until his cast-covered leg was warm, comforted and healing. And when he felt he must burn, must turn to ash, she would move him into the shade of a big cottonwood; and stirring awake in the small darkness that was the shade, he would let himself become more demanding; he wanted his late breakfast of coffee and biscuits and jelly, his later cup of tea. All day long she moved about the camp, moved quietly, cooking rice and making biscuits in a manner that was Grizzly's, changing the flannel sheet under Dawe so that he would not lie in his own sweat.

Hers was a quality that Dawe mistook for innocence, the indifference and concern of a child and woman of fifteen, and Dawe began to let himself talk to her; he let himself meditate aloud, in the sun, in the shade; he let himself speak of the clay-protected bones that lay on the bank downriver, the bone-white wrappings glaring in the sun:

"Never," he said. "We'll never make it."

Anna only listened.

Dawe let himself surrender to a new sense of despair; he groaned at the catastrophe he believed for himself, imagined; and then he discovered that it gave him pleasure as well. The tirades he allowed himself, the outcries, at the blank air, brought Anna from the tent, from the river. Unostentatiously she came nearer than she had been, and he liked that; the sense of her drawing near, protecting him from himself. He let himself cry out: "They'll find us here, Anna, you, me, all of us, bleached bones, bones bleaching in this blaze of sun; they'll find us and wonder what we did, what happened, what we looked like, what brought us to this end."

Anna burst out laughing.

"Like men, like men," he cried out, "they walked upright. And now we wonder . . ."

It was the fourth day, the fifth day perhaps, of her presence at his side. He had become careless of the entries in his field notes. Perhaps he had lost, or even gained, an entry, a day. And yet he read aloud his scribblings, harangued the listening girl, declaimed proudly and vainly the words mined from deep within his immobility, the loud words freed from the matrix of a lifelong silence into his hand, his voice:

"The cast on my leg," he read, *"a bone encasing the man. The white cast an albino lizard. A fish, a snake, devouring the manhood of the skeleton."*

Anna laughed for him again.

"I am anourous," he added, savouring the secret word, the word that exiled the girl from sharing his pleasure. Without a tail. Without tail. "As if it wasn't enough to be a cripple."

"You like it," she said.

He was at first affronted. The goddamned Indian girl telling him he liked his miserable fate. "Why should I like it?"

"It makes you special."

Dawe, not expecting to, laughed. He caught himself, stopped himself, and signalled that he needed,

189

wanted, a cup of water. And her response was not the act of a child, not clearly that of a woman; she brought him the water, made him sit up to drink.

And slyly he asked her: "You must have a husband?"

Anna was offering him the tin cup of water. She was touching his back. "He was a soldier," she said.

"A brave man," he said. Slyly.

"Would you be a soldier?" she said.

"No."

"Why not?"

"I have a hunchback."

He had never spoken that simple sentence in his whole life before.

"Ah," she said. "That is lucky for you." She reached and touched his back. To share his good fortune: the touch, sacred, magical.

And he had imagined, for three days, for four days and nights, that she would touch him.

"Why is that tree like that?" he said.

"Like what?"

Dawe indicating the big cottonwood that gave him shade: "Those thickest branches. They grow down instead of up." He indicated the thick, pitted branches that grew upward, then angled down, pointed away from the sun and bent spiky, swollen, back towards the earth. "Doesn't give me a steady shade. I ought to move into the tent, this time of day."

"The cook's tent?"

"My tent."

Anna, to Dawe's astonishment, to his secret and erotic delight, stooped to the cot and picked him up.

A goldfinch, as she moved under the tree's branches, started away from her moccasined feet. She, the woman, his own size, carried him like a boy through the sage and the dust and up the gangplank and onto the deck of the flatboat and into the tent.

And they did not speak then: he wanted to, had wanted to tell her of his wife, the woman Elisabeth Kilbourne Dawe who had married him because it was the fashion and rage to marry a man who was going away, and Elisabeth Kilbourne was not married and William Dawe said that he too was going away. Not to the east, across the Atlantic, but westward and out onto the prairies in a flatboat and down into a canyon. Anna was touching the hump on his back, touching his body. And it was the fashion and rage to marry a man who was going away to die, the deep and secret courtship becoming not only the dreamed courtship of death but the death itself. He had understood and accepted: Elisabeth needed a husband, but she did not need to have him around. Anna was touching him. All the men who might have married her and then departed had departed without proposing marriage, and she was left alone with the strange and intense and almost attractive man who was, while never a soldier, an intimate of the deadest bones; and then when he said he too was going away, was beginning a career that would take him away each spring, each and every springtime of the returning sun, she knew she must marry him and had taken him to bed, because at 35 he was a virgin who had never been to bed with a woman and she a woman of 25 was not a virgin, had been to bed with a departing soldier, had not liked it; and stiffly, with

deliberation rather than abandon, she engineered
his, the bone man's, loss of what her world had
taught her to call innocence; and he, arriving, departed, left behind him his married widow —

Whatever they had done, Dawe and the Indian
girl, he would not call it making love any more than
would she, he not having genuinely experienced that
genuine making, ever, she not having understood
that impossible concept any more than she had understood something called an ocean, an army, a
world war; she had taken his body into her hands,
had understood that, had touched him and held him
and caressed his real and pretended misery until his
body, like a muffled shell, like a distant bomb, exploded; yes, he liked the cliché, it was a good one,
accurate; the silence that he could not break with
words he broke with a long and whimpering
whipped-dog, whipped-little-boy groan of exquisite pain and welcome relief; he lay in the tent like a
broken soldier who had come on this beautiful day
to death, and the girl, quietly now, the woman, the
real and living widow, stood up from the edge of the
cot, walked as if in prayer or musing, walked out
onto the deck and bent in the sun to the water to
wash the semen from her cupped hands, from her
lips.

37. *Without a Skull*: Gorgosaurus

The crewmen, working in the new quarry, were unearthing a nearly perfect skeleton; only the skull was yet to be discovered and they would have, complete, *Gorgosaurus*. Tune carried home to Dawe, like a bouquet, a precious fragment of a tooth wrapped in his shirt. Dawe nodded. Grizzly found at the base of the butte a cave that was a natural cistern, and he carried water up the side of the butte, bucket by bucket, gallon by gallon by gallon, with his two hands and his bent back. Dawe said they were fortunate to find water so close. Tune drew a picture of the pattern of ribs he had, with a lover's patience, lifted and embossed free of their matrix with an awl, his cramped fingers alone sensing the difference between fossilized bone and bentonite. Dawe folded the piece of paper and pushed it into a pocket.

And only Web disliked him. Web whose task it was to keep the men at their task, working relentlessly in the mosquitoes, the flies, the 120 degrees of unrelenting heat. Web who reported briefly each day's activities and who knew, felt, that Dawe was not listening, as if the words he spoke passed directly from his mouth to a page in Dawe's field book without ever touching Dawe's mind. And Anna Yellowbird in her turn knew that Web knew that Dawe was not listening; in her body's bones she felt, apprehended, that Web's inviolable resistance to Dawe's dream was the inviolable and necessarily violated secret that enabled him, Web, to go each morning unwary and unafraid up the bare butte to the high, open pit.

38. *Losing Time*

Each night Anna went to her place downriver; and then in the night, hearing the coyotes, Dawe would awaken: awake he would dream her body. The darkness of her cunthair, the matted hair, so electrically black, the black focus become the focus of his night's daydream. And he told himself, in the night, in horror, I could by now have a daughter her age. And he was horrified and thrilled, would count the hours to her return, the dull ache of his twisted knee a consolation.

The sun returning, the first sunlight basting the roof of the tent, he would pretend to be asleep. He listened to Web snoring, turning in his sleep, Tune sometimes talking. The two men, quietly, half asleep still, dressing, going out on deck and rinsing their faces and hands in the river, walking down the gangplank to the cook's tent, to the breakfast that Grizzly had already prepared. Then he, Dawe, would lie motionless, listening to the birds, the catbirds, the towhees, an occasional thrasher. And he listened not for their songs, but for their silence.

These mornings, now, she came to him and undressed and almost without words she found his body in the warm blankets. He could not touch her when they were outside the tent. In the naked sun he became formal, jovial in his distant way, intense, quiet. In the tent, in the stilled air, he could lift her body onto his own; in the warming and sultry room that the tent walls made of the day, in the heat, her belly wet and sweet with sweat, he could stiffen and wait.

It was the moment of descent that came to obsess

194

him. The hot, cascading instant when, in which, she eased her body down onto his. The secret opening, the perfect mass of her cunthair yielding its secret gate, forcing his entrance; at that split second of penetration he must, he would, raise up with him into that underworld of his rampaging need the knowledge of all his life; into that sought darkness, that exquisite inundation, he would carry in his mind, in his head, the memory of wife and home, his driving ambitions that had swept him into this canyon, the furious desire and dream that had brought him here to these badlands, to these burnt prairies and scalded buttes; conquer, he told himself, conquer; and out of that blasting sun, into the darkness of her body he must, rising, plunge:

and found instead that at each moment of entry into the dark, wet heat of her body the outside world was lost, and he, in a new paroxysm that erased the past, spent each night's accumulated recollection in that little time of going in: the motion that erased the ticking clock, the wide earth:

and all the fury of his body needed, spent, to swim him back, down, to the world's surface, to the memory of the civilized east, his home and his wife.

Until he began to believe that only his humped back might save him from some absolute surrender. He told himself that he must remember to remember, asking Anna not to touch, then, appalled and thrilled, asking her to touch the magic of his clownish deformity; and Anna easing her perfect body down upon his, her quick hand taking him to the secret gate; then her mouth opening into a soft smile as she eased him into her cunthair; and Dawe, not moving at first, wanting not to move, yielding to her passion, her violence, her tenderness; his male sense of surrender surprised and violated and fulfilled:

She made him lose the past. He began to hate her for that. Sullen, then, sullen, in the last clinging gesture, absurdly, he unreeled to his mind's eye the field notes he had faked for the world from Web's reluctantly postulated observations: *Sixteen pairs of ventral ribs.* He clung to that, trying to imagine the neat bones arranged neatly, exposed to air and shellac by the stealth and pressure and art of Tune's awl. Tune's brush brushing. The bone in bloom. *The front limbs vestigial only.* He let his arms go limp at his sides. But his hands touched the sweat-filmed riding of her knees. *Thirty feet long including the supposition that the missing skull must be three feet in length; the flesh-eating reptile* . . . And then he could not remember.

Dawe was vaguely attentive, vaguely indifferent, when the three men came in from the quarry. Each night, returning weary, dirty, exhausted to the edge of collapse—each night they were greeted formally by Dawe; then Anna would set them their evening meal, wash the dishes; then Dawe would send her away: politely, coolly, masterfully, he would send her like a child, at bedtime, back to her room. Dawe the father, his daughter's guide.

Young Tune came in to supper, into the cook's tent, and said a storm was brewing in the west. And Dawe then, formally, indifferently, asking Web: "You wrapped those fibulae—those leg bones—in burlap and plaster today?"

"We finished."

196

"Did you cover them over with a tarpaulin?"

"Don't think it's going to rain," Web said.

"Did you cover them?"

"We didn't, I guess."

"*You* didn't," Dawe said.

"That's right," Web said. "We set them up on top of the butte. Lower them down with a rope the way "

"Just say it. You didn't cover them."

"Goddamned crew you stuck me with, useless. A good piece of— " Web stopped himself. "And a cold drink of water. Kill either one of them."

"I want *you* to go cover them," Dawe said.

And then he saw, noticed, the flicker of resentment in Anna's eyes. And then, slyly, conciliating and sly: "Anna. Web is going by your place. Let him cut those diamond willows you found. He can make me a pair of crutches."

*Surely he knew. Surely my father knew he risked
everything there: he could not endure Web's indifference, both to the girl herself, the woman, and to
his own, Dawe's, marvellously reckless and sinful
way of living. He could not believe that Web did not
know, and could not believe that Web, knowing,
would not demonstrate at least envy if not contempt
or scorn. And so he would tempt Web into a loss of
that supreme indifference.*

*Dawe had travelled all the way to doomsday; and
there, committing adultery with a squaw, fornicat-
ing with a child, he was being ignored. William
Dawe, leader of an expedition, hunchback, strange
husband of a wealthy and attractive woman, was not
used to being ignored. He believed, not in punishment, but in the kind of personal attention the met-
ing out of punishment involved. He should be
awarded Web's envy or contempt. And then Web
too, having succumbed to the same temptation
with the added twist that he must be denied any fruit
of his comical fall — would be, must be, treated with
an indifference as supreme as his own. For Web was
not entitled to the finely discriminated attention that
punishment involved. This from my father who, still,
years later, could cry out against Web: "He didn't
care."*

*Whatever it was they had entered that place to
rescue, they had surely forgotten. Web laboured obsessively to unearth the skeleton he did not want; my
father ignored the skeleton he wanted obsessively.
And it was Anna Yellowbird who must deliver them*

198

back to their tasks. That Anna who only knew she had walked a long distance. Had come to the promised bones. Must find and free the imprisoned ghost.

39. *Tornado*

"Web!" Tune said. "Where've you been?"

"Where've I *been*!" Web said. A bundle of torn clothes fell into the tent; the ripped and muddied and bloodied semblance of a corpse inserted itself through the tent flaps. "I've been ramming a pound of butter up a wildcat's ass with a hot poker, that's where I've been."

"Missed us," Tune said. "Tornado missed us."

"Didn't miss *me*," Web said.

"Goddamned tornado," Dawe said. "Second of September. Isn't supposed to happen."

"But it did," Web said.

"Shouldn't happen to a dog," Tune said.

"But it did," Web said.

"Missed us, but just about swamped us just the same." Dawe stretched out flat on his cot.

"Tough titty," Web said. "I was swamped, drowned, burned, froze to death, hammered and reamed."

"Tough titty," Dawe said.

Web flopping down on his own cot, sitting up again, standing up again. "Didn't miss *me*," he said. Web driven up onto his feet and moving; Web compulsive, aimless, following the words he uttered in his compulsion as if he must catch them, swallow them in again: "Two clouds. Then one cloud." Web dazed, in his wild stealth following his uttered words: Tune seated upright and silent on a cot, curious, then embarrassed, fiddling with his bare toes; Web pivoting and circling around the cot on which rested the disabled figure of William Dawe. "Two damned clouds just wham-bammed together. Thunderclouds. Sitting up there four miles high. Black as death inside. On top of the boat."

"North and west of the boat," Dawe said.

And Web, ragged, his face cut, pursuing the words that escaped him: two clouds moving towards each other even while he and Anna climbed into the first small buttes: then the shadow of the blotted sun giving down a yellow darkness into the canyon. The sticky heat that was Anna's reason, excuse, for avoiding her clump of twisted cottonwoods, gone; not into any wind but into a cooling of the stillness. Web, again, glancing back, and the clouds, contrary to all his notions of nature, moving towards each other, drawn into the towering vortex of the irresistible center: and still his determination that the bones must be covered, fleshed over with canvas, drove him plodding up onto the naked buttes.

One huge anvil-headed cumulonimbus cloud, rising, loomed over, loomed behind, the place where the camp must be; and the spun platter of surrounding cloud levelled out on every side from the black spindle of storm. And away from the sagebrush flat there was not a sound of a grasshopper or a frog or a meadowlark or an owl. Only a hiss. Only a far whisper, a hiss that was itself a part of the silence. Like the first-heard sounding of a snake.

Anna saw the butte from which the ridge ran, the ridge containing, having contained, the precious specimen.

"What?" Dawe said. Dawe not listening and hearing in the confused repetitions of the bewildered man the precious and all-holy word *specimen*. "Saw it," Web said. "What?" Dawe said. "Saw *what*?"

"The twister."

And off over on the edge of the wide base of the black cloud a funnel dropped down. A snake put down its head, came dangling down out of the cloud. The high center heaving itself forward, boiling and seething towards them; the wide black base of the cloud lighting the distant buttes, letting down a funnel.

They had found the butte, the quarry. They were certain they had found the butte they sought. Web and Anna; they climbed plodding against the clay angle of their ascent.

"And then the lightning," Web said. "Carpathian coke-sacker."

And in the stroke and web of the lightning they saw a second funnel, a third funnel, three funnels dancing, twisting and moving like spider legs that held up the black cloud from plummeting onto the earth; and out of the west the roaring came, out from under the cloud, below the growl of the distant and rolling thunder a steady and hissing roar: the cloud moved down the valley and the black and leading funnel danced onto the river. The cloud above the river not raining rain but sucking up water into the air, the cloud drawing up water into the sky; the whirl of water, the sky's whirlpool taking up with it the water and earth: the great stem of water lashing itself thick and bawdy in the canyon's long crack:

"I couldn't find the hole," Web said.

And Dawe, savagely: "Put some hair around it, Web."

And they saw, delicate and balanced on the flat top of the butte, the white plaster of paris casings of the rescued or stolen bones; Web went down into the quarry for the tarpaulin and lines and again plodded up onto the butte's crown; they were lassoing the tarpaulin down over and onto and around the collected and maybe even escaping remains of *Gorgosaurus*:

And when they looked up the air was green. They were in a green cloud. The earth was an iridescent blue under the net of lightning; the cloud was green.

And Web: "We've got to run for it."

"Run where?" Anna. Her small voice small as a bird's note under the rolling thunder.

And they leapt from the green cloud, fell down with the first rain into the quarry, onto the patterned bones, the last few bones locked in the matrix of rock, the continuous lightning lacing the sky into a vital net that held back the destruction that might in its same and repeated and recurring blind savagery have struck terror and bellowing panic and then death into *Gorgosaurus*:

"Hey," Web said. He brought himself up short, stood towering over, staring down at, Dawe's cot: Web, bewildered and shocked and staring at the cast on Dawe's right leg, at Dawe: "You're starting to *look* like a goddamned dinosaur." Web circling over the pinpointed man on the cot. "You look like a petrified tree trunk. Quartzite and schist. Theropod." And Tune: "In that there twister—" Tune sitting on his cot, his legs crossed and pulled up under him, away from the rising waters of Web's recollected disaster. "Dictionary hit him." "Wasn't no dictionary. Goddamned fish."

"What fish?" Tune said.

"Goddamned goldeyes. They were coming down like hailstones. Could have broke my back." "I thought you were looking at the sky," Tune said. "Threw myself down in that grave to protect Anna." "Come on, Web," Tune said. "You've been chewing locoweed." "Goddamned chinaman, it's the only thing he hasn't fed us." "Something hit you on the head," Tune said. Dawe saying nothing. And Web: "It was raining fish all around us; goddamned goldeyes coming down all around us, bouncing around, slapping and leaping up there and the water coming down by the bucketful; and then we were rolling uphill."

"Come on," Tune said.

"We were up on top of that butte in the sagebrush and cactus, and dozens of fish leaping around us; there was enough water up there on top of that butte, they could damned near swim." Web winded and puffing the words into the mocking stillness of the tent: "If I could do it again, I'd be a hog, wallowing in the mud."

"You look like you made it," Tune said.

"You won't believe this," Web said. "First time I came I was in a gopher hole. Fucking for dear life. Wasn't half bad."

Dawe said nothing.

"Pure accident," Web said. "Didn't intend it that way. Wind blowing fit to take the end links off a logging chain. Nothing to hang onto but cactus."

"Must have been a badger hole," Tune said.

"And then we were inside," Web said.

"Inside what?"

"Inside the twister. We were *inside*. Right dead

inside. The air was so cool and thin you could hardly get enough to breathe and I thought of the mountains: we're up in the mountains, I thought to myself, we've come to the headwaters; this is the source, the glaciers hanging up there, the moose and elk just down there below us having a drink of the mountain water; friendliest thing in the world, a grizzly, I thought to myself; the whole world was a bed: we were stretched out in the cactus, relaxing: 'Take a lot of this to kill a man,' I says; 'Makes a man horny,' I says, turning over—''

"Depriving those gophers," Tune said.

"What gophers? Oh, yuh—''

And Web, telling them, incoherent and passing in a circle around Dawe's cot, Dawe silent: the wind struck again, the hollow core of the funnel had passed over: they were in the air: Web and Anna were flying in the living air: in the ozone of the twister's swirl and roar they were raised up with a flock of cliff swallows: "Dozens of swallows," Web said. "Weaving everywhere. Weaving. Every one of them dead." Web confounded at his own recollection. "Hundreds of them. Every one stone dead. Flying." And Web describing a tree that flew after the flying, dead birds: an old cottonwood, its bare branches bent as if their bending made the tree fly: a hell-diver went past them, not a feather on it, he claimed: a fish without scales:

"And then I got the surprise of my life," Web said.

"Sure," Tune said.

"Anna and me. Don't know how it happened."

"Up there in the air," Tune said.

"Of course," Web said.

Dawe saying nothing.

"I had blue balls and lover's nuts and skinned knees; we were locked together up there like two howling dogs and the wind howling and cactus flying and us flying and the lightning like tentacles we were in this huge cave all hung with tentacles of lightning and the cave was as big as the world and me I says to Anna, 'Ever hear the one—' I says: and all that thunder, you couldn't hear yourself think: the angels roller-skating, no respect for the living or the dead, for fish flesh or fowl; playing hockey with a bunch of legs and a skull: God shooting marbles, mean and ornery, pissed off a little, aiming to get my lucky taws; 'No fudging,' I says: Anna laughing: 'I've got to come,' I says, 'I can't wait': 'Come,' she says— And just goddamned then the lightning struck us." Web in tenderest mercy caressing his own private parts. "I swear I saw it heading our way. Chain lightning had lit up the blue cloud—"

"Thought you said it was green," Tune said.

"Bluest fucking blue in the whole blue world. And then the bolt came streaking straight at us, the ball of fire came WHAM—and sweet mother of Christ the blue flames shot out of our ears, off our finger-tips, our glowing hair stood on end, my prick was like an exploding torpedo, we glowed and blossomed and bloomed like a flare, like a burning house. Like a house. Burning. We smelled the burning fish in the blue-green flame of the night. My old pecker was like a rock spigot pouring out molten lead, my balls glowing like furnace doors I could see Anna under me, on top of me: that ball or bolt or bomb of light-

ning had entered through my asshole, I could tell by
God I was scorched and burned, savaged, a flaming
pitchfork rammed out of the luminour air —" Web
trying to capture his spouting words. "And the crack
of thunder deafened us. The inverted universe and
undescended testicles of the divine, the refucking-
union with the dead—"

"You were in the air?" Tune said.

Web looked puzzled, surprised. As if he had
caught the words he pursued. "Hell no. That twister
set us down like two babes on a blanket."

They were on a white butte. The small hail came
more like a blizzard than a summer storm. But it
passed over and was gone. On the pure white butte
they stood up.

"We were sliding down that one white butte and
there it was, Dawe, in the white hail in the black-
assed tail of that early night it stuck out: the specimen. It stuck out of the hail, it had just been put
there, and trust my luck I slipped and—hell yes, it
was put there just to torment me, after a moment's
pleasure the old hammer coming down again. Not a
scratch on Anna. I sat there my aching balls caught
on that upright bone that stuck up out of the dirt, the
clay; come again I'd have spouted dust, a geyser of
choking dust; and I knew I had found it, Dawe, we
had found your perfect *specimen*—

And Tune, to Dawe: "I don't believe a word—"

And Dawe: "Get my axe, Tune."

40. *Man with Axe*

Dawe smashing at the cocoon of plaster of paris on his right leg: deliberately, with furious caution, he aimed and struck and aimed and struck again, Tune and Web and Grizzly too now watching in horrified and fascinated silence: Dawe seated on the edge of his cot his right leg stretched out in the lantern light, the axe biting away the plaster, the willow sticks inside.

And Web, savagely: "Do yourself a favour, Dawe. Cut your prick off while you're at it."

Dawe, swinging the axe: "Good riddance." And then his knee broke free and he twisted his body sideways; he stood up.

Dawe, on his feet, standing, taking a step. The last chunk of plaster sliding down like a manacle onto his ankle.

"Knock it loose," Dawe said. To Tune.

Tune couldn't bring himself to move.

Dawe raised, hoisted, his right foot up onto the edge of the cot, aimed again, struck the ring of plaster with the back of the axe. The plaster fell away; Dawe dropped the axe and bent over, tried to bend over and then motioned to Grizzly and Grizzly bent down and found a pair of trousers and held them while Dawe had trouble balancing even on his good leg; Grizzly bent down and fitted socks and boots onto the bare, tender, healed feet.

"Grizzly?" Dawe said.

"Yes?"

"You go tell her."

"Yes?"

"If she comes back here I'll kill her. With that axe of mine. You go tell her I said so."

Dawe snatched down the lantern from the hook fastened to the ridgepole; favouring his right leg only slightly he stooped out of the tent and onto deck; then, moving awkwardly in the half-light, half-darkness, he let himself stumble slowly down the gangplank, his right leg moving more easily now:

"I don't believe him," he said. To no one.

Dawe himself struck, not by lightning, struck and reeling away, blindly; Dawe groping his way up the steep bank and away from the river's edge, onto the sagebrush flat. Dawe walking on his two legs, crawling on his hands and knees up the slope of the nearest butte; Dawe in the lurid yellow and black and spent light of the tornado's wake seeing all around him the sombre and unmoved and, yes, unchanged black buttes; Dawe, in the gathered and torn and all-healing darkness seeing, against his will or wish to see, far downriver, the single preposterous unnatural white butte of Web's impossible and uncontradictable and total victory.

Anna Dawe

Yes, he was not born with his famous limp. By diligent effort, he acquired it. And by an equal effort avoided using the cane that he should have learned to use. As I learned, many years later, to sleep sitting up. To keep a weight off my chest too.

41. *Preparing to Blast*

Grizzly and Tune, in the immaculate clarity of the dawn, carried him downriver and then inland to the base of the brown butte that in the night had been white. Dawe, seated on a bench made of four hands gripping four wrists, managed all the while to be arrogant, spitefully proud, majestically impatient. When the old man, the boy, tripped and let him fall, he drew out of his pockets a pencil and his field book, he wrote quietly and almost daintily what he had been thinking to and of himself: *Dawe, cured of nothing but death, of everything but death*.

The grey-brown knob of bone that Web believed had saved him from falling was embedded in clay at the base of a cliff. The bone had saved him from nothing. But how he had come down the vertical face of the butte alive was a mystery that not even Web would venture in his extravagance to explain. "Flew down," he suggested weakly when at noon he arrived at the site, new tatters of cloth sewn onto his tattered clothing.

"Down?" Tune said. "You flew *down*?"

"Correct," Web said.

Dawe either would not or could not leave the place that would become his third quarry. Grizzly delivered to him food and his bedroll; Tune, alone at first and failing, then with Web's assistance, erected a lean-to shelter of willow poles and the boat's canvas sail. And that night when the crewmen left to return to camp Dawe was still digging, pouring shellac, brushing shellac into the exposed bone. Dawe, that first night, by lantern light, writing not of his day's dig or even of his stubborn heroism or his dull

211

pain but, egotistical, maudlin, committing one cryptic sentence to the smudged page: *I was beginning to like her*.

Whatever energy he had given to, or taken from, Anna Yellowbird, he now transferred to his own self-immolation. When the three men arrived back at the site in the morning he was already at work, as if he had worked all night. He could hardly walk and yet he was able to stay on his knees, on one knee, all day, digging, crawling, striking at the earth with his pick, swinging a hammer, driving a chisel between the fragile bones. He worked recklessly into the wall of clay, expecting his men to do likewise because if nothing else they could run and he couldn't; they could stand up and escape at the first sound of the clay's breaking. And that night, that dark second night, he wrote, curiously, in his field notes: *The sun is shining. The clay is hard.*

It was not until the sixth day of the dig that he ventured a name for his, or Web's, find. *Duck-billed*, he wrote. And added: *A crested hadrosaur*. And then he added also, with careful randomness, a series of bland observations whereby he might conclude that this crested or hooded hadrosaur was unlike any of those discovered and unearthed by his scavenging predecessors. He had located, exposed, most of the skull, and the silence in his field notes gave way to an extravagance of reason: *Nasal passage does not make characteristic curve of* Corythosaurus. *Crest above the skull roof suggests* Lambeosaurus, *but lacks the accessory spine, if we are to trust Lambe's reconstructions. Nasal tube less pronounced than in*

Parasaurolophus. And then he added, as if the mere thought had only then crossed his mind: Daweosaurus *must be recovered in its entirety.*

On the ninth day, and on the thirteenth day again, he wrote, repeated, what he had written on the second day: *The sun is shining. The clay is hard.* And on that thirteenth day, puzzled apparently by his own repetition of those simple and obvious remarks, he attempted what might to him have appeared to be an explanation: *The days shorter. Chilly last night, after the sun went down. Near to freezing.*

There was ice on the water in a basin on the morning of Thursday, September 21. Dawe was not at work when the other three men arrived at the quarry with his breakfast of bacon and biscuits and tea, with the buckets of water they lugged with them daily to make more plaster. Dawe was standing small and angry at the foot of the almost perpendicular cliff, at the mouth of the cave-like excavation they were creating.

"The tail goes straight back into the butte." Dawe addressing young Tune, Tune only, ignoring Grizzly and Web. "Eight feet in at most. But it's all this damned hill on top of it. We've got to blast."

Dawe, small, hunchbacked, daring to step in under the overhang while the others watched: "I've got a box of powder sticks stowed away in the hold of the boat. Sinnott left us a battery."

Tune too stepped into the excavation; he looked up at the tons of clay above them, looked around at the picks, the shovels. They would be here until snow fell, the river's edges and eddies beginning to freeze. And yet he would not yield to the temptation: Web recognizing that the boy was hesitating, Web, deliberately:

"How long you work in a coalmine, Tune?"

"Two weeks."

And Web: "No shit."

And Dawe, turning abruptly, not to Tune but to Web: "He can do it."

Young Tune, brown now, lean now, caught in the moment of excitement that even Web was reluctant to resist: after eighteen days of back-breaking labour, the remaining task completed in a matter of seconds. Today. The task completed today. The magic of the shale lifting itself up, scattering its exploded bulk away from the last buried bone, laying bare the sought and withheld secret, the complete creature completed, unleashed into the sun.

"We could go then," Dawe added. Slyly.

And young Tune the possessor of all their quickened hopes. Dawe, slyly, not using the word home. We could go then, he told them; and each man, then, trapped by the subtle confusion, into his own pursuit of past and future.

Young Tune in possession, the grown boy if not the young man, muscular now, his arms hardened, his hands hard. He, gone adventuring, disappearing down the river: returning a hero. Tune the explorer. The bone man. He would follow Dawe to the ends of the earth, off the map, assisting, uncovering. He, Tune, blushing behind his fallen curly hair, breaking into his boyish grin.

The day was ripe with the promise of an end; the September sun hot, but not oppressively so. They set to work with a new and last enthusiasm. Tune was given command; and Grizzly now went back to the boat to find the powder, the battery. Tune showed Web and Dawe how to begin, how they must, working with chisels and hammers instead of a drill, burrow into the clay. Web, caught up in the dream of deliverance, finding two holes, then another, made by trickling water, and reaming them out, preparing them for the charges. Dawe making up the wads of canvas that Tune might force in behind the sticks of powder and the detonators, mixing enough plaster to seal the wads of canvas tight in. They worked under the bright morning sun, Tune scrambling quick and lean up the cliffside, gauging the charge he would need to lift the matrix away and yet not smash the bedded bones. And hardly were the holes ready for the powder when Grizzly was coming into the coulee, carrying a gunny sack, a battery.

Web, yielding for a moment, turning to Dawe: "I could make up some fuses out of canvas."

"Try the battery first," Dawe said. "Maybe it isn't dead after all."

42. Daweosaurus

Anna heard the blast. It sounded to her like thunder, out of a cloudless sky. The silence that followed seemed to envelop the earth; the birds did not sing in the trees around her tipi, the river itself seemed to have been stilled. She stepped from the doorway of her house of bones, into the rigour of the light: she knew that her confrontation with the dead, the moment for which she had travelled so far, waited so long, was at last arrived.

She could no longer endure to be alone. After all those days in her tipi, convalescing, with Grizzly her only visitor; Grizzly coming to see her at night, Grizzly without words, bowing in her doorway, graciously entering, bringing in a dish, leaving food and departing. Most of the day she slept. In the night she sat by the river, the water mirroring what little light the darkness might possess; she sang to herself; she would sometimes throw out a stone, into the dark, and hear it pluck the water.

And now her waiting was over: she looked around at the bright day, the grass burned brown, the leaves of the berry bushes gone red and brown and yellow, the leaves of the trees a false green now, a yellow green against the brown of the buttes.

She could not be alone and she started inland, away from the river. Towards the place where she knew the men were working. And walking up along the crest of a low ridge she saw in the distance the long, high gash of fresh clay in a distant cliffside.

They had somehow moved whole tons of clay, the working men; she hesitated. And yet she must have their company, after the thunder that came in the empty sky. She went down off the ridge, walking through sagebrush now, through cacti; through the last yellow flowers of the summer—gumweed, broomweed, sunflowers, golden asters. . . . And up the long coulee she could see more clearly now the gash of fresh clay. She could see the heaped earth at the base of the cliff; no one was working.

In a moment of fright she believed: they had left. The men had sneaked away, perhaps at dawn when she fell asleep. She believed she had heard them going to work, had heard Tune and Web and

Grizzly marching into the buttes; perhaps they had
been deceiving her. And yet she would not go back
to the river to check; the gashed butte drew her on,
the mystery of the fallen hill.

She walked on through the silence. No birds
moved in the autumn sky; the crows, the blackbirds,
that should be gathering. The geese that should be
moving overhead.

Then, at the base of the heap of fallen clay, a
figure stirred. She saw motion, as if a pronghorn,
grazing, had raised its head. But the figure bent
down again, raised up again.

It was Grizzly, she recognized. Grizzly was alone,
working, picking up stones, slowly, deliberately
picking up stones, moving them to another pile; and
she hurried on now, willing to believe that the others
had gone, that Grizzly had refused to leave without
her.

The hot September sun itself lacked conviction; it
could not burn the small, dried figure of Grizzly
back into the dried, baked earth. Anna moved faster
against the light.

Then, moving up the incline, moving up onto a
flank of the coulee as she walked, she was able to
make out another figure. He was shovelling furiously, digging with wild, dramatic gestures, flinging clay out of the way as if he himself had made the
coulee, would make it bigger now.

And then she had a new foreboding. There was
too much clay in the heap before him, too much, he
could never move it all. Even Web, with all his energy, all his passion, could not move that much raw
clay.

Anna began to hurry forward, then checked her-

self. She did not want to know what they were seeking, Grizzly and Web, moving stones and clay away
from the fallen cliff. Her heart in her chest was
pounding now, not with the strain of walking but
with the stress of holding back. She caught the hot
air into her lungs and held it and wished for another
boom of thunder, out of that colourless, blue sky.

There seemed to be only two men; then she recognized that a third was sitting motionless, almost out
of sight, and she felt a wave of relief. The third man
was hunched down, humped down; he was almost
invisible behind a large rock. She stepped across a
dry stream bed, the sand in the bed of the stream a
webbed and hardened pattern; she glanced back and
her moccasined feet had made no imprint in the
hardened sand: there was no evidence that she had
crossed over, come up into the coulee.

She glanced up from the trackless bed of the
stream. She saw the hunched figure straighten, almost straighten. Wait. Imperiously he waited,
puffed up like a sharp-tailed grouse.

He was covered from head to foot in dust.

Anna had to laugh.

Her young girl's laugh broke out of her mouth.
Out of her throat. She began to giggle and then the
giggle burst, exploded into a forgotten childhood's
laughter. She must not laugh at Mr. Dawe. She
knew she must not laugh at the one who needed so
much humouring, and she caught the laugh, held it
back.

Dawe, solemn now, pompous, gestured at the
heaped clay.

A darkness came in at Anna's eyes. The red of the
light on her eyelids failed, and for a moment she saw

the shadow A winged shadow darted in at her eyes. Like a towhee, in the shade of a bullberry bush.

"Where's the other one?" she said.

She could not see him and could not accept that she could not see him: the boy with the pained grin, his hair hanging into his eyes as if to keep him from seeing. The boy who must be her woman's age.

"Young Tune had an accident," Dawe. Brusquely. "Buried himself."

Dawe started to make a wide gesture with his right arm and the dust rose off him like smoke. He was powdered in grey bentonite, he was covered, every inch of his clothing, his hands, his face, his humped back; he was dust and dust and more dust: Anna could not contain herself. She was trying to keep from laughing. And inside, down deep in her belly, the laugh started again, came up into her throat, burst from her mouth. She sat on a rock, holding her sides, trying to contain her laughter.

"Missed me by inches," Dawe said. "Pure luck." And added: "Buried." And added again, pompously, solemnly: "Alive."

That one last word, coming out of the man of dust, broke Anna into tears. She turned from the rock, fell down on the dry ground, lay flat on her back on the ground, her body shaking, the tears streaming from her sun-struck and shadowed eyes.

"Cry a little," Dawe said. "Good for a woman like you."

Dawe casting around of a sudden for any piece of equipment that might not be buried; and discovering again that everything except the shovel that was in Web's hand at the time of the explosion was vanished with the boy—their picks were gone, their hammers and chisels, all their plaster of paris, their burlap. Dawe's own lean-to shelter was gone, and with it his bedroll, even their next meal. Everything was under tons of clay. And Dawe himself, coated now in dust, saying pompously, softly: "Perhaps we should leave him where he is, decently buried in his own way."

And Web, brusquely, innocently: "What would we do if we found him?"

They were standing side by side at the base of the new hill, the two men; Grizzly went on moving rocks, moving chunks of clay, with his bare hands. They could not possibly unearth Tune alive. He must have died at the instant of the explosion. Web in his mind seeing the boy squatted down at the base of the cliff; he, Tune, was singing to himself, trying to repair the failed wiring when the whole wall of clay lifted, soundlessly lifted off, fragmented outward like an umbrella of stone, then itself became the rain.

"Coalminers live a hard life." Dawe tried to knock some of the dust off his hands. "Every day is fated. They die as they live."

Web, not relenting, resisting Dawe: "Mary Roper offered him a job."

"Just a boy." Dawe turning his emotion to eulogy. "Did a man's work. And then some."

"Played the piano," Web clearing his throat, spitting. "Best damned job in the world. *Hoo*-er house." And Web then, puzzled, not yet willing to believe: "I didn't hear nothing." Web touching at his ringing ears: "I don't remember that I heard . . . ."

220

"Buried deeper than ever." Dawe, checking his own quick motion, indicated the fallen cliffside. "The tail vertebrae—"

And Web, grotesquely, turning away: "One piece of tail you won't get, Dawe."

Dawe signalled to Grizzly, called him, told him to move to another spot, to the edge of the new hill. And he then, Dawe, carefully directed the two men, Web shovelling again, Grizzly moving clay with his bare hands. And even he, William Dawe, had trouble faking his surprise when they hit upon the wrapped bones they had earlier moved away from the face of the cliff. Out of the dark clay the clean, white, dusty plaster of paris appearing, and Dawe trying to say with conviction: "Jesus, we're way off."

Web, bluntly, nakedly: "Those bones that weren't wrapped must be right here beside these that are." And then adding again, to torment Dawe: "Unless they're broken."

"Let's see," Dawe said.

Dawe quiet for a while, working with his raw, bare hands, moving the clay off the clay-encased bones that were the skeleton of his precious and unique *Daweosaurus*. Then, without looking up, working while he spoke: "Sternberg . . . one time, working in Kansas . . . found some new specimens just when they were leaving the field. . . . Had no plaster or burlap left. . . . They used their last sack of flour to make paste. . . ."

"Not much use making paste," Web said. "If you don't have burlap."

Dawe working carefully, uncovering traces of the

ischium, ilium, pubis in a chunk of rock. Carefully, lovingly, he laid bare the unbroken specimen. "Used their underwear," Dawe said. "Sternberg's men."

Web went on driving the shovel into the clay, digging deeper, imagining that with one terrible stroke he would drive the blade into young Tune's face. Into his neck. The boy would sing out, mortally wounded, and Web would run screaming out of the coulee.

"We could use the last of the flour," Dawe said. Unexpectedly and expectedly too. "We'd have to get out of here right away. No food."

Web shovelling.

"Wrap these bones today," Dawe said. "By tomorrow they'll be dry enough so we can move them. Head out tomorrow night. . . . Travel all night if we have to."

Web straightening, spitting, lifting his cap to wipe the sweat from his forehead. He glanced back at Anna where she sat, ignored, dumbly waiting, like a bereaved and ever-hopeful widow. The widow widowed. Anna, the girl, waiting.

And Dawe again: "Travel all night. By morning —hit the ferry."

Web for a dumb instant aware that he could raise the shovel, smash it down on Dawe's head. They would never tell. Grizzly and Anna would never tell. The shadow passing over his eyes.

His shovel hit something rock-hard and soft too.

"This must be that skull." The muscles of Web's arms constricting, jerking the shovel free.

Dawe sensing the blind and dangerous rage in Web's arms. Web baring the wrapped and plastered skull, finding the numbers and letters pencilled in black on the white surface; Dawe not looking, resisting the impulse to touch the beautiful and salvaged code, retreating instead to the glacial boulder from which Anna had moved. William Dawe surreptitiously taking the field book from a pocket, putting it back, slapping again, loudly, at his pockets, as if he could not for the world remember where he'd put it. Anna, sitting on the ground beside the rock on which he sat. Dawe writing in the field book balanced on his knee and not writing that as he wrote he recalled the February evening, seven months before, when he sat at his desk in Ottawa and made a list and to the list added "field book." Dawe who on that February evening, the reports of the most recent and final expedition of the American Museum of Natural History spread out on his desk, Barnum Brown back in New York from the Red Deer River of ·Alberta with the finest collection of Cretaceous dinosaur skeletons ever collected anywhere in the world—Dawe, then, commencing on the back of an envelope a list he was to rewrite and revise a dozen, twenty times: flour, potatoes, beans, rice, bacon, baking powder, raisins, prunes, coffee, sugar, pepper, salt, shovels, picks, buckets, axes, chisels, nails . . . Revising and enlarging the list of the objects that would enable him to flee the comfort of his Ottawa apartment and job, his wife's summer home, his wife's family's solicitude for her unfortunate husband who might be permitted to accompany but surely never lead (because of failing health, it was duly noted in the Summary Report of the Geological Survey) an expedition. . . .

He, William Dawe, his list made up, completed, the objects purchased and packed and shipped and unpacked and hauled down a river so that he might go into the field in search of ultimate skeletons, might and would survive the mosquitoes, the horse flies, the sowbelly and beans, the occasional bout of diarrhea, the stink of a season's womanless bedclothes, and would, and had: and now they were gone, the picks, the chisels; his bedroll was gone; the food was gone or going: and still he would survive, cooking and eating his field books, if he must, living on his own last words: *Dead*, he wrote. *Tune. Dead.*

He recognized that the others were watching. Web and Grizzly were watching. They were working, but they were watching too, deciding whether or not to let an impulse make them leave, whether or not to mutiny first, kill him first, or simply to walk out of the canyon, float on out of the canyon and leave the task of killing to the canyon itself, the task of cleaning up after to the hawks, the coyotes:

And he, then, Dawe, slyly, gently, in the way of a loving father, shifted the pencil from his right hand to his left; he reached with his empty right hand, gently patted the top and back of Anna Yellowbird's bowed and motionless head.

43. *Loading the Specimens*

They left the quarry together, the four of them, Anna following close behind the three men; they walked together out of the coulee, upriver to the camp. Small and together they walked. Then Grizzly and Web each shouldered a sack of flour while Anna and Dawe found the cook's small buckets; they re-

turned together into the buttes. And when they had
mixed the flour and the water in a hole that Web
dug in the hard clay floor of the coulee, it was Web
who peeled off his shirt and threw it down into the
mixture of flour and water.

Grizzly laughed now. He unbuttoned his sweat-
stained grey flannel shirt, removed it, threw it in on
top of Web's. Both he and Web waited.

Dawe: "I'm not thinking. Should have asked you
to bring your bedsheets." And abruptly he stripped
off his shirt, stood awkward and embarrassed in his
long-sleeved underwear.

Web motioned Grizzly to follow; he and Grizzly
went out of the coulee to carry in more water, went
to bring whatever food they could find, whatever
rags they could make of bedding and clothes.

By the time they returned, Dawe had wrapped the
three shirts onto delicate specimens; he was scrambling nimbly about on the heap of clay, hardly dis-
tinguishable from the clay itself because of the dust
that covered him.

But he had made a discovery.

The blasting powder, the explosion, had exposed
more fossils: a last and furious greed came into
Dawe. He believed his own promise that now they
would leave; and now a terrible plenty assailed him.
The rocks that Grizzly had been lifting with his bare
hands were some of them fragments of a large turtle,
plates of an armored dinosaur, bones and fragments
of bone from a land crocodile, from a lizard. Dawe,
quick as a raiding animal, scurried over the huge
grave.

The rags that Grizzly and Web brought from

camp were not enough. In their fervid need of abasement the men took off their underwear. Web tore off the legs of his trousers and stood in the evening sun in his boots and a pair of ragged shorts. They wrapped the new fossils and needed still more cloth and Dawe, too, now, tore off the legs of his trousers, dipped them in the last of the flour and water, so the bones might go out of the canyon dressed and proper and secure.

Then, their specimens wrapped and laid in a row to dry, they returned to the river to break camp. Grizzly and Web took down both tents and stowed them; Dawe, trying to make room for all his fossils, suggested they abandon the cookstove, the benches and table. Web not only agreed; he dumped the camp cots, all the cooking equipment, into a dry creek bed. They loaded their saws and axes and stoneboat and their few remaining pieces of lumber onto deck and cast off; by the last light of day they let the flatboat drift downriver to where the boxed bones of *Chasmosaurus* were stacked on the shore.

Web, at the stern sweep, resisted an impulse to refuse to land. He saw in his mind the cliff exploding, lifting up, the first magical and beautiful moment when creation itself was in motion, the sun lifting the earth into a green passion. He might keep going now, ride that motion out to the first ferry, to the last ferry, to a road .... But then the butte broke, the flung rocks arced down from the sun, the bones came spewing down, came spewing down. A night of bones ...

Dawe, on shore, was waving the lantern. Web took the boat in and he and Grizzly set up the gangplank; Anna and Dawe were waiting to slide the first box from the bank down onto deck. They worked all together, quickly, eagerly; they used ropes and rollers —poles that were to have been Grizzly's firewood— to lower the largest boxes aboard, the boat yielding down into the water.

They worked by lantern light, Anna moving the lantern when they needed it first on shore, then on the boat; then they drifted, again, in the darkness, Dawe carrying the lantern along the dark shore; they landed again, this time where the bones of *Gorgosaurus* were waiting in crates; again they set up the gangplank.

The cold air took the sweat from their bodies. The damp of the lengthened night came up from the river, touched them wet, touched them stiff when they stopped working. The gangplank slippery, their bodies slick, they moved the crates and cases; they rolled them, slid them, lifted them down one by one onto the boat. By the first dawn they had loaded the second dinosaur.

Again, dreamily this time, resting in the first light, moving eerily through a patch of mist, of fog, they let the boat drift downstream, tied up this time at a point where they might easily walk up into the coulee to their last site. And when they had reached that quarry, Dawe, absurdly, seized the lantern away from Anna; he climbed up with the lit and unnecessary lantern onto the heaped clay, onto the grave, to look for still more fossils.

Web could not watch him; watching he heard the sea, the beat and rhythm of waves and tides; he had seen no ocean, ever, but the sound of the sea came up out of the exploded butte, the shell-song of the sea, the silence of young Tune.

They loaded the stoneboat, and bent like dray-horses they dragged the first block of rock and fossil down to the river, caught their breath and went back for another load; and the duck-billed dinosaur, *Daweosaurus*, moved, was moved, limb by limb, bone by bone, from the butte down to the riverbank. And the motion of its scattered body burned out the last impulse towards speech from the people who gave it legs.

By noon, Dawe was satisfied that the wrappings on all the new fossils were dry enough so they too might be moved. He and Grizzly and Web and Anna worked together, worked silently, carrying them, pulling them, the short distance down out of the coulee to the river's edge and the moving, outflowing water.

Dawe had said they would leave by this evening. Only, now, he insisted that the new, last fossils must also be packed in wooden cases.

"We'll do it on the run," Web said.

Dawe shook his head. "Not enough lumber. We're going to have to tear up the deck."

Web began to argue: in his mind the sea came up and over them, the tropical sea swamped the boat, the dinosaurs broke loose from their cases: "Weaken the boat," Web said, "if we take up the deck. Damned old tub will twist. Leak. Sink."

Dawe shook his head.

Grizzly tore up the deck, Anna carried the lumber ashore, Web and Dawe sawed and hammered, making and filling the cases. Darkness came down and

228

Grizzly, with silence and the motions of his hands, indicated they were out of kerosene for the lantern. They built a bonfire on shore so they might see, might keep warm, and they worked into the chill night, their shadows moving grotesquely, stooping down into the cases they would fill with fossils, darting into the hunched cottonwoods, preceding them down the gangplank and into the hull of what had been a flatboat.

Anna found three blankets; she fashioned for each of the men a rough cloak; she dressed them in torn grey woollen blankets, like figures emerged from the grey bentonite dust of the badlands canyon. And they went on working, sawing and hammering, into the darkness, making boxes for the hold of their scow. Making coffins, Web decided, to put down into the coffin of the ark itself, a perverse refinement that only Dawe could manage. Web, under his breath, cursing.

By midnight they had finished their task: the boat was loaded. But now it was so dark they could not see to navigate in the low water.

They had no place to sleep; they were too spent to find a tent and set it up. It was Anna then who made a suggestion: she had a place where they might lie down, a place where they might build a small fire, and she had biscuits and dried berries for them to eat.

Not even Dawe could offer any resistance.

The four of them together, Anna leading the way, walked through the darkness upriver. She found her tipi of bones and led them in at the low front door; she lit a fire while they waited, and by its small, warm light they found, each, a place to lie down. They took, each, from her hands, the food she offered; she was still busy, closing up the doorway, banking the fire, when Web and Grizzly fell asleep. Dawe staying awake.

Dawe, some last, infernal capacity for lust unquenched by the days and nights of labour, driven beyond all human limitations by some absence he would escape, compelled by some emptiness that he would fill by allowing the girl back into his arms— or maybe so absolutely tired, so exhausted beyond pain he needed the soporific of an orgasm to lull him asleep and would beg of her that pity too: "Anna, dear?" Dawe said.

And Anna: that Anna, like the wife he had days ago forgotten: that Anna motionless, feigning sleep, embracing silence.

44. *Last Night / Morning*

The sound of the pencil on paper made Web realize he was not dreaming. There was no tent over his head, no canvas diffusing the morning's first light; the old light that came through the tracery of interlocked bones made a pattern, a web of shadow across his face, his blanket. He glanced, again, at the close roof; again he glanced away.

The figure beside him had not been there when he fell asleep. The boyish figure beside him lay slim and still in a grey blanket in the grey light. The terror flooded through Web's blood and bones, rose up, through him, like a wash of chalk-heavy and lifting and choking water; he crushed his eyes shut, the

230

muscles, painfully, sealing the skin, closing off the still, grey form.

Tune, he thought, biting the word silent in his teeth. For God's sake, *Tune*.

Anna must have sensed his small motions; and Web too felt hers. Hardly a foot away from his cracked and seeing eyes her dark face appeared in a fold in the blanket. She was wearily awake; she covered her face again, folded herself into the blanket.

Web, relieved, frightened, stretching himself alive now: "Hey, Grizzly." Web sitting up beside the cold fire. "Catch us one of them goldeyes."

Grizzly had already stood up, was groping for the closed doorway. "No fish now."

"No time," Dawe said. He put aside his field book; he was pulling on his boots. "Let's get onto the boat. We'll be down to the ferry by mid-morning. It can't be more than a six-mile, eight-mile, run."

Only then did Anna speak. From inside her blanket, muffled, weary, she asked: "What about the boy?"

And Dawe: "Huh?"

"What about Tune?" she repeated.

And he had come so close too: the figure emerging from inside the fat white ghost had been on the verge of finding its adult life. He had come so close, young Tune. The lean, brown body emerging: the man's voice new and not his own, about to become his own.

We talked about the accident, my father and I. Sitting together in front of the windows of my cottage on Georgian Bay, looking across the water to the west. At first, when I brought up the subject, he couldn't or wouldn't remember. I was sitting on the carpet beside his chair. From the age of eleven I was taller than he — my better bones — and I invented no end of girlish poses that allowed me to be small. "Tuñe," I said. "Coming to life."

"What tune?" he said.

"Not tune. Tune." And I let myself be angry. For the boy, in some lost way, was the brother I never had. The boy I was supposed to have been. "The man you left there — "

"What should I have done?" my father demanded. My father, remembering, not bothering to pretend he was able to forget.

"You should have buried him."

"He was buried already. Better than we could have done it." And then, more softly, my father, more softly: "Still is, I suppose."

I had already launched my argument and wouldn't be stopped by his damned, sudden, gentleness: "You should have carried him down the river. With you."

And again, softly: "To where, Anna? Where would you take a corpse?"

I was stuck for an answer. But I knew my father was wrong, as Web had been wrong that time, in offering neither questions nor answers. Only Grizzly acted: he refused to find them so much as a bite to eat. Whatever funeral meats he might have provided, to the vanished dead, to the living, he would not serve them up without the decency of a human grave.

"Sacrifice," my father said. His awful pomposity rescuing me from any human regret. "Sacrifice, Anna. Sacrifice. . . . Something we have to do . . . for the advancement . . . the understanding . . ." He was quiet, looking at his slippered feet. "Fool that I was then," he added. "Out there on that sinking flatboat —I couldn't swim a stroke." He looked at me oddly, surprised, the old light coming back into his eyes. "Still can't," he added.

I remember clearly; it was a September day in 1962. My father had not gone into the field since the death of my mother. But that did not mean I had a father at home: on the contrary, then he was able to be gone always, for he hired himself out to the museums that bought his finds, had begun the task of chipping away the final rock and assembling the bones. He had come, unexpectedly, to visit, had caught me drinking, had criticized me like a child for it.

I dwelt on the occasion of Tune's death. Perhaps because my father reprimanded me and I wanted, in turn, to reprimand him. Or because, when I started to cry, he would not say one word, give me one *glance, that confessed he was sorry. And he looked so desperately ashen himself, almost blue; his lips less blue than purple. I asked, when I'd stopped crying, when I was sorry for both of us, why he looked so bad. He waited until I'd stopped sobbing. Then he told me the Alberta government wanted to recover Daweosaurus for its new museum. Broke his heart, he said; after he'd laboured for so many months, cleaning every bone, mounting them all together except for the tail, of course: he'd made a replica in plastic. And he felt it belonged in the east now, his finest model. I should have guessed he was lying.*

"That old canoe of yours," he said. "The red one. Where is it?"

I told him it was where it always was. Under the veranda. And then I asked I was willing to make up, finally I said: "Can I go with you, Dad?"

He had already kicked off his slippers. He leaned to an ashtray and put down his pipe. He reached and patted my head.

"No," he said.

He went, limped, in his bare feet to the door; he went outside.

234

45. *Flatboat and Waiting Birds*

They lifted themselves, hunched themselves up off the packed clay, avoiding the protrusions of bone; hurriedly, one by one, Web, then Dawe, then Anna too—they stooped through the low doorway, out of the appalling comfort of the house of bones; they joined Grizzly in the sunshine, Grizzly letting the sun warm life into his stiff body. Web, one boot on, tried to limber up, began running on the spot. "Got to piss so bad I can taste it," he said. And carrying his second boot he limped in among the twisted hulks that were the cottonwoods.

They walked in single file back to the boat. Dawe led the way now, striding small and stubborn through the sagebrush; no birds scattered up from the bullberry bushes. Grizzly followed close behind Dawe. Anna followed Grizzly, as if to stay close both to him and to Web.

But Web fell behind; he looked about him at the high, naked, scarred buttes; *mauvaise terre*, Dawe had told him, or some frog name like that; yes, they, the ridges, the pinnacles, the hoodoos, were not only worn by water but shaped by wind too, cut by the sky; there was no wind now, this morning, yet he, Web, in the stillness of dawn heard the endless nagging of the wind, the nagging sky that had worn his face almost black, his mustache almost white: time. It was over. Past. No. There was no past, never. He would not let go, remembered with loving deliberation the endless swoop and marvel of swallows out of the pockmarked banks; gone now. Time. Remembered the last cactus holding the last earth to the tabled ridge, the wind an impertinent mouse gnaw-

235

ing the bared strings of the roots; he would not leave, depart, return: the cottonwoods broken and alive, guarding him; in the cleft of canyon, hidden away from the bald and wind-cleared plains above—

Somewhere a voice calling: "Hey, Web ... Web ... Web, let's go .... Get the rag out .... Cast off ...."

Of a sudden, he ran. Web ran.

Reckless, he jumped down off a cutbank, jerked loose the lines, ran up a short gangplank:

He stood motionless, his callused hands crooked open: he watched, listened, as the two-by-ten splashed into the water:

The river, there, as brown as the surrounding buttes; the brown river bleached pale in the light and not so darkly stained as the long sandbars that swam up out of the falling water; the sandbars wave-marked and flat too, bird-tracked, the birds gone; the river wide there, shallow. Grizzly at the forward sweep. Web at the stern. They'd hardly kept enough deck on which to stand, working the sweeps, the open hull between the sweeps, between the two men, jumbled full of boxes and crates and whatever equipment they'd neglected to discard.... The boat, loaded too heavy, riding low in the brown water, moving out into the long and seemingly still reach of the river....

They hit a sandbar.

Web, intently, watching the shore, trying to see if they were moving at all; and then the dull, slow, grinding of wood on sand that told them they were, or had been, moving, would not be moving now. Might not ever move again. The water falling. The boat—he, Web, thought secretly to himself—rising off itself on a sandbar, bone-dry in the autumn sun, bleached white by the hard wind of the promised winter; white in snow—

He stepped down into the water. Before he could bend against the bow he realized he had stepped into quicksand. The sand moved out from under his boots, then sucked him downward; he pulled one boot free, forcing the other deeper in the sand; he pushed down with his free foot, that foot too sinking; he stumbled, caught at the gunwale with both elbows, the small, quick fear driving into his arms; he hoisted, rolled over and tumbled into the scow:

The boat was moving again. Web, his boots cleaned, sand working around his toes inside the boots, stood up dripping at his sweep.

"About as much chance as a fart in a windstorm." Web avoiding the others, studying the wide, long canyon behind them, the slope of brown clay down to the water's edge, the hunched, unearthly and strangely familiar buttes that were not pyramids or beehives or tables or tipis. Web, noticing: "What in Jesus' name are those things?"

No one answering.

Web pointing over the boat's stern, and up at the sky: a pair of large birds, their wings upraised too sharply for hawks or eagles, their underbellies too dark, circled slowly in the air. Somehow, motionless, they found air currents and stayed in motion, stayed far above the buttes: "Look—"

"Dead," Dawe said. Dawe straddling a long and narrow box in the middle of the scow's sagging belly. Dawe, faced to the stern, but not glancing up, hunched over his field book, writing, his right hand in its quick fury jerking itself across the long, narrow page, and, again, across the page—

"What the fuck—" Web said.

"Turkey vultures," Dawe said. Not glancing away from his paper, the pencil. And added: "Watching for carrion." And added again: "They've been around all the damned summer."

"First time I've had a chance to look up," Web said.

Again they hit quicksand.

This time, stepping carefully from the bow, Grizzly went into the water with Web. They freed the boat. They hit a sandbar again. Again Grizzly stepped from the bow, again expecting a foot of water: he plunged in over his head, came up snorting: Anna, leaning from the starboard corner of the square bow, caught his floating hat, then his pigtail.

The two men took off the cloaks Anna had made of blankets; they took off their sand-filled boots, and, that done, Web stepped out of his legless trousers. They worked almost naked, the two silent men; and now in the cool of morning the strangely warm water washed from their bodies the plaster of paris, the dried sweat, the bentonite, the dust of the explosion. The boat sat low and Grizzly and Web, instead of riding until they hit a sandbar, walked beside it, waded until they hit deep water. Then, coming to a sharp, invisible break in the sandy bottom, learning to read the break in the subtleness of the boat's cranky motion, they would suddenly scramble aboard.

Dawe did not move from the box he straddled.

Seated backwards to the boat's direction, swathed in his blanket, his black hat tipped down to hide his eyes, his scraggly beard jutting down at the box, his humped back shielding the field book from the sun—Dawe, furiously, in the outrageous silence of his writing trying to cite or fashion or penetrate or plumb or receive or accomplish or postulate or pretend the absolute truth that would give him his necessary lie: *Crushed. He must have been. Beyond.* Dawe not finding a sentence, a word, that consoled him into the community of his attendant slaves: *Will notify the proper. Hire and send in.* The sentences breaking in the middle of creation. The pencil freezing in his shovel-stiffened hand. *Dead. And buried. I found one finger. I think. I. Kicked the dirt. Over—*

Dawe, slowly, reluctantly, glaring up from his field book: "Never." He glared past Web, Web crawling naked except for his cap onto the small deck that was the stern; Dawe glowering past the unmanned stern sweep, the river behind them immensely wide, the steep brown buttes not adjoining but surrounding it, the wide river seeming to emerge from the brown clay itself:

"They've found something."

A vulture's red head flashed in the sun. They were circling down, the two birds, not onto the place the boat had left, but where the last site had been, the last digging.

Web could not watch. He went again, eagerly, into the water. He joined Grizzly in the water. Anna Yellowbird stood up on the bow deck, undraped her shawl from her shoulders. Anna raised up her arms, lifted off the dress from her body. Her shoulders, too

239

thin. Her small, dark buttocks catching the sun as
she turned, stepped down barefoot, bare-legged,
naked, into the water with Grizzly and Web. Dawe,
facing the stern, watching the vultures circle down.
Anna: a child playing in the water. At the beach.
The water swaying the seaweed hair of her crotch.
The three of them together, Anna, Grizzly, Web,
lifting up the line that trailed from the capstan on the
boat's bow.

They became amphibious. Stepping into unseen
holes. Straining against the line. Splashing out of the
way when the current briefly swept the boat down
upon them. The burdened boat, Dawe motionless
and writing in its center, seemed to move of its own:
it floated square and lifeless on its own image while
the three figures half immersed in the water themselves both fled the image and dragged it along behind them: they leaned against the line with fanatic
determination, the line at times disappearing down
into the water as if they'd hooked onto the uncreated
world itself, would pull it out of the depths. They
moved downstream, measuring the river by their
footsteps; they had become reptilian, had become
the creatures of which they would possess the dead
bones. Dawe had found his coveted skeletons and
would sink with all his findings into the quicksand
before surrendering one: Grizzly, glancing at Dawe,
looking for instructions: Dawe in a quick fury ripping out a page from his field book, crushing it,
hurling it out at the water:

The crumpled page rode easily on the surface,
stayed with the boat in the windless air, rode as easily as the boat would not: and Web let go of the line,

lunged his way over to the floating paper, bent to it, smashed it down into the water, watched for it to rise: smashed at the water itself:

"Quick," Anna shouted.

The boat had found the current. It was moving, rapidly now, moving into a deep channel and Web turned and stumbled, pushed his bare thighs into urgent, balked motion, "Hey, Jesus Christ, wait a minute," the boat moving away, too fast now; Grizzly groping, leaping his way through the tumbled crates, racing from the bow to the stern, Anna helpless, her whole weight not moving the stern sweep, Grizzly picking up a line, coiling it, flinging it:

Web caught the end of the line, was afraid of the water, was afraid to let go of the line: he was pulled out into the deep, fast current, he hung on, shouting, trying to shout against the waves he created with his threshing left arm, Web in the foam of his own sudden fear recollecting: dead is dead: his water-wrinkled white feet, afloat, lifting: Grizzly, hand over hand, pulling him towards the boat's stern:

And then Anna had his hair, not only his, Web's, wet blond hair but his cap as well and he, gasping, choking, came into the sky: "Push about half ... these goddamned ... bones into the goddamned ... quicksand ... thing might float—"

Dawe, unmoving, unmoved, on the box amidships writing: *It was an unfortunate accident.* Dawe crossing out the word, *unfortunate.* Starting again: *No doubt the boy was. Careless. Didn't follow.* He, Dawe, smashing the period down onto the page as if he would pierce it, penetrate, nail the book to the box.

Web scrambling up onto the small stern deck, gasping, cursing: "Hey."

A shadow came up darkly in the brown, translucent water. A long, floating shadow lifted up. Behind them. Following them, it seemed. Web was first to see it: it came like a body floating to the surface, about to bob to the surface—"Hey! What's that thing?"—the shadow already dissolving, into the depths—"One of them damned duck-billed—"

Dawe had jumped, leapt like a goat, was at their side, was leaning over the boat's stern with Web and Grizzly.

"Stul-jun," Grizzly said. The shadow disappearing.

"Won't catch me in that damned water again. Ever." Web swearing an oath. "A what?"

"A sturgeon," Dawe said. And added, sarcastically, "A fish, Web."

"That wasn't no damned fish."

Dawe, affecting to speak to no one: "He's an ichthyologist as well as a seaman as well as a navigator."

The three men bending down from the stern, watching the water.

"It's armour-plated." Dawe explaining. "Older than dinosaurs—"

"Look," Anna said. Anna on the bow of the boat, trying to use the bow sweep.

"Here before the dinosaurs?" Web said.

Dawe: "And after." Dawe pausing. "Damned thing. Wish I'd seen it."

"Look," Anna repeated.

They were moving around a bend. Anna was first

to see the ferry: white, motionless, it hung suspended from its cable in the middle of the river. The river narrowing there, the current beginning to carry the boat faster.

"Where are we?" Anna said. Turning her luminous eyes to the men.

"Asshole of the world." Dawe watching the water, trying to glimpse the sturgeon.

Then it was Web who glanced around, glanced to where Anna was pointing.

"Hey," he said. "What's this?"

"Asshole of the world," Dawe said.

Then Dawe saw it too. Saw the ferry. Then he went back to the crate in the middle of the boat, sat down again at his field book.

Web put his bare feet down into the hold of the scow. He bent and reached and found his boots, dumped out the sand and the water. He found his legless trousers, the grey blanket that was his cloak.

Grizzly went to the bow of the boat, crawled over the boxes. He too found his boots. He lifted onto his small body the blanket that was his shirt, his cloak, adjusted the round-domed hat on his head, straightened his pigtail.

Dawe, watching.

A black and van-like automobile was parked in the middle of the deck of the ferry. On its side was some peeled lettering in gold. Two men on the deck of the ferry were standing behind what had to be a camera on a tripod.

Dawe groped for, found, his field book. And yet he could not bring himself to glance away from the motionless ferry, down to the open book. "Goddamn," he said. "Goddamn the lucky bastard. May he vanish from the face of the earth."

The ferryman had at his side a dog. What appeared at first, for a long time, to be a dog. The boat moved steadily, rocked slightly in the quickening current, moved down upon the ferry.

Anna, on the small bow deck, helped Grizzly lift the sweep aboard, in preparation for the landing. "That's a coyote," she said.

"Goddamn," Dawe said.

Web looked up from where he was untangling, coiling, lines, glanced up from the hold of the boat and saw between Anna's spread and braced legs— she had lifted her arms to pull on her loose, red-flowered cotton dress—Web saw, before her skirt fell, the two men on the deck of the ferry: "With our luck, we'll hit a boulder."

Dawe tore another page from his field book. He bent to the new blank page, to the box; he wrote, quickly: *Saturday, September 23. Weather holding fine. The Loveland ferry in sight at 12 noon. Two wagons on the south bank of the river, each with a six-horse team. The teamsters are waving us in.*

46. *Dawe's Landing: Science Confounded*

"Hello now," Sinnott called.

And Dawe, unable to resist, shouting far across the water in reply: "We made it."

"I know," Sinnott said. Called arrogantly.

Dawe, his voice breaking loose from its stoic calm, the outrage clearing his throat of the dust of his last hours. Dawe, standing up then, standing humped on the box on which he'd ridden, Dawe shouting as he tried to slip the field book, the pencil,

244

into his pockets, found he had no pockets, only a dusty grey blanket wrapped over the fish-white indecency of his unsunned body: "We came back with everything. Everything. We got everything we went for and more."

"Hold it," Sinnott said. "Wait. Right there."

"We've got bones here, Sinnott, that will keep science guessing—Once, on this very earth——" Dawe gesturing grandly, to the sloping buttes, to the raw noon sky—"a creature walked, waded, swam; a creature so huge, so glorious, so unhumbly victorious over all creation——"

"Vanished," Sinnott called. Sinnott changing plates, readjusting his camera, then himself vanishing under the focussing cloth.

"No!" Dawe shouted. "Not vanished. Here. Now." Dawe proud, arrogant, magnanimous, victorious, beseeching, eloquently silent now, signalling his crew, his men, to assume their positions for the prophesied and providential landing.

Sinnott taking pictures. As the flatboat drifted down upon the ferry: he took pictures. The ordered and tumbled buttes from which the boat was emerging. The small, twisted hulk adrift, under the colourless immensity of sky. The stripped-down and warped and leaking boat, heavy and low in the water, drifting with the current. The four passengers slumped, spent into motionless silence, for all their grand mockery of eloquent posture: "Recovery: A Portrait," Sinnott said. Sinnott called.

"Recovery," Dawe replied. Across the water. The boat, silently, sliding down towards the cable-hung ferry.

And then, after four hours of working to make the

boat move, they, Grizzly and Web, must work to make it stop. It bore down upon the waiting ferry; Grizzly first, then Web, picked up a pole. Each tried to find the river's bottom, could not. Bracing themselves on the bow of the boat, Anna between them, watching as if she and not Dawe would give the final command, they raised each a pole—

"Now," Anna said.

The flatboat rammed hard against the ferry.

Sinnott, under his black cloth, was almost knocked off his feet. He reappeared, adjusting his black eyepatch, brushing at his white beard, "After," he added. "Night of the Journeymen."

"After what?" Dawe said.

"After before. Now ... After. Tatters and rags and old blankets. A scarecrow outfit, shouting at the air. Crazy as bats. Callused and blistered, footsore and burned. Starved till their backbones show through their bellies. Silly as loons." Sinnott again: "Priceless ... priceless shots." Sinnott raising his voice into a barker's call: "See the Monsters Returning to Life."

"We made it," Dawe said.

"Yes, folks. See him in person. Champion Bone Hunter of the Wild West. Hero of a Thousand Close Calls. The Winner." Sinnott laughed hugely. "Hold it," he added. "Just there. One foot on the scow, one foot on the ferry."

Dawe would not wait. He leapt aboard the ferry, avoiding the aimed camera.

The ferryman, the snake man, was moving both his ferry and the flatboat towards the south shore. Dawe went to the bow of the moving ferry; he called

to the teamsters on the approaching bank; they had
assumed that once again either Brown or Sternberg
was coming out of the canyon with fossils, and they,
the teamsters, had come here, as in the past, as always, to load the fossils and haul them south to the
railway. And Dawe nodding, agreeing, explaining
that no, he was Dawe of the William Dawe Badlands Expedition. The two teamsters looking upstream as if there must be more boats coming, a
whole flotilla bearing the grand title and design of
that ambition. Dawe talking prices, distances, sched-
ules, while a teamster made fast the chains attaching
the ferry's bow to the landing ramp.

Sinnott, taking pictures.

Web and Grizzly making the flatboat fast to the
stern of the ferry, securing it with lines so the
wooden cases might be lifted onto the ferry's deck,
then onto the wagons.

Anna, puzzled. Anna, puzzled, confused, had not,
would not, move from the capstan on the boat's
bow. Web needed the capstan, to pull the boat tight
against the ferry.

Web: "Go ashore."

And Anna: "No."

And Sinnott, then: "Hold it. The two of you. No,
wait. The three of you." Sinnott with a flourish in-
viting Grizzly, all three of them, to stand together on
the deck of the ferry: "Proud in your nakedness and
your rags—"

"No," Web said.

Grizzly straightened his pigtail and his hat,
brushed at the dirty grey blanket that covered most
of his small body. Sinnott moved his camera.

Grizzly, small, gracious, stepped up from the loaded flatboat onto the deck of the ferry. But he did not at first face the camera. He turned, bowed, extended a hand to Anna.

And then that Anna too stepped off the flatboat. She stopped at Grizzly's side. Grizzly dared put his arm around her waist. They stood side by side for a moment, solemn, unsmiling, the old chinaman, the Indian girl.

"Cheese," Sinnott said. "Say cheese."

"No," Grizzly said.

Sinnott squeezed the rubber bulb.

"Next," he said. "The Steersman Coming Ashore."

But Web had an idea of his own. He ignored both Anna and Grizzly. He leapt down into the scow; he tilted up onto one end the box that Dawe had ridden upon; he stood embracing it with his right arm.

Web, chest thrust forward, stood erect, the blanket falling away from his work-hardened body. He pushed his cap up off his forehead, brushed at his mustache. He embraced a leg bone of the dinosaur he had discovered; *Daweosaurus*, for that moment, was his; his conquest, his mistress, his love; proudly he grinned.

Sinnott had only time to take one picture. A teamster picked up the camera. They were in a hurry, the teamsters; they had pushed the Model-T ashore, had parked it off to one side of the trail. Now, by hand, they were backing the first empty wagon onto the deck of the ferry.

But Sinnott wanted, needed for his show, a final picture of Dawe.

248

"No time," Dawe said. Brusquely. Impatiently. Dawe stepping up onto the thick wooden spokes of a hind wheel of the wagon, forcing the wheel to roll backwards. For a moment he was taller than Web, taller than Sinnott; then the wagon moved and the wheel let him down again.

Sinnott, quietly, silently, pulled from the inside pocket of his old suitcoat a handful of photographs.

Dawe was climbing again, up the spokes of the wheel, trying to force the wagon backwards. A teamster raised the wagon pole, straightened the front wheels, waited for Dawe to move the high hind wheel across the wooden deck. Sinnott, silently, raising up the pictures, holding up the photographs so Dawe might, in his newest pride, see the original flatboat, not a fossil on board.

Dawe, suspended from the motionless wheel by one hand, one foot, saw the picture, stared, snatched it from Sinnott: the boat floating down the river below Bullpound Creek, not a box or a bone on its deck. Empty. Nothing. William Dawe of the expedition of the same name, skunked, apparently.

Dawe was pleased. He stepped down off the wheel. He smiled his approval, his satisfaction. He handed the picture along to Grizzly. Dawe, for that instant, pleased.

"Before," he said. To Sinnott.

"I know," Sinnott said. And handed Dawe a shot of Web running blurred along the top of a cutbank, dressed in a slicker on a cloudless day, gesticulating wildly. Dawe burst out laughing, was joined first in wonder, then in laughter too, by Web. They accepted the pictures, one after another, from Sinnott's

249

big, easy hands. The white tent as full and empty as a balloon in the middle of the boat's deck. Grizzly holding up a goldeye. The Model-T, a monster from the deep, its front wheels on the deck of the flatboat, its hind wheels in the river. Web repairing a broken sweep. The cast-iron cookstove on the open deck, almost buried in mud and gravel. Hawks, crowded into a tree, watching blackly against the light; a lone bird high in the sky—

"Here," Sinnott said, pushing, forcing still another photograph into Dawe's hands.

Dawe only glancing at the picture.

Dawe pushing the photograph in turn into Anna's hands. He turned away from Sinnott. He ordered Grizzly and Web to begin lifting the crates and boxes onto the deck of the ferry. "Let's get on with the job I hired you bunglers—"

Anna staring at the picture of a boy, a comb and a piece of paper pressed to his mouth. She turned the photo over and looked at the blank side, then looked again at the young face framed in its mop of curly hair, the two almost pudgy hands. She straightened her drying red dress over her hips. She took the picture to Sinnott; Sinnott busily moving his camera.

"But he's dead," Anna said.

"I assumed as much," Sinnott said. From under the cloth.

"You can bring him back—"

Sinnott moving out from under the focussing cloth, straightening. "It's only a picture—" Sinnott, then, seeing her luminous eyes, the unfeigned praise of his magic, the simplest hope recovered—

He was framing a picture. The teamsters had unloaded three poles from the wagon; they would set up a huge tripod, as if they had imagined some camera vaster than his own: he bent to find the frame, the picture. He moved.

Anna followed after him, carrying, clutching to herself, the handful of photographs. "You can bring him back?" she was asking, softly, in her plain wonder, her soft Indian voice hardly heard under the din of the men's activities.

"Just be natural," Sinnott shouted.

And he vanished again, under his black cloth. Focussed. Took a picture. Began again in abstracted silence to study the frantic activity.

Web had put a sling around a large crate, had fastened the sling to the pulley that hung from the tripod. Three men pulling on a rope raised the crate into the air, up into the air, so the wagon might be backed under.

"Just be *natural*," Sinnott shouted. He ducked under the cloth.

"Wait," the ferryman said.

And Dawe: "What's the matter?" Dawe vexed, frustrated.

The two teamsters and Grizzly stopped pulling on the rope; the crate swung free, suspended in mid-air.

The ferryman took off his cowboy hat. He stood, unmoved by Dawe's impatience, studying one of the poles that made up the tripod, fingering the skin of a garter snake that was his hat's band. "One pole— cracked. Going to kill somebody here." He slapped his hat onto his head, turned, went running ashore.

"Going to die of hunger and thirst right here at the end," Web said.

The ferryman, the snake man, running upriver to a pile of old lumber and driftwood. He began shifting, moving poles, looking for one that wasn't rotten.

"Son of a bitch looking for a bottle of moon," Web said. "Take the edge off our total misery."

"Hoi." The ferryman gave a whoop, swore.

He was flailing his cowboy hat as if he rode a bronco; he went running through the tall, thick grass near the river's edge, swatting at something invisible in the grass. He was going away from the ferry, and the men on board at first were irritated at being left with the raised and suspended crate; then they were intrigued, watching the ferryman's race with an invisible contender, watching him swat his way into some preposterous combat; and they tied the rope that held the raised crate, gathered at the low cable that was the ferryboat's railing.

The ferryman glanced up, shouted over his shoulder: "Rattlesnake."

His coyote, tethered to a wheel of the second wagon, gave out a howl. The two six-horse teams started up, neighing, their harness jingling, ready to tear: both teamsters ran to calm them.

"Better help," Dawe said. To Sinnott. "Kill it."

Sinnott pointing down. "Ruin my new shoes." Sinnott indicating his white buck shoes, whiter than his beard.

Dawe led the way ashore. Dawe in the lead, seizing up a stick, Web following at a decent distance, Grizzly, as he stepped off the ferry, as he stepped ashore, remembering that he didn't understand, and then not following either.

The ferryman puffing, shouting, explaining, directing: he'd never found a rattler this far upriver. Unbelievable. Fantastic. Unique in the history of the place. He needed the trophy, just to prove it: the rattles, the skin. Do or die.

And Web, then, following, staying close to the invisible snake, staying out of its way, too, had visions of a whole new splendid costume. For the snake man. No, for Dawe himself. Raiments never before imagined. Send old Dawe back east with his hump covered in tanned snakehide. Must be as old as dinosaurs, those snakes. Hundreds of years. Here in this muck and mud, looking for skin for his bones, old Dawe. Hump on his back celebrating its millionth birthday. Need some gladrags myself, vest made of the skins of sixteen gigantic rattlesnakes, all of them captured, strangled and skinned with my bare hands. Row of fangs worn around my neck: had to bite them out of those skulls with my own teeth. A brave man and true, yes, by God, a jockstrap made of the whitest bellies of nine deadly females, the rattles of four males tied to my prick when I get into town. Bone-on I had last night, didn't have enough skin left over to close my eyes. How the hell do snakes screw? Get warts—no that's a toad. Web, carefully, cautiously, swatting through the tall grass in a direction parallel to yet distant from the imagined course of travel of the snake: get my prick bit now, it'll swell up; just when I might have some use for it, the damned thing fall off—

It was Dawe who found the snake. Or at least, once the snake had been found, it was he who tracked it down.

Dawe did not want the snake's skin. He made that clear, after; before he'd even caught his breath, before he dared touch the moving, lifeless body. He wanted simply to be photographed, holding in his left hand the rattler itself, in his right the stick he'd used to kill it.

It was then they discovered that Sinnott was gone. And with him his Model-T, his tripod, his camera—

"Where're those pictures of me?" Web yelled.

Anna had had them. They looked for Anna, those two men, Dawe and Web. They cast about as if she, holding the precious photographs, guarding them, presenting them, must materialize out of nowhere. She must appear as surely as she had vanished, must provide those worthy men not only with the photographs of themselves but with the food they absolutely required, with the clothes they desperately needed, with the applause their success so intimately invited and so richly deserved.

It was Grizzly who pointed at the dust, the tracks made by the Model-T.

They stood together on the riverbank by the ferry, the ferryman, the two teamsters, Web and Grizzly and Dawe: those six men together looked up the road and they could see nothing, only a prairie trail that seemed to vanish into the nearest butte, then reappeared, then vanished again, up over the coulee wall.

"Not here now," Grizzly said.

Web, still gasping for breath, went back onto the ferry; he went to where the first crate of fossils hung, suspended, in the air:

"Give a dog's ass the heartburn."

"Go get her." William Dawe, to no one, and no one moving either. "Go find her, eh?"

And no one moving . . .

The pathos of their winning through. So brave and so stubborn and so proud, those men. And yet how sad, to think they had risked their days, their lives, everything, for that little ceremony of success. There at the landing: my father holding in one hand a stick, in the other a poor creature that had tried to escape down to the water rather than do him any harm: and no one to take the necessary picture.

But I did go looking, after all . . . . Forty-five years after I was born. Fifty-six years after the event . . . . We live in time, we women. And, yes, when I found her, she had some photographs.

In the end it was Anna Yellowbird who got them. She had a half dozen, still, when we met — there in that godawful, sun-smashed, wind-ripped town on the prairies — where I entered the Queen's Hotel to rent a room and more by chance than by daring found myself asking questions in the beer parlour. Where I met that Anna who said she would go with me.

We drove together to her shack, bouncing over the railway tracks, onto the Blackfoot Reserve. I assumed she wanted to pick up her toothbrush, a change of clothes. Instead she came out of her dirty shack in her dirty blue sweater and her canvas shoes, carrying in one hand a case of beer, in the other the photographs she would show me, she promised right after we'd had a drink. She settled at my side; deftly she tore open the beer case, lifted out two bottles, used one to open the other.

Our plan, when the three brightly painted grain

*elevators, the water tank of Gleichen, disappeared
behind us, was obvious enough. We did not at first
intend to go west to the Rocky Mountains, to look
for the river's source. We would drive east to the
edge of the Badlands of the Red Deer River and stay
overnight in a small country hotel; in the morning
we would look for the site of the Loveland ferry.
Then I would drive her home again, go home myself.
It was to be that simple.*

*And we found it too: not the ferry, but the place
where the ferry had been. The river itself is unchanged; the trail down into the canyon is almost
obliterated and surely unusable. Only the ferryman's house remains, where my father's glorious expedition came to its fit conclusion: a decaying log
shanty hoists up its rafters out of the wild growth,
out of the weeds and the buffalo-berry bushes, like
the last roof of a vanished civilization.*

*A rancher let us drive in on his land; we had to
walk the last two miles down through the coulees.
And while we huffed and puffed in the summer heat,
Anna told me of Michael Sinnott. Sinnott who
wanted her youth as much as she wanted his pictures
of Tune, of the others; and how they made the trade
no questions asked, beginning right there at the top
of the first coulee—we were come in our weary
walking to the place itself: on the flat edge where
the prairie broke and became a badlands, they made
love; in his darkroom, she explained: "He wanted
me," she explained; and together they traded, trans-
acted, in the absolute darkness that was necessary
to his profession: and then they drove on again, in
the afternoon sun*

And after we'd seen the river, the ferryman's shanty, we did not go back to the lunch that was ready for us in Frenchie Leroux's hotel.

By then we had formulated a new and drunker plan, agreed to it. And that night I did not drive her back to her shack. Because, in the sun by the river, reading in my father's field books, we began to look at those abrupt notes as he had looked at his prized skeletons, wondering and wondering. We looked at his secret record of boundaries crossed, of secret terrain laid open like a foot with an axe and healed again by limping fortitude—

Like his dream of my mother. My mother and her lover, swimming, seeing the snake in the water: You saw a snake, *he wrote of his dream,* not seeing that it was he who saw—

The strange thing was, she did have a lover. Had had one, before she met and in her hurry married my father. Her lover was a soldier and believed he was going overseas to die and therefore would marry no one. And he went overseas, survived St. Eloi, survived Vimy Ridge, survived Amiens. He looked everywhere for death and could not find it, could not even get a scratch while all his comrades died around him. And alone he returned home after the war, and my mother, in her pride, and maybe in her shame too, would not ever see him. At least she gave him that version of death—

We drove upriver, Anna and I, starting from where the flatboat had landed. We looked for other gravel roads, other dirt trails that would enable us to approach that river which is as unapproachable today as it was in the season of my father; we drove to isolated ranch buildings and corrals where polite old cowboys sized us up in quiet disbelief, the white woman in white, too well-dressed for either the weather or the place, her only companion the old Indian woman carrying a bottle of beer and stinking to high heaven; then they indicated where we might follow the service road to a gas well, a berry pickers' trail, even a cowpath, that would get us closer to an outcrop or a riverflat mentioned in William Dawe's cryptic field notes. And then, permission granted, directions given and repeated and sometimes mapped out on the back of an envelope found in a hind pocket, we would drive over the rough prairie, a hawk swinging high above us, the gophers dodging out of our way, the two of us passing a bottle of Gordon's London dry gin back and forth while I drove, that other Anna following a swig of gin with a sip of beer from the brown bottle of Labatt's Blue that she carried in the side pocket of my Mercedes-Benz. And we drove and talked and sometimes laughed outrageously, that Anna so unthinkingly and absolutely obscene that I could only stop the car and laugh until the tears ran down my cheeks; and then I dared it too, tried those words on my mouth: and glanced at her face and saw she was letting me try in the same way that my father had stopped me—

We drove, one day, and then another, and then, as I recall, another still. We were happy, and yes, we were drunk, gloriously drunk, most of the time, finding little prairie beer parlours where we might have a beer and tomato juice, the smell of cowshit rich and delicious on the air. And one evening two old *cowboys tried to pick us up; they wished, they said, to show us what the prairie was like at night; and Anna said, "I've seen the stars before, and that's the only damned thing we'll see. Let's do it"; and I wanted to — sweet dear Jesus, how I wanted to. Wanted to lie out there on the prairie, looking up at the stars, getting fucked by a man whose name I did not know, whose face I could not quite remember, and would never see again:*

And I shook my head and bought a case of La-batt's; and we went up to our little room and opened two beers and a bottle of gin and the field books, planned:

And all the time we were working our way upriver, looking for the Steveville ferry and finding instead a new bridge; looking for Bullpound Creek, for Crawling Valley. We drove and we talked; and if that corridor to the afterworld of hers, to the hell of mine, was lined and commanded and domineered by rutting men, then she knew what she must do; re-membered the folly of each man's hunger and pos-ture and body's outline; Web like a madman gone into his agonized paroxysm of joy — "What hap-pened to him I wonder?" she said; "I know this," I told her. "He joined the army that fall, went over-seas. He gave my father as his only next-of-kin" "And Sinnott," she said: poor dear Sinnott wanting pictures of her in the nude — a vanishing life, a van-ishing dream, he explained, Travelling Emporium of the Vanished World, This View Men Only: 25¢ Extra; and she lay naked on a bed in a small coun-try hotel and let him photograph her naked young body, which he then kissed and entered with his

260

tongue, then muttered over or into, his precious word, vanished, then kissed again and photographed again, and in the morning he too, himself, had vanished—

"Did you have any children?" I asked her. One morning over a western breakfast of steak and eggs and fried potatoes and coffee.

"Four," she said. "Or five." She raised the fingers of one hand, counted, hesitated over the thumb. "All sons."

"What did you call them?"

"Billy Crowchild."

"And the others?"

"No," she said. "All of them. I called each one — Billy Crowchild."

She laughed and then we both laughed.

And that morning, driving again, we entered Drumheller. The coal mines are closed. The few remaining miners, too old to move on, sit in the little beer parlours and sip a beer and remember. We had a drink, too, and talked with an old man who remembered Mary Roper's place and who said, bowing graciously, "Excuse me, ladies, but I must tell you— I was a customer 144 nights in a row, and the money well spent." And he sent us to walk across the swinging bridge where the Old Star Mine used to be; and we stood in the middle of the bridge, the wind around our ears, the water rough below us, and we spoke of Web, at dawn, rowing out into the current, nothing on but a shirt and his cap and stove polish, my father both hating the man and needing him; and the old town, baked to its bare bones in the hot valley—

We drove, looking for Ghostpine Creek and the

*place where Claude McBride had enough sense to
jump ship, looking for the Bleriot Ferry and an old
stone house that might have belonged to a rancher ···
and, drinking again, I repeated:*

"Did you have any children?"

That Anna began to laugh.

And I said what I'd wanted to say before:

"Any relations of mine, mother?"

*We were laughing so hard I had to stop the car;
and while we were stopped we got out to relieve ourselves, and we squatted there on the prairie ···
"Watch out for thistles," Anna said ··· and we were
peeing and laughing, the tears running down our
cheeks. And I told her then: that time when he came
home from the field; I was fifteen, my mother was
dying: he showed up on a blustery day in late October, pretending he had only stepped out to buy a
quart of milk, pick up the morning paper, and he
could not understand how the door had locked itself
behind him: and he came to my room instead of
going to my dying mother, his dying wife; and he lay
down on the bed beside me; he held me in his arms,
held me, and "Anna," he said, "Anna"; and then, in
the midst of his maudlin crying he told me; "You
were named for that Anna, and she was fifteen, then,
too; your mother dying then, too, always dying ---";
and he kissed my neck, my shoulders, my young
breasts. And I told that Anna. "I was frightened.
But I touched his back. And he kissed my
breasts—"*

*And Anna interrupted me. "He was a great one
for the nipples." She was standing there in the heat,
in the unrelenting sun. She put her hands under her*

old, sagging breasts, raised them up against the sun. "I let him suck by the hour. If that's what he wanted."

And I had to ask her then. I was pulling up my panties, straightening my white skirt, when I saw against the glare — the sun shines in hell too — a deserted stone house, a brown, stony house, near the river, on a field of spiky grass. We had found the old house after all, the place where the woman had seen the men come off the river, out of the mud, had gone from love to silence. "What was he — like?" I asked her.

"He?" Anna said. That Anna.

"He. Him. It. That." We'd been drinking hard. "Christ, Anna," I blurted, "I'm a goddamned virgin. I'm forty-five years old and I wouldn't know a prick —" She was silent, watching me out of those old black Indian eyes of hers, and I thought my God, she doesn't know what virgin means, and I started to shout —

"Grizzly," she said. Softly.

She, Anna, knowing all the time which he I had meant. "Little Grizzly," she said, playing the words on her old mouth . . . . She had saved me; in that instant had brought me back, turned me around, somehow. She had let me say it, and beyond that, beyond even the saying, she had let me see that I had had nothing to fear. And maybe even nothing to regret.

"Little Grizzly, he wasn't like that Billy, crying out, 'Mammal,' in the middle of it all." And I was ready to laugh then. I was not laughing, but I was ready to laugh. Not the pained and uneasy and nervous laughter of a lifetime of wondering, of trying to

263

recover and then reshape and then relive a life that wasn't quite a life. I was ready for real laughter. And Anna was saying: "He never talked about it, that old man with the pigtail. Couldn't talk. Just did it."

And it was then, it was there, we decided there beside the old stone house, the windows broken and gone, the man with the shotgun gone too, and the woman he thought he was protecting; there where my father could write in his field notes How can she endure the silence *while he did not see she was held prisoner, as was Anna, as was I; there where he cowered and sulked on shore when he should have stormed the fortress, smashed down the doors, freed her—*

Right then we decided to go, not to Tail Creek and the place where Anna, seeing four men approach her, had leapt into her sham grave; we decided we would go to the source. To the high source of the river.

"Let's do it for Web," I said. To Anna.

"Fuck Web," Anna said. "Let's do it for us."

And that is why, now, I am staying—living—here in the mountains, where I can look to the east, and downward, to where it is all behind me. And each morning I go to the desk clerk and the servile little pup says, "Checking out today, Miss Dawe?" And each morning I think about it, decide for myself, tell him or tell him not to put another day on the bill.

And then I was crying while I drove. A crying jag, Anna told me, and patted my arm; and while I cried and then whimpered and then sobbed, she sang a Blackfoot lullaby. And we took the road to the

*mountains: we stopped in those little Alberta towns
and asked where the chinaman's was, and we had
coffee and a sandwich, then coffee, then supper, in
those awful places, watching as if the ghost of
Grizzly must appear from the back room where we
heard the alien, indigenous speech that we could not
understand; and we saw only the shelves of groceries
for Sunday shoppers, the stacked cases of soft
drinks, the booths where the vanished kids carved
their names in the tabletops.*

*We drove into the night, and somewhere we pulled
off the road and slept in the car, and next morning I
felt cramped and dirty and smelly and good and
Anna sat up and chuckled and said to me: "This is
how it was. In the old days"; and she opened a beer
for each of us, we had our breakfast there in the cool
and warming sun. We got out of the car, we
stretched and shouted; and God we had turned the
Badlands upside down, we were in the Rockies;
"Let's have another," I said, and found two beers in
the open case on the floor of the back seat: "Let's
go."*

*And we took a gravel road up to a place where
skiers, in winter, parked, and left the car, each of us
carrying a shopping bag that rattled and clinked and
embarrassed the proper passengers on the VW bus.
I alone carrying a field book. And at the log chalet
we made inquiries, were told it would take a day to
hike in, over the passes, to the Red Deer Lakes, a
day to hike out. Were told it was too far for two
middle-aged women. And Anna, loudly, to me, to be
heard by the others: "But is it too far for two drunk
women?"*

And we had been walking for hours, against the sun, against that cool, deceptive sun of the mountains: and some hikers on the trail told us, "Yes, Boulder Pass, you're in it, almost through"; and they watched and worried and then called out after us, "Don't take the wrong turn into Deception Pass . . . ."; and their voices faded or we would not listen; and we were into Skoki Valley and missed the last lodge where we might have given up, turned back; a hiker stopped us and pointed up at Oyster Peak and spoke of mystery and beauty and peace; and in an hour, in all the time I could remember, I had seen nothing but my own feet; my feet were blistered and raw, every bone of my body aching, and that other Anna, remembering her longer walk, the creeks she crossed, the cliffs, the maze of buttes, the blazing sun:

And when we stumbled around the shoulder of Skoki Mountain, when we emerged from the spruce forest, onto the scrub-covered meadow, and saw the first lake, we were not elated at all.

We saw the source, the still and unmoving source, the visible rim of a glacier far to the west; to the east the high peak of a mountain, where the river must, somehow, fall away to the foothills, down to the plains.

We were there and I wanted to cry. Only because my feet were bleeding.

And that other Anna was as spent as I. She sat down by the water and opened another bottle of gin and we drank, not to get happy or maudlin, not to kill the pain, even. I held the gin in my mouth and scooped water with my hand from the lake into my mouth and mixed them and swallowed. Anna could not stand on her legs to get to the water; she was looking for a bottle of beer to chase the gin with. In rooting through her brown paper shopping bag, she found the photographs.

She raised in her hand the photographs she had meant all those days to show me. She was about to show me those last surviving pictures of all our lost men:

"Listen," Anna said. She pointed, the pictures held loosely in her raised left hand.

I listened and shook my head.

"Listen," Anna said. "What's that?"

And then I saw it too.

A helicopter, yellow as the sun, was coming up the valley. And my first fear was the fear that we, already, were missing, the searchers come to seek us. Too late, too late. The searchers come to rescue our living and defeated bones. And even that hope to be defeated; the pilot not seeing, would pass straight over.

That Anna was first to laugh.

"A grizzly," she said.

The fear that had first possessed me turned in my bowels to terror.

Anna straightened, sat straight and proper on the fallen tree where we'd collapsed to rest, to drink at the water's edge.

And then I too saw the bear that she had, already, recognized.

The grizzly was in a nylon net, slung beneath the helicopter. I saw it, clearly, and yet in the moment of perception I believed in the apparition too, believed all my pointed and hurt senses and believed too that I had drunk too much, walked too far through boulder-strewn fields and soggy alpine meadows, climbed too high against the thin air, against the rising and descending sun.

The great, hunched, shaggy beast dangled down from the helicopter, about to be born into a new life, away from garbage cans and tourists' tents. Once its umbilical cord was cut, the sac opened, it too could run free; on the high avalanche slopes it could dig and eat and fatten and fight and breed and sleep.

But the grizzly had awakened too soon.

The grizzly had stirred itself awake against the tranquillizing shot, had kicked itself loose, was foaming at the mouth, was shitting.

And now we knew the pilot had seen neither us nor his bear; unknowing, indifferent, he would pass over; the hammering, thudding noise of his machine would violate our tongues into dumb silence. But we laughed; we could see now the grizzly's crotch; he was suspended upright by his head and upper limbs in the tangled net; his hind legs swung free in the air, galloped straight at us in the empty air, his sharp claws scratching for the gone earth, his testicles following crazily after.

He was running in the air, straight overhead, so comically human and male that Anna fell backwards, laughing, off the fallen tree; Anna lay fallen, her skirt up, her legs spread, her body shaking with laughter; and I was laughing too, unheard and laughing, against the thudding passage of the yellow machine; I held out my arms, my fists, to the galloping, flying bear; we laughed ourselves into a tear-

glazed vision of the awakening old grizzly, lifted
into the sun, his prick and testicles hung over us like
a handful of dead-ripe berries.

Anna raised up her photographs; she flung them
out at the approaching helicopter. She flung them up
at the bear's balls. I believed she would signal our
rescue. But she was laughing: she flung up the pictures into the moving air: like so many vultures they
hung, descending, onto the still water of the river's
source.

And then I could do it too. I opened my purse,
took out the field book I had carried like a curse for
ten years. For that was the craziest thing of all: he
had kept making field notes for the twenty years
after his last trip into the field. While he laboured
and hid in the museum, when he might have been
remembering, or regretting, or explaining, or planning, or dreaming, or hating, or even loving I suppose, he was busy putting down each day's tedium
and trivia. Shutting out instead of letting in. Con-
cealing.

He had written on the last page of his last field
book: I have come to the end of words. Yes, and the
fucking bastard had let me prepare the canoe, had
let me send him out onto the water. And we found
the canoe all right; at least we didn't lose eighty
dollars worth of canoe. But we never found the body.
Thank God for small mercies. Oh the government
was efficient, they searched high and low, the police-
men, the guides, for their famous man. But they
found nothing.

And I took that last field book with the last pompous sentence he ever wrote, the only poem he ever

269

wrote, a love poem, to me, his only daughter, and I threw it into the lake where it too might drown.

And I turned around on my blistered, bloody feet, and I walked out of that place, as I had walked in. Anna and I walked out of there together. We walked through the night, stumbling our way by the light of the stars; we looked at those billions of years of light, and Anna looked at the stars and then at me, and she did not mention dinosaurs or men or their discipline or their courage or their goddamned honour or their goddamned fucking fame or their goddamned fucking death-fucking death.

"Like pissing in the ocean," she said; that Anna, who had never seen the ocean.

We sang together, that awful song about rolling over in the clover, because that was the only song we both remembered and could sing long enough to see us through. We walked out of there hand in hand, arm in arm, holding each other. We walked all the way out. And we did not once look back, not once, ever.